DYME

HIT LIST

← A Curtis Alcutt Novel →

Black Pearl Books Publishing

WWW. BLACKPEARLBOOKS. COM

HIT LIST

A Curtis Alcutt Novel

Published By:

BLACK PEARL BOOKS INC.
3653-F FLAKES MILL ROAD – PMB 306
ATLANTA, GA 30034
404-735-3553

All Black Pearl Books titles, imprints and distributed lines are available at special quantity discounts for bulk purchases for sales promotion, premiums, fund raising, educational or institutional use.

Special book excerpts or customized printings can also be created to fit specific needs. For details, write to Black Pearl Books: Attention Senior Publisher, 3653-F Flakes Mill Road, PMB-306, Atlanta, Georgia 30034 or visit website: www. BlackPearlBooks. com

FOR DISTRIBUTOR INFO & BULK ORDERING

Contact: **Black Pearl Books, Inc.**
3653-F Flakes Mill Road
PMB 306
Atlanta, Georgia 30034
404-735-3553

Discount Book-Club Orders via website:

www. BlackPearlBooks. com

ISBN: 0-9766007-1-4 LCCN: 2005923838

Publication Date: May 2005

Cover Credits

Photographer: CHARLES BROWN

← A Curtis Alcutt Novel →

Black Pearl Books Publishing
www. BlackPearlBooks. com

ACKNOWLEDGEMENTS

First of all, I have to give thanks to the Higher Power that laid my path before me and provided me with enough sense to follow it.

I dedicate this book to two people I love VERY much; my Granny, Georgia Taylor and my Grandpa, the late Booker T. Emery. Thank you both for providing me with all the wisdom and "old sayings" I gleaned from you. Even when I didn't act like it, I did listen to you… Thank you two for creating my mother, Betty Alcutt.

Dear Mother: I can never, ever, ever repay you for all you have done for me, your hard-headed first born. There is no way I can put a price tag on the love and guidance you have given, and still give to me. I love you, Momma…

To my father, Pierre Alcutt: Thank you for your discipline and guidance. There's something I want you to know…I love you.

To my wife, Lisa: Thank you for being my rock, my confidant, my critic, my consultant, my everything. I'll love you 'til the day after forever…

To my kids: CuSandra, Curtis, & Logan: I want to let you guys know I love you very, very much. Don't you EVER give up on your dreams, no matter how far off they seem. Aim as high as you can; you may land within walking distance of what you desire…

To my brothers: Yo! Tony and Pete! Thank you guys for all the fun we had as kids and now as grown men. I was blessed to have you as brothers… I love y'all…

To the rest of my family, the Alcutts, Emerys and Lartigues: I thank the Almighty for blessing me with such a loving family tree. I'm gonna do my best to make you proud!

To my extended family, the 5-2 Boys: although we are not a "gang," you had better bring a lunch if you mess wit us! All kidding aside, in no particular order, I'd like to acknowledge the fellas I grew up with. Booker aka "Poochie", Donnell, Horace, Steve, Ray, Archie, Marcel, Vincent, Richard, Kelvin, Gary "G-Fly" Martin, Gary Sweat, Phillip, Ronnie and Johnnie Gaddis, Kirby, Frazier, Kenneth, Chris, Joe, Anthony, Luke, Stephan, "Woodsy," and your families. I apologize for those I can't recall at the moment, so please forgive me and remind me so I can put you in the next book. I wouldn't trade your friendship for anything in this world… FIVE-DEUCE! 52nd street, North Oakland, Ca.

To Black Pearl Books: Felicia, you are a godsend. Thank you for taking a chance on a new voice in this crowded literature landscape. I'm going to do my best to make our relationship positive, profitable and peaceful.

To Winston Chapman: Thanks for helping open the door for me at Black Pearl Books. I owe you BIG!

To Eric Pete: My man! Thank you for introducing me to Winston. I will forever be in your debt. Remember, drinks on me when we meet!

To Deatri King-Bey of "T.D. Critiques": Thank you so much for being my mentor and GOOD friend. Many times you held my hand over rough terrain as I made this writing journey. Your kindness and evil red pen will always be in my heart…

To Carla Dean of "U Can Mark My Word Editorial Services": What can I say? Thank you for the great editing job you did on my manuscript. I can't wait to give you a big ol' hug!

And finally, I want to thank EVERYONE that bought my book. I'm going to work harder than ever to keep you as a customer by providing you the best books I can possibly write. I *do* realize I need you more than you need me… Peace.

CHAPTER ONE

"Check ball, fool," I said to my homeboy Dominic Harper right before I slammed on him.

"Nigga, you lucky I twisted my ankle earlier or I would've swatted that weak ass dunk," he shot back, as he glared at me.

"You know damn well you didn't twist ya ankle. Besides, you couldn't stop me if you were on a ladder," I laughed, as I tried to catch my breath.

"Whatever. I'm through givin' you basketball lessons for the day, Rio," Dee said as he bent his lean, brown, six-foot frame over and gripped the bottom of his shorts. I called him Dee for short, he hated being called Dominic. Sweat dripped from the ends of his neck-length cornrows as he gasped for breath.

I surveyed the fans around the basketball court to see if any honeys worth gettin' at were in attendance.

Mosswood Park, Oakland's version of Rucker Park in New York, was a tree-lined park located a couple miles north of downtown. Three full-length basketball courts, swings, monkey bars and a sandbox, stood off to the side of a large grassy area where outdoor concerts and other events were held.

Streetball had become so popular that people would circle the courts and watch us play. Players from all over the area—including Dee and me—came to show our skills on the weekends. There were many streetball groupies there, eager to get with the best players on the court.

"You see any hotties?" asked Dee. He knew by the way my hazel eyes swept the crowd what I was up to.

"Nah, just a bunch of the regulars," I answered.

Dee tapped me on the shoulder and pointed. "Ain't that ya girl, Yo-Yo, over there by the hotdog cart?"

"Oh shit!" I picked up my tee shirt and pulled it over my head. "If she sees me, she's gonna fuck up all my action. Let's bounce before she brings her ass over here."

Nearly all the fellas were shirtless on that hot August Sunday. Appreciative glances trailed my 6'1", 205 pound, athletically-built frame. Nearing thirty-years-old, bald headed, sporting a neatly trimmed goatee, most women considered me a black Adonis. In my mind, they were exactly right.

As we strolled past the sandbox, toward the parking lot, the hairs stood up on the back of my neck. Just when I thought I'd shaken Yo-Yo, I found out I was wrong.

"Rio… Rio! Wait a minute," she yelled, her raspy voice echoed across the basketball court.

Dee laughed. "Well, you almost made it to your car."

"What up, Yo-Yo?" I turned, held my arms out to her for a hug and played it off like I was glad to see her.

"You," she said as she placed a blatant, territorial kiss on my lips. "Where you been, Sexy?"

I thought quickly of a good excuse for dodging her.

"I've been workin' crazy overtime at the phone company. Ever since DSL came out, it's been off the hook."

"So, do I have to order DSL to get you to come see me?" she asked, horniness in her eyes.

Yo-Yo's real name was Yolinda Fortenberry. She was a twenty-six-year-old, black, sexy bombshell of a woman. She reminded me of the singer Brandy—but she wasn't in the upper echelon of my stable. Yo-Yo worked as a cashier for Albertson's grocery store on MacArthur Boulevard in East Oakland. She had almost freakishly large breast on her petite frame. Her ass was shaped like the basketball I held under my arm.

"I can't help you there, chick. I work in the office, not in the field. I'm the one that throws the switch and turns on your DSL service."

"You need to throw *my* switch and turn *me* on," Yo-Yo said with nasty intent while shielding her eyes from the late afternoon sunlight.

"Damn, homeboy, it sounds like you got work to do. I'm gone. I'll holla at you later." Dee left me standing alone with Yo-Yo the Freak.

She and I had been screwing each other for over a year. We met in a club in downtown Oakland called The Spot. Our classic one night stand grew into a yearlong "fuck-o-rama."

Her boyfriend was in Folsom Prison doing the last few months of an eighteen-month stint for a parole violation. We agreed to have a purely sexual relationship: no kissing, no feelings, no personal information shared; just straight, hot, monkey sex.

"I wish I had time to service you, but I have a dinner date tonight," I said.

"With who?"

"Somebody."

"Do I know her?"

"Who said it's a female?"

"Nigga, I know you." She adjusted her black and white striped half shirt. I loved her tits.

"Yeah, yeah, yeah. Well, I gotta go. I'll call you tonight."

"What time?"

"I dunno. Just be there."

"You are so full of shit, Rio."

"Yeah, but if you didn't like it, you wouldn't be standin' there smilin'." I picked up my red and black Nike gym bag and left.

I was a human dildo in her eyes. A dildo she didn't get that night. I had a rendezvous with my Puerto Rican girl, Angelina, in Pinole. She *definitely* outranked Yo-Yo. I went home to get dressed for my meeting with the freakin' Puerto Rican.

"What took you so long, Papi?" Angelina asked as we stood in the doorway of the two-bedroom townhouse she shared with her pregnant cousin, Carlita.

I kissed her thick, pink lips. "You know how traffic is on I-80 this time of day, baby."

"Hey, Rio!" Carlita said from the kitchen.

"Wassup, girl? When you gonna have that baby?"

"Any day now. I'm a week overdue."

"No shit! You need to be sittin' down somewhere." I handed Angelina my coat and took a seat on the tan and brown-striped couch. Their place was furnished from the high-priced, low-quality ghetto furniture store called "Frankie's Furniture". According to Frankie's cheesy commercials, "all credit is good credit".

The fake "brass and glass" décor was commonplace in the homes of welfare recipients throughout the ghetto. Even though Pinole wasn't exactly "ghetto," some of the people (like Carlita) were. Carlita asked Angelina to move in with her four months ago after her baby's Daddy, Renaldo, left her claiming the baby wasn't his. He took all the furniture except for a mattress and box spring. Since Angelina's bank teller job didn't pay enough for her to afford a nice place like Carlita's, she gladly accepted her offer.

♦♦♦♦♦♦♦♦♦♦

"What are we havin' for dinner?" I asked as unfamiliar but appetizing smells filled my nostrils.

"We're having *un pollo completo, arroz con gandules, ensalada* y *tostones,*" Angelina replied as she massaged my shoulders.

"Now, baby, you know I don't speak a word of Spanish. Can you break that down for me?"

"You don't need to know what it is. Just try it."

"You know I don't eat just anything."

"That's not what she told me," Carlita said as she walked past us on her way upstairs. "She told me you eat one thing *really* well."

"You should've had Renaldo eat your meal instead of him spilling in it," Angelina replied as she took a playful swipe at her cousin with my jacket.

"That's a three hundred dollar leather coat your swingin', woman," I said.

"I know that, smart ass. I'm the one who got it for you, remember?"

"Oh yeah, I guess you did, huh?" I pulled her down into my lap. Angelina was a lovely Puerto Rican hottie. She made J-Lo look like Biz Markie.

"When you gonna stop playin' and marry me, Rio?" She lifted her eyebrows in anticipation of my answer.

"You know damn well Marty ain't *ever* gonna sign your divorce papers."

"He might."

I stroked her short, bobbed haircut. "No way in hell, especially not after he's found out you're datin' a brotha."

"I don't know why he's trippin'. He can have that fat white bitch I busted him with last year."

"I guarantee you, every time he looks at a picture of you and then looks at her, he knows he messed up." I played with the small gold crucifix that hung around her neck.

"Oh well, the hell with him anyway. Are you ready to eat?"

"Yeah, I'm starvin'. Now tell me in English what we're havin'."

"Okay, it's Puerto Rican style rice and chicken casserole, peas, and fried plantains."

"That'll work. Go hook me up a plate." I lifted her short and shapely body out of my lap.

After dinner, Angelina and I sat on the couch and watched her favorite show, "Fear Factor".

"Would you eat those cow eyeballs for $50,000, Rio?" Angelina asked.

"Hell naw!" I turned towards her and unbuttoned her Tampa Bay Devil Rays baseball jersey. I wanted to get to her small pretty tits.

"What you think you doin'?"

"First, I'm gonna suck your nipples till you get wet, then I'm gonna put this hardness in you." I unhooked the front of her baby blue bra.

"Oh, you gonna do all that even though Carlita's right upstairs?"

"You scared?" I pulled off my white Polo shirt.

"No… but… mmmmmmmmm…," Angelina moaned.

I rubbed and kissed her nipples. Her breasts were her hot spot. All I had to do was touch them and she'd get heated. I continued sucking them as I simultaneously unsnapped and unzipped her denim shorts.

"Baby... not here... mmmmmmm... stop... Rio...," she whispered as she lifted her hips to aid me in removing her shorts. Her actions betrayed her words.

I listened and heard Carlita in the midst of a loud phone conversation behind her closed bedroom door. The danger of her catching us excited me. I reached into the pocket of my cargo shorts and retrieved the condom I'd brought with me. Angelina went into a frenzy of passion and clawed at my zipper. Two minutes later, I slid her baby blue thong to the side and my latex covered penis collided with her Puerto Rican muff.

I pounded Angelina so hard, I had to repeatedly put my hand over her mouth to keep her quiet. The couch squeaked in rhythm with my strokes. One of her legs was on the floor, the other draped over the back of the couch.

"Ouch! Stop that shit! I told you about tryin' to give me monkey bites," I hissed as she released her mouth from my neck.

"You scared... one of your... other bitches... gonna... see it?" she uttered between my thrust.

"Be quiet and gimme my pussy." I gave her a hard "punishment fuckin'" after that. I tried to ram my dick into her uterus.

We screwed for almost half an hour before my goo filled the rubber reservoir. Soon after, we both heard Carlita tell whoever she was talking to she was gonna go eat and that she would call them back in a few.

"Dammit, Rio! Carlita's on her way down here!" Angelina reached for her shorts which hung from the coffee table.

I pulled up my shorts, grabbed my shirt, and ran to the bathroom downstairs. Once inside, I disposed of the jizz-filled condom in the toilet and washed up.

Meanwhile, Angelina had opened her living room windows and lit a stick of rose-scented incense. She then joined me in the bathroom.

"You could have at least taken me to your room if you wanted some dick *that* bad," I said as I put on my shirt.

"That ain't funny. We almost got caught." Angelina lowered her shorts and sat down on the toilet.

"Damn, I've barely known you five months and you're already comfortable enough to pee in front of me?"

"Negro, please. I've watched you nut all over me. You can stand to watch me pee." She wiped, flushed, and washed her hands.

"You're off the damn chain, girl." We left the bathroom and found Carlita busy fixing a plate of food in the kitchen.

"What you guys doin' in the bathroom together? Y'all been in there gettin' freaky?" Carlita waddled out of the kitchen with her overloaded plate of food. The incense did a good job of masking the residual aroma of sex.

"You know Angelina ain't gonna gimme none unless I marry her." I lifted my coat off the loveseat.

"Save that drama for ya Momma. I heard y'all breakin' her bed down last week." Carlita smiled as she shoveled food into her mouth.

"What she talkin' about, Angelina? Who were you with?"

"She must've been high. She knows I'm celibate."

Carlita pointed her fork at us and said, "Both of you are full of shit. Keep it up and you gonna have a belly full of baby like this, Angelina." She patted her swollen tummy.

"At least we'd have some fine kids," Angelina replied as she looked lovingly into my eyes. Those words were my cue to leave. Lately, she'd been hinting she wanted kids soon.

"Well, I hate to cut this short, baby, but I gotta go. I have to stop by my mother's house before I go home."

Her smile morphed into a frown as we walked to the door. "You always cut me short."

I hugged her tight. "You know I have a busy schedule, boo."

Angelina really was a sweetheart and would be a good wife for the right man. Even though I'd found myself tiring of the player life—and pondered giving it up—she had too much baggage, like her psycho-estranged husband and lack of ambition, for me to consider settling down with her. I loved the way she pampered me, but she had *no* chance of becoming "Mrs. Rio Clark".

The fatigue, time, expense, and lies associated with juggling several women at one time began taking its toll on me. I'd proven to myself I could handle multiple lovers, but I secretly desired to have a serious relationship. First, I'd have to find the right woman, but that seemed harder than finding ice on the sun.

♦♦♦♦♦♦♦♦♦♦♦

Angelina blocked my exit. "When am I gonna see you again?"

"Soon, I promise."

"That's what you always say."

"Have a little faith, Mrs. Espinoza." I kissed her between her mocha brown eyes.

"I told you my last name is Morales. I *dropped* Marty's last name when I *dropped* him."

"The laws don't give a damn about what you say. All that counts is what's on your marriage certificate."

"Rio, I'm not playin'. I'm not gonna wait for you much longer. Remember what I told you when we first met that morning at the car wash?"

"Yeah, I asked if you were lookin' for a new friend, and you said, 'No, I'm lookin' for a new man.'"

Angelina folded her arms across her chest. "I meant that, Rio. I don't wanna be just another piece of pussy to you."

"We haven't even been kickin' it for a year. How serious you think we ought to be?"

Angelina sucked her teeth as dejection replaced her passion. "Just forget it, Rio."

I bent my knees so I could look her straight in the eyes. "Hey, you know you my girl, right?"

"I guess." She gave me a mini smile.

"You love me?"

"You know I do, even thou--." I interrupted her answer with a soft, warm kiss.

"Get outta here before I forget I'm mad at you," she said as she opened the door.

"I'll take you to dinner next weekend, a'ight?"

"Okay, you better call me, too."

"I will. I'll holla at you later." I turned and left. Angelina was becoming a little *too* clingy. I was gonna have to cut her loose soon.

CHAPTER TWO

"Mmmmmm, there she is again, and looking good as hell, too," I said to myself while sitting on my balcony, entering notes into my journal.

I first started keeping a journal at the age of ten, after learning my Uncle Lee kept one. No one, except Uncle Lee, knew I kept it. I had about sixteen of them in my safe, all chronicling the events of my life for the past nineteen years. I grew up a very shy and quiet kid, with writing being my only outlet for verbal expression. After losing my virginity at thirteen, things changed. I became one of the most extroverted kids in my neighborhood. Even after "*getting some*", I found I enjoyed writing, so I kept on writing to this very day.

Anyway, back to my gorgeous neighbor. Each time I watched her walk past my building, my dick moved. She was the kind of sister that made the average fella say to himself, "Damn! She's fine as hell!"

She was about 5'7", 130 pounds, had quality ass, not just quantity, and hair to her shoulder blades. You could tell she always kept her hair and nail appointments. From the heels she wore, I noticed she had a high, sexy arch. She had the calves of a dancer, well-toned thighs, and skin the color of a gold nugget.

Her eyes were dark brown, almost black, so dark you couldn't see the pupil unless you were lucky enough to be given the time to look into them. They were slightly almond shaped and conveyed a look of high intelligence. Her eyebrows were severely arched, giving her the appearance of a mean ass bitch. But the smile I once saw told me she could love you 'til you cried if you were the chosen one.

She had a well-sculpted nose, like that of an Indian princess. She had a heart-shaped face that framed all those beautiful components. Her sexy, slightly pointed chin was just the right shape to caress as you kissed her.

I'd lived on the top floor of my three-story apartment for the past six years. Last Tuesday and Thursday evenings, I saw her walk down my street from the corner bus stop at about 6:00 p.m. She usually carried a large purse or one of those backpacks on wheels.

I thought she might be a student at the community college downtown since I saw her wearing a Laney College sweat suit one Saturday morning while she was out jogging.

I remembered wishing I could have been one of the beads of sweat that ran down her neck, between her breasts, picking up more moisture on the way to her navel, and finally ending its sensual journey in her pubic hairs, which I presumed were soft, straight, and well-groomed.

She lived about four buildings down from me in another apartment on the same side of the street.

I first noticed her about three months ago. I'll never forget that day. It was a Sunday morning and I was on my way to the Laundromat to wash my clothes.

I *hated* going to the damned washhouse. Since I was down to my last pairs of drawers and socks, I had no choice. So, I stopped bitchin' and went.

When I got to the washhouse with my load of clothes, there she was standing at the Big Boy washer adding soap to her load. She wore headphones and an iPod on her hip. I assumed she was listening to a song she liked a lot because her lips moved slightly as she lip-synched the words to herself.

I stood there next to the change machine staring at her like a muthafucka. I would've stayed there gawking at her if this kid hadn't run by me—breaking the spell—threatening to beat her brother up over some kid shit.

She wore some comfortable looking old jeans that molded to her well-shaped hips and ass, an Oakland Raiders tee shirt, and a black bandana with her silky hair cascading out the back. Her black, open-toe sandals revealed her brick red painted toenails. She couldn't look bad if she wanted to. I bet she even looked good throwing up.

I would've got my mack on then, but I was wearing my "washhouse gear", which consisted of a pair of old ass sweat pants, an old ass tee shirt that had been washed so many times it was damn near transparent, and equally old Nikes that were down to their last few miles.

After taking a self-assessment, I decided it wasn't the best time to try to get with baby girl. Instead, I went to the opposite corner, hoping she didn't see me. That way I could watch her undetected.

It was hard to believe a woman *that* fine was there doing laundry. I imagined her on some African compound with servants at her feet begging for the opportunity to wash her clothes.

As it turned out, she was almost finished with her wash. I watched as discreetly as I could while she folded her towels. I wondered how many times the large black one she held had the good fortune of surrounding her dripping wet, sexy body.

I walked to the change machine again and noticed she had already washed and folded her undies. Not that I'm an underwear pervert or anything of that nature. It's like when you see a car you like and you want to see how the interior looks, even though you may never get it.

By the time I finished with my first load, she was gone.

Don't get me wrong, I did date and always had women that were 7up—on a scale of one to ten, they were all sevens or better—but "Ms. Mean Eyes" was definitely a nine, and that's only because *no one* is perfect.

♦♦♦♦♦♦♦♦♦♦♦♦

I toyed with the idea of putting away my journal and going outside to get at her, but after a quick look over my balcony, I saw she was nearly home. It looked as though I'd have to wait until at least Thursday evening to try and get with her.

Fortunately, good luck was with me the next day. After finally finding a parking spot damn near half a block from home, I spotted her about a hundred feet away striding toward me. I stood in the doorway of my car and watched her approach. She had a "please-don't-bother-me-I-don't-have-time-for-your-bullshit" walk.

I didn't give a damn. No way would the opportunity to speak pass me by. I bent into the car—acting as if I was looking for a CD—and stalled for time. I heard her steps nearing and stood, CD in hand.

Our eyes connected and I got at her. "Hello, lady, how you doin'?" I said over the roof of my black 1996 Impala SS. I walked around the back of the car to face her.

"I'd be better if the cleaners wasn't about to close on me. Besides that I'm fine."

"Which cleaners are you on your way to? Do you need a ride?"

"No thanks. It's the one right around the corner. They close at 4:30 p.m., leaving me only ten minutes to get there. Hopefully I'll make it."

I lost myself inside her nearly black eyes and snow white smile.

"Yeah, maybe."

"Huh?" I asked. She was talking to me and I hadn't even realized I asked her a question.

"You asked me if I come back this way, and you just so happen to be going to your car again, if we could finish this conversation," she said with a slight grin as she checked the time.

I noticed she wore no wedding ring when I followed her eyes to the watch on her left wrist.

"Oh yeah, right. Okay, I'll let you go, but I'm gonna hold you to that."

She half-smiled and said, "I'm not promising anything," then continued her quick pace to the cleaners.

CHAPTER THREE

Should I wait for her to come back or not? My instincts told me to let her wait, while my dick said, "Nigga, you'd better try to get with that fine bitch!"

The last time I listened to my "little head," I ended up hooked up with a fine broad named Naomi who was as dumb as wearing two left shoes. I decided to listen to my "big head" for once and just chilled.

I knew if I stayed in the house I would end up out there waiting for her like some sprung bastard. So instead, I went downtown, picked up some Chinese food, and brought it home.

I picked at the shrimp fried rice and broccoli beef on my plate, unable to stop thinking about her. Then it dawned on me—I didn't even get her name. I was slippin'. My mackin' techniques were a little rusty. No longer hungry, I put the food away and swore the next time I saw her I'd be ready.

♦♦♦♦♦♦♦♦♦♦♦

It didn't take long for our next meeting. A week later, I was having lunch at Sam's Hofbrau down the street from my job when a herd of females strolled in.

Amongst the crowd was my sexy neighbor. She was dressed in a beige business suit that couldn't hide her femininity.

Her hair was full of Shirley Temple-like curls that hung well past her shoulders. A couple of women from her crowd noticed my gape and assumed my attention was meant for them.

Evidently, the word spread through the herd as they all took peeks at me. "Ms. Mean Eyes" glanced in my direction and did a double take when she saw who I was.

I put down my pastrami sandwich, wiped my mouth, and walked over to her.

"You just keep popping up like a bad penny," she said as she turned to study the menu on the wall.

"I was expecting you to say you missed me."

"Oh really? Is that the affect you have on your women?"

"You can answer that question yourself when you become my woman." She picked up a tray and silverware. Seeing that my attention wasn't meant for them, her friends moved right along.

"I don't think you'd want me to be your woman. I'm allergic to bullshit." She ordered a turkey sandwich on rye. I detected a slight country accent in her voice.

"Are you this mean to all your friends?"

"You can answer that yourself when you become my friend."

"Touché. Where can I pick up one of those 'new friend' applications?"

"I'm not accepting applications at the moment. I'll let you know when I am."

"Well, just for the record, my name is Rio Clark. What's yours?"

"Carmen," she replied as she paid for her food.

"Carmen what?"

"Just Carmen."

"Fair enough, 'Just Carmen.' But if I was your friend, I would've warned you to never eat the turkey here. It's nasty as hell." I left her there to ponder her lunch choice.

Leaving my half-eaten sandwich still sitting on the table, I went back to work. Carmen was gonna be a tough tit to lick, but I loved a challenge. Her demeanor was that of a woman equipped with what I called "Playdar", the ability to detect a player a mile away.

CHAPTER FOUR

After work, I went to The Spot for a drink. It was a former small business complex, converted into a split-level club. Downstairs, there was a large dance floor encircled by several tables. Upstairs was a smaller dance floor and bar.

The Plexiglas and wood encased DJ booth downstairs was located next to the twenty-foot long bar. Massive black woofers and other speakers mounted high on the walls could shake and rattle the club at the DJ's whim. Mirrored walls surrounded both dance floors. Huge mirrored disco balls hung from the ceilings. Both upstairs and downstairs, several colored spotlights surrounded the dance floors.

Lola, the bartender, smiled when she saw me. She'd been trying to get me in her bed since she started working there three years ago.

"Hey, baby, what you drinking tonight?" she asked.

"Wassup, Lola? Hook me up with a Long Island Iced Tea."

Lola was sexy for her age. She had long black hair with a gray streak that lay on the left side of her head when she parted it. Large, firm breasts, a matching firm butt, and brown gravy colored eyes added to her attractiveness. She was in her late forties, with the body of a thirty-year-old.

"Rough day, Rio?" She placed my drink in front of me.

"Yeah, you could say that."

"Anything you wanna talk about?"

"Nah, just work stress." I took a swig of my drink, which was strong as horseradish. That's how she always made them for me.

"I have a cure-all for that," Lola replied with a wink as she rinsed a wine glass.

"Is that right? Well, hook me up."

"You'll have to wait until I get off work."

"Why is that?"

"If I gave it to you now, all the men in here would want a dose." She mixed an apple martini for a waitress to deliver.

"You must have that bomb shit."

"Nuclear, baby." She smiled, and then sauntered to the other end of the bar.

Happy Hour at The Spot was the place to be. The crowd consisted of mainly workin' folk from downtown Oakland. Many of my co-workers were there, drinking their way into oblivion.

"I knew I'd find you here," Dee said as he sat on the stool next to me. He was still wearing his AC Transit bus driver's uniform.

"What you doin' here this early?" I asked.

"I switched to an earlier route." Dee grabbed a handful of snack mix from the bowl between us. "Man, I hooked up with this bad bitch on the bus today. She lives out in San Pablo."

"Is she a big Momma?"

"Why you think all I mess wit' are fat hoes?"

"Because most of 'em are."

"Don't hate. I know you fuck with big girls on the sly."

"Bullshit! You know me better than that, homeboy. They have to be less than 150 pounds to make my team," I said to my long-time friend.

We met about eight years ago through a mutual friend of ours named Qualen. Sometimes I felt like kicking Qualen's butt for introducing me to Dee's crazy ass. Dee was a damned good friend, though. He'd been there for me when I was in a pinch more than once.

Dee was married to a woman named Brenda. She had a good job at County Hospital as a medical clerk, and they had a five-year-old son named Rakim. Dee seemed to be a good father most of the time. He always took Rakim with him to sporting events and shit like that, but I'd seen Dee get at women with the boy right there. That bothered me. Sometimes it seemed he only messed around as much as he did to compete with me.

♦ ♦ ♦ ♦ ♦ ♦ ♦ ♦ ♦ ♦ ♦

"Let me get a shot of cognac," Dee said to Lola.

"Why you play around on Brenda so much?"

"I don't trust her no more. Last year, she went out with some of her friends and didn't come back home until eight in the morning." He wiped snack mix crumbs off the front of his shirt.

"What'd she say happened?"

"She said they went to San Jose and got too drunk to drive all the way back home. According to her, they got a room at a Motel Six and crashed there."

"Sounds legit to me." I removed the red drink stir stick from my glass and laid it on my napkin.

"Not to me. The dude she was datin' before she met me lives in San Jose." He swirled the cognac in his glass before downing it.

Damn, was trust in a relationship *that* fragile? That subject was a little too touchy and depressing to keep pressing him about, so I stopped. Besides that, I was distracted by thoughts of Carmen. It was funny how we lived so close but I rarely saw her. Part of the reason was because I was hardly ever home. I was a nomadic player. There was no telling which one of my girls' houses I'd end up at on any given night. Sometimes I'd have dinner at one chick's house, have sex at another one's place, then sleep it all off at a third.

♦♦♦♦♦♦♦♦♦♦♦

"What you gettin' into this weekend, Rio?"

"I'm supposed to go to Reno with my uncle. What you gonna do?"

"Brenda and Rakim are spendin' the weekend at her aunt's house in Sunnyvale. I'll be all alone," he said with a devious grin. The sound of a wine glass crashing to the floor drew our attention. Lola scowled at the rookie waitress who had loaded too many drinks on her delivery tray, thus loosing the glass of Chardonnay.

"Why don't you come to Reno with us?"

"No thanks. I got pussy lined up from here to Santa Rosa."

"Boy, you a fool. Brenda's gonna cut ya balls off one day."

"As long as I get to bust a nut first, I don't give a damn."

"A'ight, I'm outta here. Call me if you change your mind. We're leavin' early Saturday mornin'."

"I'll be knee-deep in some kitty at that time, homeboy. I'll holla at you later."

CHAPTER FIVE

On Friday, Carmen and I bumped heads again. I'd just left work and was driving down Telegraph Avenue when I spotted her at the bus stop on Telegraph and Twentieth Street.

"Hello, Ms-not-my-friend," I said out the window of my car, after I pulled up to the curb, in front of the bus stop.

"Hello to you, bad penny," Carmen replied with a half grin.

She was stunning in her peach, knee-length dress and copper lipstick. Sunlight bounced off my twenty-inch chrome rims onto her dark sunglasses. A slight breeze pushed her long hair into her face.

"I'll give you a better ride than the bus for the same price."

"What makes you think I want a ride?"

"It looks to me like you could use a good ride."

"You assume too much." Her half grin expanded to a three-quarter grin. However, she still seemed to struggle with trusting me.

"Look, if you don't agree that the ride I'll give you is better than the bus, I'll give you your money back."

"I could lie and say I didn't like it, even if I did."

"You could, but I bet you won't."

"You don't even know where I'm going."

"It don't matter. Do you tell the bus driver where you're goin'?"

Damn, she was fine.

I looked in my rearview mirror and saw the bus about two blocks away and closing in. From behind her shades, she considered my proposition.

"Okay, I'll take the ride, but I intend to get *all* my money's worth," she said with a full grin.

Carmen picked up her black briefcase and entered my car.

"Ahem." I put my hand out, palm side up.

"What's your problem?"

"Where's my fare?"

She reached into the Coach bag that hung from her shoulder and deposited $1.50 into my hand.

"Where are we off to, princess?"

"Carmen will do just fine, driver."

"Okay, *Carmen,* where are we goin'?"

"Fisherman's Wharf."

"Uhh, that's in San Francisco," I responded hesitantly.

"I know. Is that a problem? You're the one who said it didn't matter where I was going." She fastened her seat belt.

"But you live no more than ten minutes from here."

"Did I say I was going home?"

"I guess you didn't." I put the money in my ashtray and pulled away from the curb.

We sat in Friday bumper-to-bumper, rush hour traffic en route to the toll plaza. She seemed to enjoy our peril.

"What's so funny?"

"Men."

"What about men?"

"The lengths you'll go through when you think you're going to get what you want." She gazed out the window at the sailboats on the bay.

"Are you referrin' to me?"

"Are you a man?"

"Hell yeah!"

"Case closed."

"What you think I want from you?"

"You tell me."

"Maybe later."

"Suit yourself."

Carmen was as complex as she was beautiful. One minute, she smiled, and the next, she looked as though she wanted to fight somebody.

We arrived at Fisherman's Wharf over an hour later.

"Here we are. Where you want me to drop you off?"

She looked at me wide eyed with shock. "Drop me off?"

"Yeah, you paid for a one way trip." That was the first time she didn't have a quick comeback.

"In that case, you can drop me off right here."

"You need to do like Michael Jackson and lighten up."

She stifled a laugh. "And what you need to do is get a new joke writer."

Her smile was magnetic. I wanted to kiss her full lips for hours on end.

"On the real, where you goin'?"

"I *was* going home, but since I'm here, I'd like to get some fresh crab so I can make some gumbo this weekend."

"What you know about gumbo? You look too good to know how to cook."

"You can't be that shallow." She wrinkled her eyebrows and smoothed out her dress.

I fanned her with my hand. "Take it easy! I was just messin' wit' you, girl."

We pulled into a parking garage across the street from Pier Thirty-nine.

"Let me put your briefcase in the trunk." I popped the trunk's release before exiting the car. After walking to the rear of the vehicle, we both laid our eyes on a pair of black, size eight pumps.

"Nice shoes, Rio. You have good taste."

I'd forgotten Angelina had left them there last weekend after we went to Alameda Beach for some late night fornicating. When she found she couldn't walk in the sand in them, she asked if I would put them in the trunk for her. Once we had returned to her place, and in preparation for round two, we didn't bother to get her shoes. I simply carried her inside her place as we kissed and groped each other.

♦♦♦♦♦♦♦♦♦♦♦

"Those are my sister's."

"Yeah. Sure, playboy."

"They are. You wanna call and ask her?"

"If I cared, maybe I would." The look of wanting to fight somebody reappeared in her eyes.

A change of subject was needed. Badly.

"Do you put okra in your gumbo?" I asked, closing the trunk.

"Yes, but I fry it first so it's not slimy."

I rubbed my abs. "Damn, you're making my stomach growl with all this food talk."

We walked down the sidewalk, stopping periodically to see what the street vendors offered. Carmen bought a pair of huge silver hoop earrings from a white woman with a Scottish accent. The sun dipped down enough for Carmen to remove her sunglasses.

"Ah, there go those evil eyes."

"What are you talking about now, Rio?"

"Your eyes. You can look mean as hell sometimes."

"I *am* mean as hell."

"That's okay. I'll change that soon enough." I watched as a tiny wind-up toy dog did flips on a vendor's table.

She patted me on the back. "Your arrogance is showing, dear."

"See, it's workin' already. You called me 'dear'."

With a roll of her eyes, she responded with, "Whatever."

Time flew by as we meandered down Beach Street. A glance at my seven-hundred-dollar Tag Heuer steel watch—which Amanda gave to me last Christmas—informed me it was nearly 7:00 p.m.

"Aw man, I guess I'll have to get my crab from the high-priced grocery store," Carmen said, noticing that most of the food vendors had closed shop for the day.

"How many crabs you need?"

"Three, why?"

I'd spotted a tiny Chinese man halfway down the block hooking up his seafood cart to the back of his pickup truck.

"Stay right here. I'll be right back." I jogged quickly on a mission to obtain crustaceans for my damsel.

"I'm so sorry. I just locked up," the ancient Chinese man uttered.

"Look, I'll give you ten dollars extra just to unlock your cart."

He thought about my offer for a fraction of a second, and then broke out in a jagged-tooth smile.

"Okay, mister, okay." He opened his cart. The ice inside was littered with delicious looking Dungeness crabs.

"How many you like?"

"Gimme three. No, make it four."

Ten minutes and thirty dollars later, I showed Carmen two white plastic grocery bags crammed with the biggest crabs I could find.

Carmen fought to contain the smile that grew on her face.

"Thank you. How much do I owe you?"

"A bowl of gumbo and some tongue."

"What?" Her face went brake light red.

"All right, just a bowl of gumbo."

"That's what I *thought* you said." Her blushing face returned to normal. "I only wanted three crabs. Why'd you get four?"

"I wanted to make sure there'd be enough left over for when I came by for seconds."

She shook her head and smiled. "You're impossible, Rio."

"Not impossible, irresistible." Carmen lowered her head in defeat.

The fog rolled in and the temperature dropped. The smell of the salty sea air became more noticeable. I could tell by the way Carmen's nipples reacted that she was chilly.

"You ready to go?" I asked as she rubbed her arms.

"Yes, it's getting cold."

Once inside the car, I turned on the passenger side heated seat to warm her until the car warmed up.

On the way home, I found out she was single with no kids, born and raised in Alvintown, Alabama, received a MBA in accounting from Howard University, and was a financial analyst for Pacific Gas and Electric Company.

Carmen had no car at the moment, loved sushi, hated bugs and cigarettes, loved the Oakland Raiders' toughness and any other team that had her favorite color—purple—In their uniforms. Overall, she didn't care much for sports. She tried to hide her southern accent, which slipped out every now and then and I loved it.

♦♦♦♦♦♦♦♦♦♦♦♦

"End of the line, lady," I said as I pulled up in front of her building. "Was the ride cool?"

"It was all right, I guess." Carmen unfastened her seatbelt and placed her hand on the door handle.

"Is that it, just all right?"

"Yes, it was okay."

"Just for that, I'm not gonna kiss you goodnight."

"You know, I'm really disappointed. I was going to kiss you till your toes curled." Her reply oozed sarcasm.

"It's not too late to change your mind."

"Thanks, but no thanks. I enjoyed the ride and appreciate you getting the crabs for me, though."

"No problem. Does that mean I get my kiss now?"

"Rio, just open your trunk so I can get my briefcase and the crabs, please?"

"When's the gumbo gonna be ready?"

"Sometime this weekend. Give me your number and I'll call and let you know when it's ready." After she entered my number into her Palm Pilot, I turned on my flashers, hopped out, and retrieved the items from the trunk.

"Here you go."

"Thanks. You'd better get those shoes back to your girlfriend. They look expensive, and I'm sure she wants them back."

"You mean my *sister* wants them back."

"Whatever, playboy." As Carmen walked toward her lobby door, she turned back to me and said, "Oh, by the way, the turkey at Sam's Hofbrau is *terrible*."

"Does that mean we're friends now?"

"No, you haven't filled out an application yet," she responded while unlocking the lobby door.

"Well, are you accepting applications?"

"Not yet, but there may be an opening soon." She smiled and entered the lobby.

I looked over the roof of my car at the lobby door until it closed with an inaudible click of the latch. Part of me hoped she would open the door and invite me up.

She didn't.

I went to Yo-Yo's house and screwed Carmen vicariously through her that night.

CHAPTER SIX

Uncle Lee and I rode up to Reno the next morning after having breakfast at Nation's Giant Hamburgers. They specialized in enormous hamburgers, but served a damn good breakfast.

"Since I got your room covered, you can drive," Uncle Lee said as we exited the restaurant.

"That's cool," I replied as we reached the side of his two-year-old Caddy. "Hey, wait a minute! I bet you got the room free from your girl Tonya who works at Harrah's."

Uncle Lee just smiled. "What's that got to do with anything?"

"That means you get a free trip."

"Don't hate on ya uncle, young buck. Follow me to my house so I can drop off my car."

"A'ight." I followed him home.

Uncle Lee was my mother's brother. He was my height, about ten pounds heavier, and had the same hazel eyes as me. He had a sprinkle of gray hair in his perfectly trimmed short afro. There was also a tiny bit in his Billy Dee Williams-styled moustache.

He used to take me all over the place when I was a kid. He exposed me to plenty of shit a seven year old didn't need to know.

Uncle Lee took me to places like Stubby's Pool Hall, The Black Aces Motorcycle Club, and many of his girlfriends' houses. It seemed to me that he knew everyone in the world. Everywhere we went people would call his name or flag him down. I thought he was the coolest nigga on the planet.

His car of choice wasn't a Lincoln like my father's. It was a Caddy. Back then, he had a long, sky blue 1969 Coupe DeVille, not one of those tacky ass '70s pimp movie Cadillacs. His was all stock, just like it rolled off the showroom floor. He kept it clean. I don't remember a single time that car ever had a speck of dirt or drop of bird shit on it. He purchased a brand new Cadillac every few years.

I saw my first tits while I was with him. He had a girlfriend named Valerie who was a dead ringer for Pam Grier. She had the same big tits, big ass, and big hair as Ms. Grier. After taking me to the store to spend my allowance on some new baseball cards, we stopped by Valerie's house on the way home.

He insisted I come in with him. Once inside, he told me to have a seat, then he and Valerie went somewhere in the back of the house. They came back a little while later smelling funny, like fish or somethin'.

I don't remember how long we were there, but I do remember watching Gilligan's Island on her TV which had a clothes hanger for an antenna.

"Rio, come here," Uncle Lee said with a grin. "I wanna show you somethin'."

The next thing I knew, he lifted Valerie's shirt before she could react, and I saw the biggest, scariest, strangely interesting breasts of all time. The areola was dark brown like the top of a chocolate cupcake with nipples that looked like brown pinkie fingers.

"Stop that, Lee," Valerie said, swatting his hand away. "You gonna have that boy walkin' around here with a little hard on." Not knowing what a "hard on" was, I didn't trip. I did find it funny that she had those little pinkies sticking out of her things, though.

Uncle Lee slapped her on the ass, kissed her lips, and then we left. In the Caddy, he told me not to tell Momma what we did, to just say we went and got some baseball cards and a hotdog from Doggy Diner. We had a good time that summer day, Uncle Lee and me.

He had never been married. One of the things Uncle Lee said which stuck with me was, "It's a poor rat that has only one hole to crawl into." When I asked him what he meant, he just grinned and said, "Keep livin' and you'll find out." He had what I considered the ultimate bachelor life. He was able to quit his job as a salesman for Mother's Cookies in Oakland about twenty-five years ago, thanks to a settlement he received from Olsen Oil Company.

He was rear-ended by an Olsen Oil gas truck on Market Street in West Oakland. It was proven that the driver was legally drunk. Uncle Lee was able to parlay his back and neck injuries into a large cash settlement, which I heard was in the high six figures. He also became eligible for a lifetime disability check from the government.

He wasn't as dumb as my mother tried to make me think he was. He had the vision to sink a substantial chunk of his cash into internet stocks before the bubble burst and the stock market took a shit. He dated a sista who worked for Charles

Schwab in Frisco. She gave him some good investing advice. He took some of the money and purchased a couple of apartment buildings in Pittsburg and Antioch. Although he never actually told me how much he made from his stock purchases, I was at the real estate office with him when he told the agent he wanted his house, which he paid cash for. Between the rents he collected and the profits from his lucrative marijuana sales to his limited clientele, he didn't need a job.

When I asked him why he used to take me with him all the time, he told me it was because I was his protégé, a mack in the making. Man, I had a hell of a teacher. Uncle Lee still had a way with the females. He was fifty-one years old and still fuckin' chicks half his age.

♦♦♦♦♦♦♦♦♦♦

After gassing up my Impala, we hopped on eastbound I-80.

"So tell me, what you been up to, Nephew?" Uncle Lee asked as he removed his black stingy brim hat and put it on my backseat.

"Same ole shit, managin' my stable."

"Oh yeah? How many girls you workin' with now?"

"I have about six regulars and workin' on lucky number seven." I handed three dollars to the middle-aged white woman at the Carquinez Bridge tollbooth.

"Seven, huh? Now, are these hardheads or Stella's?"

"What you talkin' about? What's a Stella?"

"Well, a hardhead is just that, but a Stella does what you tell her!" He winked a hazel eye at me and smiled. Every time I thought I'd heard it all, Uncle Lee would break out with a gem, like his definition of a Stella.

"You said you're workin' on number seven. Have I met her?"

"Nah, I'm still tryin' to reel her in."

I didn't wanna tell him I wanted more from Carmen than to get fucked, fed, and financed. Uncle Lee wouldn't keep a woman longer than a minute if he felt he couldn't get the triple F's from her.

After all the years he spent grooming me to be a world class player, I couldn't find a way to tell him I was thinking of trying to settle down with one woman. The sham of a relationship I'd had with my ex Amanda didn't count. I only stayed with her as long as I did because I needed a place to go when I wanted to get away from my other girls.

Uncle Lee and I bullshitted about women, music, and football as I drove us through the Sierra Mountains and into downtown Reno.

"Pull up to the valet parking," Uncle Lee said.

"Shit, I can park down the street in that parking lot cheaper than parking here at the hotel." Obliging, I entered the Harrah's Casino valet parking area.

"You can be cheap on your own, but when you're with me, you're gonna show some class." Uncle Lee pulled a solid gold money clip out the pocket of his seven-button, ivory-colored, Baroni suit trouser pocket. The money clip held a two-inch thick stack of bills. He had to peel back at least half an inch of hundred dollar bills before he found a stray twenty.

After he tipped the valet, we went inside and located Tonya Marblethorpe, the assistant tourism manager.

"Hello, Lee! How was the drive up?" Tonya asked as she tossed back her long, straight, blonde hair.

"Hey cutie, the ride was real nice," Uncle Lee replied right before they hugged. Tonya's ice blue eyes examined him from head to toe.

"This is my nephew, Rio."

I shook her creamy hand. "Wow, I can see the resemblance. You're both quite handsome. If I didn't know any better, I would've mistaken him for your son or younger brother."

Those kinda remarks, regarding him and me, *always* made him smile.

"Thanks, I'm pleased to meet you, Tonya."

"It's a shame you guys are only spending one night; your rooms are *really* nice."

I could tell it was hard for Tonya to be professional there in the lobby with Uncle Lee. The looks she gave him divulged her lust.

"Is it like the last room you put me in?" Uncle Lee asked.

She went through her purse. "Nope, since you told me you were bringing your nephew, I fixed you guys up with adjoining spa suites at the Peppermill." Moments later, she handed us two cardkeys each. I put mine into the breast pocket of my taupe, three-button Bettola suit jacket.

"What time do you get off, Tonya?" Uncle Lee asked.

"I'm doing the 8 to 4 shift today. Since it's only a little after one o'clock now, I'll see you in a few hours." She adjusted the collar of her blue blazer.

"Okay, gorgeous, you have my cell phone number, right?"

"Yes, I'll call you when I get off. Don't be too hard to find." Tonya all but skipped back to her office.

"Damn, she was glad to see you," I said as we walked through the spacious lobby towards the valet parking. Dozens of people of every ethnicity crossed our path. The sounds of coins falling from the many slot machines into metal trays filled the air.

"Yeah, it's been a while since me and Tonya hooked up. We first met here the last weekend of April. She and some of her friends were celebrating her thirty-fifth birthday at the Calypso Club in Harrah's. I spit at her and ended up fuckin' her that same night. I usually come up and see her at least once a month. All I have to do is let her know when, and she gets me a room."

"Why didn't she hook us up with rooms in Harrah's where she works?"

"They have rules against management fraternizin' with the guests." We waited for the valet to retrieve my car.

"How you guys doin' so far? Did'ya break the house, or did the house break you?" an intense-looking, older white man asked. His leathery face and beady gray eyes led me to believe he had lived a very stressed and cigarette-filled life. He studied us in our expensive suits from behind his horn-rimmed glasses. Homeboy smelled like a walking distillery.

"So far, so good since we haven't started yet," Uncle Lee answered.

"Take my advice and run while you can," he said. "I've been here for two days, and I'm already down five grand."

"Thanks for the advice," I responded.

"Not a problem. I just wish somebody had told me the gamblin' here was so lousy," he said with disdain as he entered his blue Buick sedan.

"You hear that, Unk? Old dude lost five g's. You still gonna try your luck here?"

"Oh yeah, I always do my serious gamblin' here at Harrah's. Guys like him are always talkin' shit. I bet he let 'em pump him full of free alcohol before he started losin' all his money. That's why I never drink while I gamble. I smoke some good weed to relax, and then I go get 'em." My car finally arrived.

"Speaking of that, did you bring any bud?"

"Got it right here." Uncle Lee patted the breast pocket of his jacket.

Tonya had hooked a nigga up. We each had a suite with all the trimmings. It had a Jacuzzi, sitting area, wet bar, refrigerator, king size bed, and a spectacular view of the downtown city lights. The bed was covered in a thick, royal blue bedspread. The wall behind the headboard was completely mirrored, making the room appear even larger than it was. There was a dwarf palm tree in one corner that reached the ceiling. Lamps seemed to be everywhere.

"What you think of your room?" Uncle Lee asked as he entered from the adjoining door that separated our suites.

"It's tight as hell! Baby went all out."

Uncle Lee stretched and yawned. "Yeah, it's all right."

"All right? Man, this is the shit! You need to make sure you keep Tonya on your roster."

I explored the large bathroom. The bellhop arrived with our bags as we gave our rooms the once over.

"Hey, Youngblood, I'm gonna take a short nap, then go gamble. I'll check with you before I go," he said, taking his bags to his room.

I decided to take a nap, also. I, too, wanted to be fresh before I hit the tables.

A knock at my door woke me up two hours later.

"Wake up, Rio. It's time to go."

"A'ight, hold on," I spoke in the direction of the front door. It took a minute before I realized he was talking to me from behind the door which connected our rooms. I put my suit back on and joined my uncle in his suite.

"How many changes of clothes did you bring?" I asked. Uncle Lee had changed into a gray Gucci mélange wool three-button suit.

"You know how I roll." He adjusted his stingy brim hat on his short afro. I got a whiff of his Hugo Boss cologne as I stood next to him in the mirror and checked myself.

"What you gonna play?" I asked.

"I'm gonna shoot some craps to warm up, then work my way to the blackjack tables."

"Cool, let's go do this."

"First, I need to get my head right." Uncle Lee went into the closet, opened the room safe, and pulled out a fat sack of Indo weed.

"That's what I'm talkin' about!" I exclaimed. He rolled a fat bomb. We went into the bathroom and sparked it up.

"Turn on the exhaust fan, Rio." Uncle Lee puffed on the spliff. The familiar aroma told me it was the high octane shit. Twenty minutes later, we were both mellow.

"You ready?" Uncle Lee asked as he extinguished the remaining third of the joint into a complimentary Peppermill ashtray.

"Yeah, I'm good. Let's roll."

After placing the rest of his stash inside the safe and squirting a few drops of Visine into our eyes, we returned to Harrah's Casino. Uncle Lee's demeanor changed once we stepped inside. He went from "jovial" Uncle Lee to "game-faced" Uncle Lee. We walked by five different crap tables until he found one he liked.

"Let's get paid." Uncle Lee reached into his right front trouser pocket and pulled out his thick bankroll. He plucked two hundreds off the top, cashing one of them in for four twenty-five dollar chips and the rest in for five-dollar chips. I went to my wallet, pulled out a c-note, and cashed it in for five-dollar chips.

The table was surrounded by about eight or nine people. The shooter was a Boss Hogg lookin' white dude in a black cowboy hat, hubcap-sized belt buckle, black jeans, black shirt, snakeskin boots, and black leather vest. He had a modest-sized stack of chips under his protruding belly, which hung over the table as he rolled the dice.

Uncle Lee's eyes followed the dice until they landed on eight. Then, he put the twenty-five dollar chips into the field bet section of the table and waited for the fat man to roll again. At the last minute, I placed five of my chips on the same bet as Uncle Lee.

"Shooter rolls twelve. Pay the field," the table controller announced as he gathered the dice with his long, curved stick. The bet paid triple for rolling twelve or 'boxcars' as rolling double sixes was sometimes called. Uncle Lee removed all his chips from the field and tossed a five-dollar chip to the guy with the curved stick.

Before we could bet again, Uncle Lee's cell phone rang.

"Hey Rio, I'll be right back. Watch my chips." He walked away with the cell phone on one ear and his hand pressed against the other to block out the background noise.

"Tonya said she got a little sidetracked, but should be here about eight. She wants us to meet her at the Steak House restaurant inside the Peppermill for dinner," Uncle Lee informed me after returning and wedging himself in between the fat man and me.

"Cool."

Uncle Lee gathered up his winnings. "Let's go play a few hands of blackjack 'til she gets here."

I followed Uncle Lee to the fifty-dollar minimum blackjack tables. We sat down at a table occupied by a sixty-something Japanese woman with diamonds on every finger on one end of the table and a white boy that looked like he belonged to the Hell's Angels on the other end.

"This table's a little rich for my blood," I said as I pulled two of the remaining four hundred-dollar bills out of my wallet.

"Just follow my lead, and play like I taught you." I took the seat to his left. I always played behind him.

We usually played blackjack well together. Uncle Lee taught me different strategies to use, depending on how many people were at the table, how they were betting, and what the dealer's hand looked like. I sometimes had a habit of getting greedy and betting too much, too soon. My first hand was a pair of Queens. For some reason, they reminded me of Carmen.

"Would you like to hit or stay?" the dealer asked as I stared at the cards in my hand. The Japanese lady and the Hell's Angel glared at me impatiently as I daydreamed.

"Oh…I'm good," I said, snapping out of my trance. "I'll stay." I placed my cards facedown under my bet.

"Keep ya head in the game, Rio," Uncle Lee reminded me as the dealer busted with twenty-three.

Two hours later, I was broke as the Ten Commandments. The gruff lookin' white dude left, disgusted, but the Japanese lady hung right in. Uncle Lee had parlayed the three hundred dollars he'd won from the crap table to nearly four grand.

"That's my last hand, Unk. I guess I'll go back to my room." I was pissed off that I'd let my greed get to me once again.

"Sit down." He slid me a stack of twenty-five dollar chips. "This time follow my lead, knucklehead."

By the time his cell phone rang again, some three hours later, I'd managed to win enough to pay Uncle Lee back and pocket over twelve hundred bucks.

"Tonya's at the restaurant waiting for us," he said after ending the call. It was good timing because a new dealer had come to relieve the one we were having good luck with. Uncle Lee had three trays full of fifty and hundred-dollar chips.

"Thank you, sir!" the departing dealer said as Uncle Lee tossed him a hundred-dollar chip. The hawk-eyed Pit Boss, who looked like a hefty, well-dressed Mafia type, seemed relieved to see us leave. After cashing in our chips for crispy new bills, we drove back to the Peppermill.

Uncle Lee smiled and counted his swollen bankroll. "I don't know who or what you had on your mind, Rio, but I'm glad you got over it." I couldn't tell him it was Carmen who dominated my thoughts.

Instead, I said, "I was just buzzin' from that good ass weed." After arriving back at the Peppermill, we got out my car and I handed my keys to the red-vested valet.

"Do you have a reservation?" asked the hostess at the steakhouse.

"Yes, we're part of the Marblethorpe party," Uncle Lee said.

"Please, follow me. They're right this way," the short, cheery brunette said.

"They?" I asked in a clueless tone.

"They," Uncle Lee said with a wily grin.

When we arrived at the table, I saw Tonya times two. A carbon copy of her sat directly across the table.

"Hello, guys." Tonya stood and hugged Uncle Lee.

"How you doin', Sonya?" Uncle Lee asked Tonya's clone.

"I'm great. Is this your nephew?" Sonya asked, placing her blue eyes on mine.

"Yup, this is my nephew, Rio."

She offered me her tanned hand. "How are you, Rio?" Her blood red nail polish matched her lipstick.

"I'm real good now." I took a seat next to her. The twins were dressed in identical black halter top dresses that hung to their knees and Franco Sarto black pumps.

"What you ladies have planned after dinner?" Uncle Lee asked as he sliced a piece of his rib eye steak.

"Gamble a little, party a little," Tonya replied after swallowing a bite of salmon.

"How you like to party, Sonya?" I asked.

"Any way I can, as long as it doesn't hurt too much or require my lawyer to bail me out of jail," she said with a smile. Her eyes never left mine as she took a sip of her Merlot wine.

"In that case, you can skip the gamblin' and come party with me in my suite."

"Is that right?" she asked with a naughty grin as she circled the rim of her wine glass with her finger. I normally didn't get too fired up over white girls, but she was fine as a muthafucka. Both Tonya and Sonya looked like *Baywatch* cast members.

"Yeah, that's right." I gazed at her—maybe not all natural—breasts.

"That's the best offer I've had all day."

The restaurant was packed. A thousand different conversations, along with the sounds of utensils striking plates, resonated throughout. A few curious passersby looked twice when they saw us, two handsome black men and two white starlets, having dinner. Waiters dressed in mock tuxedos scurried about like ants on a sugar cube.

"Can I get you guys anything else?" the mid-twenties Italian waiter asked.

"We're okay. Could you please bring us the check?" Tonya asked.

"I got it," I said, handing the waiter six twenty-dollar bills after he returned with the check.

"Thank you, Rio," the twins said in unison. Uncle Lee just grinned and gave me his "good move" wink.

"Tonya wants to play some roulette. What are you two gonna do?" Uncle Lee asked as we stood up.

"Me and Sonya are gonna go to the room and have a drink."

"Be careful, Rio. She's an animal when she gets too much liquor in her," Tonya teased.

"How much is too much?" I asked with a cunning smile.

Sonya looped her arm around mine. "You'll have to find that out for yourself." Her heels made her just my height.

"Well, if the gambling doesn't go my way, we'll be joining you two real soon," Tonya said as she took Uncle Lee's hand.

There was a table with two black couples across from us. The women looked at us with open contempt displayed on their faces. The men wished they *were* us. In my eleven-hundred-dollar suit, and that bad-ass white girl on my arm, I felt like a star in *American Pimp, Part Two.*

"Let me holla at you for a minute, Rio," Uncle Lee said.

"Have a seat. I'll be right back," I told Sonya as Uncle Lee and I walked toward the restrooms.

"Here's the combination to the safe in my room in case you wanna get some smoke. Here's my extra card key, too." He handed me both items.

"Thanks, Unk. I'm gonna tap that snow bunny ass."

"You better," he said with a chuckle. We went back to the girls, and then went our separate ways.

♦♦♦♦♦♦♦♦♦♦♦

"Nice view," Sonya said as she parted the drapes and peered out the window of my suite. "What do you do for a living, Rio?"

"Did you really come up here to talk about that kinda boring shit?" I responded while placing my jacket on a hanger.

"You know, as a matter of fact, I didn't." Sonya walked over to the bar then slid her feet out of her pumps.

"What you wanna drink?" I stood at the wet bar and examined its contents.

"You have any vodka?"

"Yeah, there's some Absolut here." I placed the bottle and two glasses on the counter. "You want ice?"

"Please. God, I wish I had a joint." Sonya sat down at the counter and brushed her hair out of her face.

"I ain't God, but I can make ya wish come true, baby." I poured her a double shot of vodka.

"No way! Do you really have some?"

I poured myself a shot. "Yeah, I have to go next door and get it, though."

"That would really put me in a party mood." Sonya leaned on her elbows toward me. I put my hand in her long, golden locks and massaged her scalp.

"I got plans for you tonight." I threw back my shot of vodka.

"Well, if you go get that bud, we can discuss your plans." She took my hand out of her hair and kissed the palm.

Before I opened the safe in Uncle Lee's room, I looked at the red lipstick kiss left in my hand by Sonya and reflected on my current situation. I was a young black man with a pocket full of cash and a fine white broad waiting in my pimpish suite to fuck and suck me to death. Most men would have been in seventh heaven, but I was gettin' tired of hit and run sex. I wanted to try some stick and stay lovin'.

Inside the safe, beside the bag of dope, were a stack of new bills Uncle Lee had won at the blackjack table and a fresh pack of Zig Zags. I rolled two fat joints, closed the safe, and went to rejoin Sonya.

"I'm bac--," I started to say, but was cut off by my shock at seeing Sonya butt naked in the Jacuzzi.

"I decided to warm the water for us," she said as she sipped from her glass of vodka. She had also turned out all the lights except for the lamp on the right side of the bed. I noticed the bottle of vodka and my glass were next to her. Sonya had pinned her long hair up in a bun.

"Good idea." I handed her a joint and my gold Zippo lighter. "Here you go. Fire it up."

She exhaled a lung full of smoke. "Oh! This is great." I took my time undressing. I didn't want her to think I was too anxious.

"You like that?" I asked as she took another hit.

Sonya exhaled and replied, "Yes, but not as much as I like *that*." She pointed at my black pipe.

"You gonna have to show me how much you like it, later." I entered the warm water, sat down next to her and took the joint as she poured vodka in my glass.

Sonya laid her head back, closed her eyes, and said, "Mmmmmm, I have a great buzz."

I watched her nipples poke out of the water like tiny, pink periscopes. After three long tokes of the ganja, I passed it back to Sonya.

"I don't need anymore of that, honey. You go ahead." She put her wet hand on my wrist.

"A'ight." I took one last puff before putting it out. The warm water and the soothing jets made me emulate Sonya. I kicked back, eyes closed. Soon after, I felt a hand on my thigh, then on my Johnson.

"Don't mess with that unless you're ready to take care of it."

"I'm ready." She stroked me to an erection. I leaned over and sucked one of her nipples which protruded out of the water. I massaged her unnaturally firm, augmented breasts.

"God, that feels good." She gripped my dick harder. Sonya got up and straddled me so that her enhanced tits were mouth level for me and my dick was pussy level for her. She fumbled around before finally inserting me into her bald cunt.

"Ohhhhhh… yes…," she gasped as she took all of me inside her. Her pussy was as hot and wet as the Jacuzzi water.

After splashing gallons of water over the edge, I said, "Let's get outta here and do this right."

We dried off and had another shot of vodka each. I then led her to the bed.

"I want to taste it," Sonya said as she licked her way down my chest to my monster.

"Get busy then." I unpinned her hair and let it fall on my thighs.

Her tongue moved like a whirling dervish on my genitals. I looked down and watched as my dick pushed her cheek outward. I pulled her hair and fucked her deep in her small mouth, ready to skeet. When I shot my load, she relaxed her throat muscles and swallowed every drop.

"You have sweet cum, Rio." She lay next to me, massaging my balls.

"I got more for you, baby," I said, stroking the side of her face. Just then, I heard laughter in the hallway and the sound of the door, next door, open and close.

"Sounds like Tonya and Lee are back," Sonya said.

"Never mind them. You got more work to do." I rolled her over and put my dick deep inside her. She squeezed her eyes tight each time I slammed into her. I let my dick fall out of her and find its way to where it wanted to go.

"That's the wrong hole, baby."

"No, it's not." I guided the fat, mushroom-like head of my dick into her tight, hot ass. I felt Sonya's hand rubbing on her clit as I gave her a brown-eye swab. She came about three times before I filled her ass with hot sperm.

At 11:49 p.m., Sonya staggered to the bathroom to clean up. Upon hearing a knock on the adjoining door, I put on my Peppermill courtesy robe and opened it.

"What y'all up to?" Uncle Lee asked, wearing his robe.

"Take a wild guess." Sonya came out of the bathroom draped in a white towel and a smile.

"Where's Tonya?" she asked.

"Here I am." Tonya sat up in Uncle Lee's bed with the covers pulled up over her breasts.

"You boys talk while I go speak to my sister." Sonya slipped between Uncle Lee and me.

"Those hoes are off the hook!" I opened a Coke from the bar.

"Oh, I know." Uncle Lee grabbed and opened a Coke, also.

"How'd y'all do at the roulette table?"

"Tonya didn't do too well at roulette, but she did hit a three-hundred-dollar jackpot on a dollar slot machine." He downed his soda and burped.

"I see you tried fuckin' in the Jacuzzi." He stepped over the puddles of water surrounding it.

"Yeah, that shit was crazy. I took her to the bed instead and hit that pussy right."

"That's what you supposed to do." We laughed and high-fived each other.

"Okay, break it up, fellas," Sonya said as she entered the door, still sporting her towel.

"I'll see you guys in the mornin'." Uncle Lee closed the door behind him.

"So, where were we?" Sonya asked. Her face was full of excitement.

"Oh, you want some more of this?" I lay back on the bed so she could ride me. She looked at my dick like she'd never seen one before.

"Mmmmmm, I can't wait to get that inside me." She climbed up on it and rode me like a madwoman. Her bald, wet pussy sucked my dick well. She put her hands on my chest and bounced up and down on me fiercely. That is when I noticed something peculiar. She had French-manicured fingernails. At dinner, they were blood red.

"Tonya! Is that you?" I asked as she continued to ride on my dick.

"I'm busted," she said with a grin as she swept her hair over her shoulder. "Do you want me to leave?"

"Hell naw, we got some fuckin' to do."

"Good." She proceeded to fuck my dick raw deep into the night.

That turned out to be one of the best "player runs" Uncle Lee and I had ever shared.

CHAPTER SEVEN

We got back from Reno late Sunday night. I checked my messages and all my girls had called except for Carmen. I guessed the gumbo was a no go. Instead of dwelling on it, I took a hot shower and went to bed.

The next morning, I had a pleasant surprise under the windshield wiper of my car. It was a note from Carmen.

The note read: *"Hey you! I apologize but I must've entered your number incorrectly in my Palm Pilot. I looked for your car all weekend, but I guess you were busy returning your girlfriend's shoes. (smile) Anyway, I'll be having lunch at Sam's again (but not having the turkey!) at noon. If you want your bowl of gumbo, you'll be there. Ciao, Carmen."* My Monday started off with a huge grin on my grill.

The minutes crawled by. I must've looked at my watch a thousand times. At 12:12 p.m., Carmen looked at her watch and said, "I'm glad to see you're *almost* on time."

The sight of her pleased my eyes. She wore a raspberry skirt with a sexy split in the back, a white sleeveless button-up blouse, and a pair of low-heeled shoes that matched her skirt. Her mane was teased and rested on her shoulders.

I took a seat across from her. "If I'm here, I'm on time."

"Is there enough room in your place for you *and* your ego, Rio?"

"If you're nice to me, you might get to see one day."

"Enough already." She made me talk to her hand.

I noticed some of the same herd Carmen was with last time were in line ordering lunch. Carmen had a diet Mountain Dew in front of her. The aroma of roasting meats triggered a pang of hunger in my gut.

"Where's my gumbo?"

"Did you really think I was going to bring it with me to work? I only asked you to meet me here so I could get your number again." She pulled her Palm Pilot out of her purse.

"How about I call *you* this time?"

"No, I'll call you."

I didn't ask her again. I just gave her my number.

"Well, I'm outta here. Call me when it's time for me to get my gumbo." The look in her eyes told me she didn't expect me to leave so soon.

"You're not eating?"

I grinned and stood up. "Nope, I had a taste for gumbo." Two of the herd members were on their way to join Carmen, food trays in hand.

"Here you go, Carmen. I got your chicken salad," said a heavyset, dark-skinned woman, handing Carmen her food.

"Thank you, Kim."

The two ladies glanced from Carmen to me, as though they wondered if they had interrupted us.

"Enjoy your lunch." I walked out slowly so she could relish my mack stroll. I ended up in the McDonald's drive-thru for lunch that day.

Two days later, Carmen left a message along with her cell phone number on my answering service letting me know I could pick up my gumbo.

I hated fuckin' cell phones. I refused to own one or any other kind of leash. The way I saw it, if I wanted to talk to you, I'd call you or you could leave a message on my voicemail.

♦♦♦♦♦♦♦♦♦♦♦

That Friday, Dee called to tell me one of his hoochies was reading poetry at the Rasta House on Grand Avenue.

"What time do the poetry readings start?"

"About eight o'clock tonight. Do you want me to pick you up?" Dee offered.

"Yeah, that'll work. See ya."

I hadn't talked to Carmen since Monday at Sam's. I refused to call her on her cell phone. If she couldn't give me her home number after I'd given her mine—twice—she didn't wanna talk to me too damned bad.

Dressed in tan linen pants, black square-toed gators, and a black silk muscle shirt, I waited in front of my building for Dee to arrive.

Dee's red Jeep Grand Cherokee pulled up at about 7:45 p.m. with the sounds of rapper E-40's latest hit blastin'.

Dee wore oversized brown jeans, a matching jean jacket, and a San Francisco Giants tee shirt.

"You are forever late," I said as I jumped into his jeep.

"What you talkin' about, fool? It ain't eight o'clock yet."

"Now, who's readin' tonight?" We rolled towards the Rasta House.

"It's my girl, Nina. She's been all over the Bay Area readin' poetry. Last weekend, she was in Portland."

Nina was this thick, yellow girl Dee met a few months back on his bus route. He met most of his women on the job.

"Well, at least she's decent and not one of your usual whale women," I said, messing with him.

"There *you* go," he said. "I'm gonna have one of my big ones turn you out one day."

"Nigga, there ain't enough alcohol in the world for that to happen."

We had to park two blocks away and walk to the club. The night was warm and breezeless. The sun gave its final wink as it set. The end of summer was fast approaching.

The streets were filled with people on the go. There were plenty of outdoor cafés, bookstores, and ice cream parlors in the area to lounge in. There was a line to get inside the Rasta House. An ex-Oakland A's baseball player owned it, another example of a black person who'd made it and gave back to the community.

"Damn, it's off the chain tonight," Dee crooned as he gawked at the many women in line.

"No shit. Lots of booty out here." I took inventory of the females in attendance. The last time I was at the Rasta House, I ran into my ex, Amanda. We broke up seven months ago after an off and on relationship. I had no desire to see her again.

Dee and I got in just as the first poet began to read. He was a dreadlocked white dude named Major. The Rasta House was tiny compared to The Spot. It had a dance floor the size of a living room and about a dozen round tables. Bob Marley and reggae concert posters decorated the walls along with a huge Jamaican flag. The only alcohol they served was beer and wine. Major stood on a portable stage in the middle of the dance floor, microphone in hand.

Dee found two seats near the back of the small venue, close to the restrooms.

"You want a beer?" Dee asked.

"Yeah, a Corona."

He nodded and worked his way across the crowded club to the bar.

Female eyes sought my attention from every direction. Some of them I'd seen before. Fortunately, Amanda wasn't among them.

Dee came back minutes later with two beers and Nina on his arm.

"Nina, you remember my boy, Rio?" he asked, holding out a beer for me.

"Yes, how are you, Rio?"

"I'm good. Did you already read?"

"Not yet. I think I'm fourth on the list."

Dee sat down on his stool and pulled Nina toward him so she was standing between his legs. For a married man, he had brass balls. Any of Brenda's co-workers or friends could have been watching him.

Dee and Nina flirted as Major wrapped up his poems. A tall, slim, olive-colored chick in overalls and a tight blue tee shirt stopped at our table.

"Wassup, Nina?"

Nina stood, gave her a hug, and said, "Hey, Opal. What you doin' here, girl? I thought you were in L.A."

"I just moved back. I got tired of the phony people and bad tasting water." Opal had a short, blonde afro. Her diamond nose ring sparkled in the faint light.

"Who are you here with?" Nina asked.

"I came with my brother and his fiancée." She nodded toward a couple sitting three tables across from us.

Her brother looked just like her, sans the gold hair.

"I'm so rude," Nina said. "This is my friend, Dominic, and that's his friend, Rio."

"How you doin'?" I asked out of politeness and shook her hand.

"I'm great," she said with a predator look in her amber eyes.

Dee gave me his "Jump on that pussy, boy!" look. I liked slim women, but baby girl was nearly emaciated. Her tight tee shirt revealed her lack of tits and her baggy overalls told me she had no ass to hold onto.

Meanwhile, the second poet, a sister called No Love, began an electric rant on the ills of society.

I wasn't feeling Opal at all.

"Have a sit down," Dee said to Opal. I gave him my, "I ain't down with this" look. He just flashed his sly grin and went back to flirting with Nina.

That son-of-a-bitch!

I was stuck with entertaining Opal.

"So, how long have you known Nina?" Opal asked as she admired my arms.

"I met her through Dominic a couple of months ago," I said in a tone of voice used when a person didn't want to continue a conversation. Opal, nonetheless, continued on.

She squeezed my right bicep. "Do you work out a lot?"

"Not much these days."

"You look like you could be in one of those Bowflex commercials," she remarked, trying to butter me up.

"Thanks. Hey, I'll be right back. I gotta use the bathroom." I left without waiting for her acknowledgement. I wanted to whoop Dee's ass. That wasn't the first time he'd used me to take up the slack for him. At least when I had him do it for me, we would have a huddle beforehand about what was goin' on.

After going to the restroom, I stepped outside and walked to the end of the building.

A group of two men and three women stood in the shadows. The two dudes shared a joint and the three women talked amongst themselves. The smell of ganja smoke aroused my nostrils. I wished I'd brought some with me.

"Kim, quit being so loud!" I heard a familiar, slightly country voice say followed by laughter. When I turned around, the owner of the voice emerged from the shadows.

Carmen.

She was dressed in ass-hugging jeans, a long sleeve button-up purple shirt, and purple pumps, with her hair in a Sade style ponytail.

She was with two of the lunchtime herd members and two dudes. She saw me and momentarily stopped in her tracks before composing herself.

The rest of her group nearly bumped into her before she continued walking toward me.

The big girl named Kim recognized me and elbowed Carmen.

She didn't speak and neither did I. We were in a Mexican standoff of sorts. Our eyes locked for a few seconds as they walked my way.

"Hurry up, Carmen, so we can get a good seat," one of the two weed smokers said to her as he put his arm around her shoulder.

She looked me in the eyes again as they walked past me. I nodded my head and mouthed, "Okay," making sure she could read my lips.

She pressed her eyebrows together and mouthed back the word, "What?"

I stood in their wake and said to myself, "Playa, Playa," before following them back into the club.

"Where you been, dude?" Dee asked. He was at the table alone.

"I told you about dumpin' ya dead weight on me without lettin' me know what's up."

"Damn, nigga! Calm down. I didn't know Opal was gonna be here."

"Where'd they go?"

"Nina's about to go on stage, and Opal went to get a drink." Dee waved his empty beer bottle at me. "It's your turn to make the beer run."

I zigzagged through the crowd to the bar. The line to place a drink order was five people deep. I felt someone bump into me, but ignored it. I felt the bump a little stronger a second time. I looked out the corner of my eye and saw a purple arm sleeve preparing to push me again.

"What's your problem, Mr. Bad Penny?" Carmen asked.

"I don't have a problem."

"Then why didn't you speak?"

"You looked a little busy with Mr. Weed Man."

"Weed Man?" she asked, perplexed.

"Never mind. What you doin' here at the bar? Can't your man get your drink for you?"

"That's not my man. He's a friend." The line moved forward a bit.

"Whatever, that's your business anyway."

"Why didn't you call me back? I've been trying to reach you so you can get your dang gumbo."

"I don't do cell phones. I gave you my *home* number and you gave me your *cell* phone number. What's wrong with that picture?"

"I need to establish a certain comfort level with a person before I give out my home number. Besides, you could've given me *your* cell phone number instead," she countered.

"Like I said, I don't have nor do I use a cell phone."

I tried to give her my hard look, but her beautiful, mean-looking face made it difficult.

"What can I get you?" the Nigerian bartender asked.

"Lemme get two Coronas."

Carmen leaned against the bar. "Are both of those for you?"

"No, one is for my *friend,*" I said with a hint of sarcasm.

"Ha-ha, very funny."

"Uh-oh, here comes homeboy now." Her friend worked his way through the crowd toward us.

Carmen looked in his direction and exhaled between her pursed lips.

"Have fun. I'll see ya around." I meant to just leave her there, but her words stopped me.

"5-5-5-9-7-1-1," she said as dude closed in.

"What?"

"That's my home number."

Immediately, I committed the number to memory, studied her face one last time, and then left her with her friend.

When I got back to Dee, he was craning his neck to see Nina. She had just walked on stage.

"Thanks, dude," he said, not taking his eyes off the prize.

"It's about time you made it back. I thought you'd slipped out the back door on me," Opal said as she beamed at me. Opal had taken the seat right next to me, invading my personal space.

"I ran into a buddy of mine and got hung up."

Carmen and her crew were two tables over in front of us. Her "man-friend" ran his mouth a mile a minute as she feigned interest. She was positioned at the circular table in such a way that I could look into her face and see the back of his head.

Nina read her surprisingly good poetry as folks clapped and snapped their fingers. Carmen still hadn't noticed me. I read her lips and they occasionally said, "Really?" or "That's nice," as homeboy rambled on.

Carmen lifted her head, stretched her neck, and found me during one of the "Rambler's" few pauses. I maintained my gaze as she let her eyes go from his face to mine.

"Do you ever read poetry here, Rio?" Opal asked. She played the "touchy-feely" game, placing her hand on me whenever she asked a question. Opal rubbed me like she was reading Braille.

Out the corner of my eye, I saw Carmen watching like a hawk.

Opal had to go.

"It's my turn to go to the restroom. Unlike you, I'll be *right* back," she said.

"Opal, I'm sorry I didn't tell you earlier, but I'm waitin' for my friend to get here. She might trip if she sees us together, you feel me?" I said with false regret in my voice.

Opal put her hand on mine. "I should've known a fine brotha like you had a woman. If things change, get in touch with me through Nina." She then disappeared into the crowd.

Carmen was still engrossed in the one-way conversation with "Mr. Talk-a-Lot". Her eyes narrowed in a look of disapproval when she caught my eye.

I turned away from her, sipped my beer, turned back, stuck my tongue out and crossed my eyes. What followed was comedy.

Carmen sucked her lips into her mouth and bit down on them in an attempt to contain a laugh. The "Rambler" happened to be looking at her and was confused at her reaction.

When he turned around to see what Carmen was looking at, I lifted my chin up and gave him the "Wassup?" nod. He turned his head sideways the way a dog did when it heard a high-pitched noise.

I thought for an instant he might want to chit-chat with me, but he didn't. He turned back to Carmen, who looked at him and shrugged her shoulders like she didn't know what was going on.

Unbeknownst to me, Dee witnessed the entire episode. "What the hell you doin'?" he asked with a bewildered look on his face.

"Just markin' my territory." I turned my attention back to the stage to watch Nina.

Carmen and I played eye tag the rest of the evening.

Nina completed her set to a standing ovation. In mid-clap, Dee said, "Uh-oh, we gotta go!"

"What's wrong with you?"

"Brenda's sister Alicia is here," he said, eyes wide with fright.

"Where?"

"She's the one shakin' hands with Nina."

Nina was talking to a medium-sized, cute, dark-skinned sister with big lips and long braids, and who looked just like Brenda.

"So, what's the problem?"

"The problem is I'm supposed to be at Albany Bowl with the rest of my bowling team."

"Since when have you been in a bowling league?"

"I'm not. I told Brenda I joined the AC Transit bowling team so I could get out the house on Friday nights." Dee waited for Alicia to turn one way so he could go the other.

"Come on, nigga, before I leave you," he whispered and ducked his way through the crowd. I was barely able to keep up with him. I laughed at my boy all the way to my house.

CHAPTER EIGHT

I had an appointment on Saturday at a place I had come to hate: the D.M.V., Department of Motor Vehicles. I was there to pick up my car registration. Since I had neglected to mail it in on time, I had to pay the cost—in more ways than one—in person to avoid late payment penalties.

I couldn't believe my eyes. Standing three people in front of me was Carmen.

I could tell it was her by the way her form-fitting, yellow and white flowered blouse tapered away to her shapely hips.

She was bowlegged. The yellow Capri pants she wore revealed that fact to me. Her hair was tied back into a ponytail. A throw of hair curved around the right side of her face.

Carmen and I were both in the information line. As though the Gods had heard my mental wishes for Carmen to turn around, the woman behind me dropped her keys. The loud noise caused a few curious heads to turn, including Carmen's.

I was thrilled at the instant recognition that registered on her face when our eyes met.

"Not you again," she said and blessed me with a smile.

"You gotta quit followin' me, woman."

"Don't start with me." She approached the counter.

It turned out Carmen was there to apply for a California driver's license. As I continued to ear hustle, I found out she had just moved here a couple years ago from Alabama and that her last name was Massey. She was Carmen Massey.

As it turned out, we were going to be in two separate lines. I had hoped we would be in the same line so I could kick it with her.

"What are you doing here on a Saturday? Shouldn't you be recovering from partying all night?" Carmen asked.

"I recover quickly. You might wanna remember that."

"Now why would I--. Never mind, I forgot who I was talking to," she said with mild exasperation in her voice.

I told her I was there to renew my registration, and she told me what I already knew from my eavesdropping.

Since her line was considerably shorter than mine, I asked her if she would wait for me.

"Why should I wait for you?" Carmen asked as she put her paperwork in her black Prada bag.

"So I can get my gumbo."

"Oh, so *now* you decide you want it, huh? What happened? Your girlfriend didn't cook for you?"

"As a matter of fact, she did. She made me some gumbo." Cockiness seeped out of my voice.

"Get over yourself. I'll think about waiting for you." She walked her sexy walk to her line.

When she was done with her test and the rest of the D.M.V. bullshit, she promptly found me in line. I was six people from the counter when she snuck up behind me and poked me in the back with her finger.

Startled, I looked around wondering, "What the hell," and then her smile washed all malice from my body. I was immediately taken out of the mental confines of the D.M.V. to a world where only she and I existed.

We talked about everything under the sun while I waited in line. In no time, I found myself at the counter, and damn near got mad because I'd gotten there *too* fast. After I paid my fees and received my tags, we walked slowly toward the door.

"What you have planned for the rest of the day?" I asked.

"I'm supposed to go get some groceries with my friend."

"You mean homeboy from the Rasta House?"

"No, *definitely* not him. I have other friends."

"Do all your other friends hug up on you like he did?"

"If you must know, he's a guy I work with that's been trying to date me." She hitched the strap of her bag up on her shoulder.

"I see. He's just one of your many fans, huh?"

"I don't have fans. I have friends."

"No doubt about that. I heard about you southern girls."

Carmen tilted her head and looked at me like I had three eyes.

"What are you talking about?"

"I heard southern girls are freaky," I said with a contrived serious face.

"You've been watching too many rap videos." Just then, a red-headed white guy squeezed past us with an annoyed look on his face.

"How about I take you to the store instead? I need to get a few things myself."

Carmen dodged another departing D.M.V. customer. "I don't know. How much is it going to cost me this time?"

"A smile."

"Deal," she said, then paid my price.

I felt my heart swell and a tingle deep inside my ball sac as my primal urges stirred. As we walked to my car, I viewed her natural walk. I loved the way her hips swayed. It was sexy and natural and made me imagine how they would move with my dick deep inside of her. When I opened the door for her, I got a faint whiff of her perfume. It was exotic and fitting.

She sat back in the spacious front seat of my car, enjoying the way the leather hugged her. It made me wish I was that seat. I took the long way to the grocery store, my excuse being the store in the "rich, white" neighborhood would have a better selection.

I wished the ride would never end. As I looked over at the gorgeous woman in the seat next to me, a Boney James song played on the radio. It was just right for the mood.

We pulled into the Safeway parking lot in Alameda, a city literally on an island in the "rich, white" neighborhood. I watched as she got out of the car, arched her back, and stretched. I stalled closing the door as I put my keys in my pocket and deftly adjusted my swelling meat. I didn't want Carmen to see what was on my mind.

I was determined not to turn our budding friendship into just another "sex thing".

After having dealt with Amanda for about a year and discovering we had little more in common than sizzling sex, I vowed to spend more time getting to know my next number one female. Currently, that spot was wide-ass open.

I took the shopping cart from her. "I got this."

"What are you doing?" she asked, amused at my insistence on pushing the cart.

"It's a man's job to drive the cart."

"Is that some California rule?" Carmen stood with one hand on her hip.

"No, that's a Rio rule. I have a lot of 'em, so you'd better get use to it." We began our walk down the cereal aisle.

"Rio, you have issues." Carmen rifled through her bag for her grocery list.

"You got it wrong. I have subscriptions to issues."

She laughed and agreed to let me navigate the cart. Little did she know, it offered me the opportunity to watch her ass percolate as she selected her groceries. The store was sparkling clean and fully stocked. They had things like caviar, goat cheese, truffles, and pumpernickel bread, items not stocked in the "hood" grocery stores. All the checkers wore clean white shirts, black bowties, and crisply-creased black slacks.

When we reached the detergent aisle, I rushed behind her to lift the economy-sized box of Tide she wanted into the cart. I purposely brushed up against her booty. Feeling no resistance, I got a little bolder.

"Mmmm, you smell nice," I whispered in her ear.

"Thank you." Her whisper was just as low as mine. I fought off the urge to kiss her neck, even though the soft baby hairs there seemed to wave me on. I tried to back off before she felt how hard I was, but it was too late.

I knew she felt the head brush up against her butt cheek when I attempted to turn away. Her hand "accidentally on purpose" brushed against my crotch area. It wasn't blatant. In fact, it was done with a smoothness and innocence that rivaled my own.

Was she really feeling me? It was hard to believe a woman that fine, southern-raised, and regal looking had copped a feel on me.

When we arrived at the produce section, she picked out grapes, apples, celery, and potatoes. I noticed when we got to the squash section Carmen paid a little more attention to detail in her selection.

She picked up a cucumber and looked at it as though she was sizing it up for something besides cooking. If I didn't know better, I'd say she purposely put that show on for me.

In the checkout line, I decided to take her free hand in mine, and was happy as heck when my advance was met with no opposition. Carmen and I continued our small talk as we stood in line, ignoring the conversation our fingers was holding.

As I pushed the cart, we walked to the car. It felt like we'd been together for years instead of only a couple of hours. On the way to her house, I scanned my brain for ideas on how to prolong the day.

After arriving at her place, I asked if she needed help taking her groceries up.

"I don't know if I should let you in my place," she said while digging in her bag for her keys.

"Why not?"

"I don't think I can trust you."

"I see. You can trust me to be your chauffer, but not your pack mule."

"It's not that. I just have a hard time trusting guys like you."

"And what kind of guy is that?"

"You look like one of those 'pretty boys' that are nothing but trouble." Her face hardened for a few seconds after making the remark.

"So, if I was ugly, you would trust me?"

"Maybe." She switched her keys from hand to hand.

"Let me get this straight. You think I'm cute?"

"I didn't say all that. You know what I mean, Rio." Her face softened.

"Just pretend I look like Whoopi Goldberg in *The Color Purple.*"

Carmen exploded with laughter.

"Oh my God, Rio! You're going to hell for that!" she said between laughing fits. "Come on, crazy man. Help me take these bags up."

Yes!

Since she was accustomed to cooking for one, there were only a few bags. I took the heaviest of them and left her one to carry.

Watching her walk up the steps to her lobby door was a real treat. The way her butt cheeks moved in unison created enough friction to draw a nut from a dead man.

When she opened the door to her apartment, I saw a place that was still in the decorating stages, but had started taking on the personality of the tenant.

There were a few African and Asian landscape paintings on the walls and many plants. A few boxes were stacked neatly in the corner, labeled "Living Room," "Carmen's Stuff," "School," and a couple others.

She lived in a one-bedroom apartment with a nice size kitchen. The living room contained a tan leather couch, a few beanbags, two bonsai trees and a leather winged-back chair with matching ottoman. I could tell she had spent many hours in the winged-back chair listening to the huge CD collection which surrounded the entertainment center. Her place smelled of aromatic incense and good cooking. From the looks of the kitchen, she was no stranger to the stove. She had matching pots and pans, unlike the crazy mix I had accumulated over the years.

After taking a quick look at her place—and imagining all the spots I'd love to *do* her in—I thought it would be best not to push my luck on the first visit, and decided to leave.

"Aren't you forgetting something?" Carmen asked from behind her kitchen counter.

My mind imagined her wanting a kiss.

But her words said, "Here's your gumbo," as she sashayed over to her freezer. She pulled out a blue, two quart Tupperware bowl crammed with frozen gumbo.

I relieved her of the bowl. "This'll make a good little snack."

"You have got to be kidding. You consider that big bowl a snack?"

I ran my finger under her chin. "Remember what I said about lightening up?"

Her skin was as soft as an angel's whisper.

For a few seconds, she totally relaxed, and time ceased as my finger held her chin up.

It was as though our souls were hugging. I don't recall breathing for those few seconds. I blinked, she blinked, and then reality resumed.

I reluctantly let my hand fall from her chin. "I'd better get this food home."

As I reached for the doorknob, I turned and caught Carmen checking me out. She was surrounded by late afternoon sunshine that radiated through her patio windows. The sun framed Carmen in her bowlegged stance. It gave her the appearance of a bronze goddess. I almost forgot what I was going to say to her, I was so mesmerized. It appeared she was just as shocked that I'd caught her.

"What's your schedule like during the week, Carmen?"

"I'm usually free after four o'clock in the afternoon, except on Tuesday and Thursday. I teach a jazz dance class at Laney College those nights and don't get home until about six o'clock in the evening."

"No shit? You teach jazz dance?" Thoughts of seeing her in a leotard invaded my mind.

"Yes, I do."

"I guess there's a lot more to you than a big butt and a smile."

"A *whole* lot more, Shallow-man." She walked with me to the door.

Before anything else crazy could happen, I opened the door, said goodbye, and bounced with the image of her burned into my retinas.

CHAPTER NINE

Later that night as I wolfed down Carmen's good-ass gumbo and made entries in my journal, I wondered what she was eating and wished it was me.

I couldn't believe I was jockin' her so hard. Was it because that pussy was only about two hundred yards away? I doubted that. For me, sex was only a phone call away at any given time. Carmen offered all the things in a woman I had begun to desire. She was career oriented, self-sufficient, a good homemaker, sexy as hell, intelligent, and she made me laugh. She was the first woman I'd met with all those qualities. The more I thought about Carmen, the more I wanted to be with her.

I took a break from entering the day's events into my journal and looked over at the clock. It read 8:45 p.m. It wasn't that long ago I had left her apartment. If I called, I would seem too anxious. Damn, the game had some crazy rules.

Instead, I called Angelina and invited her to the movies. Before I got in my car, I looked down the block at Carmen's building. Lots of lights illuminated the building, but I couldn't tell if any of them were the ones in her apartment.

Surrendering to my craving for her, I briskly crossed the street and called her from the payphone.

After three rings, my call was forwarded to her answering machine and I left her a brief message.

Angelina and I went to see the new Ice Cube flick. Normally, I would've enjoyed it, but it was hard to concentrate on the movie when all I could see in my mind's eye was Carmen's face.

After the movie, I dropped Angelina off and went straight home. I picked up my phone and heard the familiar stutter tone of the message center letting me know someone had thought about me.

Two messages awaited my return. *"Hi, it's me, Carmen. I was just calling to see what you were up to and thank you for helping me today. Well, give me a call when you get this message. I should be home. Talk to you soon. Bye."*

The second message came at 11:11 p.m. *"Hello, it's me again. Sorry I missed your call, but after I called you earlier, a friend invited me to the movies. I was bored, so I went. Well, if it's not too late for you, give me a call. I tend to be a night owl on the weekends. Bye."*

I wondered who in the hell she went to the movies with. It was 11:36 p.m. *Should I call her or not?*

Before I knew it, I had dialed the first five digits of her number while the mental debate continued inside my head.

"Hello?"

"Hi, may I speak to Carmen?" I asked, using my suave, baritone phone voice as I shifted into romance mode.

"I thought maybe you were gone for the night," she said.

"Nah, I decided to come on home. I went to the movies, too. What did you go see?"

"Kim and I went to see our monthly 'chick flick'."

It eased my mind knowing she didn't go to the movies with another dude. Or so she said.

"I hope I didn't wake you."

"No, you didn't. As a matter of fact, I thought this would be a good time for me to paint my toes." I could almost see those cute feet and smell her nail polish over the phone lines.

"Need any help?"

"I don't know. You might charge too much. When I get my toes done, I usually get a foot massage, also."

Oh yes, it was on. That's all the opening I needed.

"Well, I can show you better than I can tell you, and the first visit is on the house."

"How many times have you used that line, Rio?"

"You're the first one I used it on *this* week." I paced the floor, grinning.

"I believe you."

"Why don't you gather up your pedicure stuff and come on over?"

"Will I need to bring a pit bull to protect me?"

"I'll give you a three-foot circle of safety."

"All right, I'll stop by."

"Cool. How long before you get here?"

"How about fifteen minutes? Is that okay with you?"

I looked around at my place, wishing I could tell her, "Fuck yeah!" Instead, I responded by saying, "Uh, can we make it thirty minutes?"

"Okay, how 'bout a little after midnight?" Carmen suggested.

"Cool, see you then. Just press buzzer 3308 and I'll let you in."

"Oh, and Rio, I have to let you know this upfront: This is *not* a booty call."

"The thought never crossed my mind."

"Good, I'd hate to have to use my stun gun on you."

"It's a good thing I got some nookie earlier tonight so I won't be tempted."

"Keep it up and you'll be doing your own toes," she said and hung up.

I needed to make sure my place was presentable. I couldn't risk her finding an empty condom package, one of my other girl's underwear, or anything like that.

I rushed to the bathroom, brushed my teeth, washed my balls, put a fresh roll of TP (toilet paper) on the holder, cleaned the toilet bowl, laid out fresh towels, and cleaned the bathroom mirror all in twenty minutes flat. The living room was decent. I checked the kitchen…a few dishes, but not bad. Luckily for me, I ate out a lot.

Now, to the bedroom. I slept under one comforter and a fitted sheet on my California king-sized bed. I shook the comforter out and laid it evenly across the bed. I stashed my basket of clothes from the washhouse—along with an assortment of other stuff—in my closet.

The bewitching hour arrived. I lit a stick of Sandalwood incense and placed it in the holder that sat on my speaker.

I switched the radio to the smooth jazz station, otherwise known as "the fuck music channel". Then, I turned the ringer off on my phone.

I got the buzz at 12:19 a.m.

"Hello, it's me, Carmen." I buzzed her in after giving her directions to find my door.

Minutes later, there was a knock at my door. I knew once I opened the door, it was going to be the beginning of a whole new round of "sexcitement" in unit #3308.

After a deep breath, I opened the door and was greeted by a Black Venus. Carmen was dressed in denim shorts that hugged her hips appreciatively and a black, short-sleeved knit shirt that revealed curves I'd somehow missed earlier. Her shirt was just long enough to touch the top of her shorts.

Carmen's slightest movement exposed her bronze-toned abdomen. To my surprise, she had a small hoop with a tiny purple bead on it which pierced her perfectly formed belly button.

Her open-toed shoes revealed unpainted, perfectly trimmed toenails. All that loveliness was underneath her three-quarter length leather coat. She still wore the ponytail I saw her with earlier in the day.

I invited her in, took her coat, and gave her a tour of my spot. My place was decorated with dark green shag pile carpeting, a celery three-piece sectional sofa, black leather recliner, a beige overstuffed chair—big enough for two, a twenty-gallon tropical fish aquarium, dark green marble-topped coffee and end tables, and a 32-inch TV. My huge entertainment center took up nearly my entire east wall. My place lacked the feminine touch Carmen's place had, but I got the feeling she was comfortable when she asked me if she could remove her shoes.

She handed me a black leather bag which contained her toenail polish, cotton balls, nail file, and some other stuff.

It was amazing how comfortable we had become with each other. I realized I didn't just want to screw her badly. I genuinely liked her as a *friend*.

I guess there's something to be said about a woman raised in the country. She didn't give off any airs of a slut, hoe, or freak. She gave me a vibe that said, "The ball's in your court. Play right and you score. Make a foul and you lose."

I invited Carmen to sit on the sofa, then went to my kitchen and got a chair. I sat facing her and placed her foot on my thigh. Her heel was just above my knee. Carmen had total control of my stereo's remote control.

"Play, DJ, while I work on these sexy feet. As I recall, you said you get a foot massage with your pedicures."

Carmen smiled. "Yes, as a matter of fact, I do."

Noticing the baby oil in her bag, I grabbed the bottle and squirted a small puddle in the palm of my hand. I rubbed it together until I felt it warm up, then I grabbed her foot and massaged her Achilles tendon.

"Damn, your skin's soft," I muttered as I slowly worked the oil in. She uttered a muffled sound as I worked my way down to the heel of her foot. I used both hands to knead the oil into her skin, paying special attention to her high, sexy arch as I massaged oil into the sole of her foot.

Carmen's foot relaxed in my hands. She put the remote control down and leaned her head back. Her eyes closed as we listened to Chaka Khan's "Everlasting Love".

I tenderly massaged each toe, starting with the baby toe. I pulled, stretched, and rolled them between my thumb and forefinger.

"Mmmmm, that feels good," Carmen moaned. The sound of her voice was so low and sexy I thought it was a part of the song.

I said nothing in response. I just continued giving each toe the attention it deserved. Before I moved from the right foot to the left, I massaged her calf muscle. She sensually inhaled, letting me know I'd hit the right spot. As I massaged every inch of her lower leg, I noticed my breathing had increased.

Carmen's heel was only five inches from my rising nature. I moved over to her left leg and duplicated my technique—but with a little more expertise since I'd learned her sweet spots.

When I finished massaging, some forty minutes later, I offered her a drink.

"No, thank you. Your hands have me intoxicated enough." We both laughed. "Can I use your restroom?"

"Sure. It's the second door on the right. The light switch is on your left." As she walked down my short hallway, I watched her ass until she disappeared into my bathroom.

"Would you like some water or juice?" I offered when she returned.

"Okay, I'll have some water. Just make sure you don't spike it," Carmen said in a lighthearted, accusatory tone.

"Damn, it took me all day to find these knockout drops," I replied with a grin full of devilment.

After killing the un-spiked glass of water, she thanked me and handed me the empty glass. A yawn escaped her.

"Tired, sweetheart?" I asked.

"Kind of, but you're not getting out of doing my toes that easily."

I noticed her southern drawl became more prominent as she relaxed. She repositioned herself on the sofa and gave me a choice of three polish colors: Fire Engine Red, Pale Pink, or Liquid Gold. My choice was Fire Engine Red. I placed her foot back on my thigh as I began my art project entitled, "Carmen's Toes".

Starting with her big toe, I took my time and stroked the red paint onto her perfect, white toenail. The color exploded onto her foot. After completing the first toe, I blew on her nail. She giggled as the breeze from my mouth tickled her foot.

"Now that's something I never got with my pedicures." A radiant smile escaped her.

That inspired me to put a lot more effort into the remaining nine toes. After I finished the first foot—even putting cotton balls between her toes—she leaned over and rubbed the top of my bald head.

"Thank you, Rio. You did a good job. Your girlfriend's lucky to have a man who does her toes."

"There you go with that girlfriend stuff. You're the one tied down, not me."

The feel of her nails on my head sent a pleasant jolt down my spine.

"Tied down to who?" she asked.

"You know who. Homeboy you were with at the Rasta House."

"His name is Bernard, and he is *not* my man. He's a guy from work."

"He sure looked like he was more than that."

"Are you jealous?" Carmen grinned and rubbed my cheek.

"Why should I be jealous?"

"Because Bernard was where you wanted to be."

"Where the hell did you get *that* idea?"

"You couldn't take your eyes off of us the entire night. Ray Charles could've seen that."

"You got it twisted. You're the one who was lookin' at *me*."

Carmen's company was refreshing. There was no pressure. We were free to be ourselves.

"Whatever, Rio. You were busy with your girl, anyway."

"Who?"

"That skinny girl with the nappy gold afro." There was a hint of resentment in her voice.

"You must be high. She's hardly my flava."

"Well, it looked like you were *her* flava."

"Oh, you jealous?" I said with a huge grin.

"Please, jealous of you and that nappy-headed wench? I don't think so." Her body language told me otherwise. She avoided my eyes during her answer.

It was 1:33 a.m., and I was getting both anxious and nervous after realizing the time. Not wanting to bring it to her attention for fear she would leave, I asked if she wanted to watch a movie.

"What kind of movies do you have?"

"It depends on what you like. Take a look at those DVDs over there next to the television."

We got up at the same time, me to take my chair back into the kitchen and her to walk over to my movie collection.

At that moment, there was only a foot of space between us. She made a weak attempt to bypass me. Before I knew what I was doing, my hands grabbed hers at waist length. Our fingers interlocked.

I looked into those black eyes. They told me it was okay; everything was all right.

The heat between us was almost visible, like heat waves on the street on a hot summer day.

The only sound was the sweet sax of Candy Dulfer, which drifted out of my speakers. The notes were like ropes, tying us together.

My thumbs rubbed hers as we held hands, letting nature take its course.

"You wanna dance?" came out of my mouth.

"Now?"

"Yeah, I love this song." I pulled her a little closer to me and put my arms around her waist. Carmen's arms wrapped around my shoulders and closed the gap between us.

"I have to tell you somethin'. I don't know how to slow dance," I said.

"You're doing a good job so far, Mr. Slick." Her smile was inches from my face.

We relaxed and drifted along with the music. I felt as though God had sprinkled a blessing on me.

I recalled many nights I'd had women in my place for a typical booty call. That night with Carmen was far from it. Being with her was actually *fun,* not just the mechanical "drink, smoke, talk, fuck, get out my house" type of date. After those encounters, I would wake up with a hollow feeling in my heart and a stranger in my bed. That shit was gettin' old.

When the song ended, we made no effort to separate.

I felt her finger slowly travel the length of my neck. I returned the favor by rubbing the small of her back.

I let the tip of my thumb sneak under the bottom of her blouse and rub back and forth across her spine.

Carmen rested her head on my shoulder as I combed her hair with my fingers. Soft, black, and silky was the only way I could describe her hair. I marveled at how easily my fingers worked their way through it.

More of her fingers went to the back of my neck, rubbing and massaging. I reached further up her warm back and traced the outline of her silky bra strap. I didn't attempt to unhook it, although I was tempted.

I opened my eyes and saw her neck and ear just below my hungry lips. She had a little mole right below her earlobe. I targeted it.

The dance turned into a slow sway, and her neck became my playground. I kissed her earlobe, tracing the outline of her ear with the tip of my tongue, mixing in nibbles between licks.

I tossed her scrunchie to the floor, freeing her from her ponytail. I placed both hands in her sexy tresses and spread her hair out evenly over her shoulders.

My hands fell from her hair to the sides of her face. At that moment, she opened her eyes halfway and looked into mine. There was no need for verbal conversation at that point. Nature had taken its course. I saw her lick her lips just before my eyes closed and her mouth opened.

My lips melted into hers, much like the way two drops of rain formed as one on contact. Our tongues, eager to please, wiggled and danced in each other's mouths.

She sensually stroked the back of my neck and head, as though she had read my mind and knew what made me throb.

Her hands went under my shirt as she caressed and faintly raked my bare back with her nails. Seal picked up as our background music when Candy Dulfer's mini concert ended.

I slipped my hands under her blouse and felt the warm skin of her back. I started at her slim waist and worked my way up to her 38c breasts. The feel of them through the soft, smooth fabric of her bra was almost unbearable.

I moved my hands further up and let my thumbs rub the tips of her hard nipples. The rest of my hands cupped the warm, soft flesh of her tits.

She gasped at my touch. Driven with desire, she attempted to take my shirt off. I gave her a hand by pulling my arms out of my shirt and letting it hit the floor.

As we kissed, I unbuttoned her shirt and lifted it up over her head. Carmen's shirt fell to our growing pile of clothing on the floor.

The feel of her skin against mine was electric. Her nipples were hard for me. I could feel them through her purple satin bra. Something about feeling her bra against me aroused me even more.

Her hands traveled from my waist to my ass as she pulled me closer to her magnificent body. Since I was wearing sweatpants, I knew damn well she could *feel* me. My dick was like granite. Between the crooning of Seal and my increased breathing, I heard her moan for my touch. I bent my knees and placed my leg between hers. She accommodated my move by straddling me. We both quivered as I grabbed her ass and pulled her down on my knob.

We kissed and rolled on each other in rhythm. Never had I felt so hot for a woman while we were still in clothes.

Our inhibitions turned to animal lust. Even though Seal was singing his ass off, the only sound we heard was our mingled moans. I lifted her up and she wrapped her legs around my waist as I carried her to my bedroom. En route to my room, our tongues intertwined.

After I sat down with Carmen in my lap facing me, I noticed a few of the cotton balls from between her toes had left a trail to my bedroom. It reminded me of the bread crumb trail left by Hansel and Gretel.

The only light in my room was from the streetlight outside. It gave the room a strange, but romantic orange hue through my blinds.

I worked to undo the top button of her shorts. Sensing my difficulty, Carmen placed her hands on top of mine, and seconds later, they were completely undone.

I rolled her on her side and untied the drawstring of my sweat pants. They hit the floor, starting a fresh pile of clothes.

While lying on her back, Carmen's eyes sparkled in the low light. I saw in her eyes that she was meant to spend many nights with me.

I reached for the hem of her shorts and removed them. Then, Carmen positioned herself in the center of the bed. I lay next to her and kissed her cloud soft lips as I rolled her over on top of me.

Her long hair fell down on my face and tickled my nose. Our lack of words was almost as erotic as our kissing. We were quickly learning what each other liked. Feeling her on top of me made my manhood rise like a cum-filled cobra.

I had an urge to *do* her without penetrating her. When we were kids, we called it getting some "panty juice."

The way her matching purple undies looked on her, Carmen could stand up to any of Victoria Secret's models. Our toes played with each other as she lay stretched out on top of me.

I reached between us and moved my swollen member so it rested against my stomach. I grabbed her butter-bowl ass and guided her down on it, causing her clit to line up with my pulsing dickhead. Judging from the long, low moan that escaped her, I'd hit the target.

Carmen rolled on my penis as I sucked her hard nipples through her satin bra material. I bit and nibbled them as Carmen let me in on a secret: She was a screamer. My biting her nipples and grinding my stiffy on her throbbing clit drove us both crazy.

Fighting the urge to add her purple French-cut panties to the pile of clothes on the floor, I rolled her over and kissed my way down to her tummy. On my voyage down south, I kissed her navel and played with her tiny hoop. As I approached her waiting pussy lips, I heard a low whimper.

Before I even began licking, I noticed a wet spot had already begun to spread. I licked her lips through her panties, tasting her sweetness through the purple screen.

Her hands were on my head as she forced, guided, and begged me to continue. Her whimpers stoked my fire.

I traced the split between her pussy lips with my tongue after seeing the outline and indentations of her wet, hot box through her panties.

There was no longer any top-level thinking between us, only a pure animal passion. Her legs spread W – I – D – E so I could have full access if I wished.

The only bit of control between us was the fact that I wanted to make her cum without going inside her. I poked my tongue in as far as the satin barrier allowed. Carmen writhed with pleasure. I believe the idea of being so close to penetration made us both wild.

My monster jumped as she pumped my tongue. I rubbed my hardness through my draws as I licked her, feeling fullness in my balls.

"Come here," she said in a low, sexy, animal-like whisper. That was all I needed to hear. I rose up and saw her hair spread like a fan on my comforter. Her legs were wide open, waiting for me to fill the void. Her hand replaced mine and stroked my cotton-covered penis as I maneuvered myself between her outstretched legs.

Her years of dancing showed in her flexibility. She placed the steel between my legs on top of her hot forge. It seemed as though there was a sexual telepathy between us.

I began thrusting my dick against her clit, trying to see if I could break through her panties and enter that heavenly hole.

"Please tell me you have a condom," she whispered in my ear.

"Not this time, princess. This is just foreplay," I whispered back. "I... like you... too much... to turn this... into... a... booty call... sweetheart," I said between soft kisses on her lips.

"Mmmmm... Rio... baby," Carmen moaned as she wrapped her legs around me.

"Don't move, don't... mooooove, Mmmmmm..." Carmen whimpered right before her body shivered. She let out the most passion-filled moan I'd ever heard.

Her legs vibrated like a too-tight guitar string. The stinging sensation on my back told me her nails were firmly in my flesh. The head of my manhood was right on her hole, with just a half inch of material separating us from true bliss. I felt my pre-cum drip. She knew I was close to climaxing as I pumped faster and harder. She nibbled my ear and opened her legs ever further, giving it all to me.

After seeing my face contort in ecstasy, she sucked my tongue, which caused my sperm to gush. I moaned with pleasure and jerked, releasing the final drops. I put my hands in her hair and felt a trace of sweat on her forehead. I then kissed her like there was no tomorrow.

As we drifted off to sleep, I felt her hand on my penis, squeezing the wet, warm cum spot on my draws she helped produce and knowing next time it could end up inside her.

CHAPTER TEN

As we lay together in the famous "spoon position", I thought about how it was some of the most intense sex I'd *never* had.

Her breathing was silent, soft and precious, like that of a newborn baby. I glanced at the glowing blue letters on my alarm clock and discovered we had been asleep for approximately four hours.

When I moved to pull my comforter over us, she stirred and pushed back against me, seeking the combined warmth of my body heat and that of the comforter. I pulled the cover up over her shoulders and watched her sleep. Her hair draped over the side of her face brought back memories of the passion we'd shared a mere few hours ago.

In the past, I would've been waiting for the moment when the female would wake up—sometimes with my help—and tell me she had to leave.

I'd pretend like I wanted her to stay, saying some shit like, "Awww baby, can't you just stay a little while longer?" as I prayed like hell she didn't change her mind.

With Carmen, I felt the total opposite. I intentionally didn't move much so I *wouldn't* wake her.

I woke out of a dreamless, dark sleep to find Carmen gone.

My first thought was: Is any of my stuff missing?

I guess I was so used to dealing with scandalous hoes that I had become conditioned to think the worst.

I looked at my clock and it told me it was 7:37 a.m. From the bathroom, I heard the sound of running water. My toilet was refilling after a flush.

The sound of the door creaking told me she had finished her business. Just then, the craziest image popped in mind of Carmen sitting on my toilet, smoking, and dropping shit in my toilet. What the hell was I on?

My muffled laugh damn near blew my cover of faking like I was still asleep. I cracked my right eye and watched as she picked up and examined her black top.

A cute smile crossed her lips as she looked at her shirt. I would've given my left nut to know what she was thinking at that moment.

She pulled the top down and shook her hair into place, as I'd imagined she had done many times before. Next, she placed her hands in her hair as she looked around for her scrunchie.

She found it under my coffee table. I'd hoped she wouldn't find it. I had plans on adding it to my sexual conquest trophy collection.

She reached into her seemingly bottomless bag and came out with a purple comb and black brush.

I watched as the comb effortlessly maneuvered through her hair as if she was combing it with the handle instead of the teeth. A few brush strokes to neaten it up, and in one quick motion, the scrunchie put a strangle hold on her hair, producing a ponytail.

After watching that ritual, I suddenly wanted her to hurry and get the fuck out my house. How many other niggas got that same treatment? I had a feeling I wasn't the only fella she was kickin' it with.

Was I set up from the git go?

I no longer felt the urge to feign sleep. I just lay on my side and watched as she slid her feet into her shoes.

There was an irrational anger brewing in me that I had to suppress before she came to my bedside to say goodbye, unless she decided to just sneak out the door.

The bitch.

I guess I was gettin' a taste of my own medicine. Usually, *I* was the one who left without saying goodbye after I'd gotten what I wanted.

To my surprise, she didn't pick up her coat and bag. Instead, she took a breath and walked toward the bedroom while trying to be as quiet as possible.

"Hey, how long have you been watching me?" she asked as that sunshine some would call a smile flashed in my eyes.

"Long enough."

"Oh. Are you okay?" Carmen asked as she sat down next to me with a look of concern on her face.

"I'm all right. I'm just weird when I wake up sometimes."

"I slept so good I almost forgot I have to be at church this morning. I know I won't make the nine o'clock service, so I'll have to attend the one at eleven o'clock."

"Sorry I made you late. It won't happen again."

"It's okay, Rio. I'm just as guilty," she said with a soft laugh.

Both of us sat there in silence, waiting for the other to make the next move.

"What time you get out of church?"

"Hmmmm, about one-thirty if I attend the late service and the preacher isn't too fired up. If not, it could be about two o'clock."

Since I don't attend church, I didn't want to give her the impression that I'd like to join her.

"I told my sister I'd come by this morning and take a look at her car. She said it's making some kind of noise. You know how you women don't know anything about cars," I said as my anger receded.

She pushed her eyebrows together. "What's that supposed to mean? Don't tell me you're one of 'those' men that think a woman doesn't know how to take care of a car."

It would be damned scary if she was really mad. Because as sweet as she looked, I bet she could be just as evil if provoked.

I sat up on my right elbow and rubbed her back. "I'm just messin' with you, Boo."

Carmen looked at my clock and sighed.

"I had a wonderful time, honey, but I have to go home and get ready for church." She rubbed the five o'clock shadow that covered my bald head.

Boy, if she was playing the role, it felt good.

"Okay, I'll walk you home."

"You don't have to. It's not like I live across town."

"No date of mine is walkin' home alone, even if it is daylight," I insisted. Before she could protest, I put my finger to her soft lips and shushed her. I grabbed my sweat pants and tee shirt as I went to the bathroom.

After brushing my teeth, I wiped the toothpaste from around my mouth, threw on my tee shirt and sweats, and opened the door. Sitting there like a good little girl, Carmen was watching TV.

"I didn't think you watched TV," I said.

"Why you say that?"

"I didn't see one in your place."

"Oh, I'm waiting for it to be delivered. I ordered a Phillips plasma screen TV, and it's taking forever to get here. Can you believe I ordered it a week ago?"

A plasma TV cost a few bucks, which had me thinking she must've been grating a lot of cheese at her job at PG&E.

"Yeah, I hate that, too. When did they say it would be delivered?" I couldn't wait to see that TV myself.

"Tuesday at the latest," she responded.

When Carmen got up and grabbed her coat, I got the feeling once again she does what we did that night every weekend. Before my anger could manifest itself, I grabbed my keys and walked her to the door.

As we walked down the hallway to the elevator, my nosy ass neighbor, the widow Mrs. Cleveland, walked toward us. She had lived in my building for as long as I could remember, at least six years, but I bet it was closer to a thousand. She looked like an evil and older Della Reese.

"Hello, Mrs. Cleveland," I managed to say as I tried to get to the elevator with Carmen as fast as I could.

"Good morning, you two," she said as she stopped in front of us, impeding traffic. "How y'all doin'?" she asked.

"Just fine. We're on our way out to get some morning air."

"Yes Lord, that's good for your soul. And who's *this* lovely lady on your arm?"

I couldn't believe Mrs. Cleveland tried to bust me out like that. It was true, she'd seen me with several different women—hell, a *lot* of different women—and more than a few times we'd met in that same scenario.

"Hi, Mrs. Cleveland, I'm Carmen. Pleased to meet you."

"Did you say your name's Carmen?"

"Yes."

"Do you attend St Lawrence's Church on 8th Avenue?"

"As a matter of fact, I do."

"Oh child, you don't remember me? We attend the same church!" Mrs. Cleveland said.

Ain't that a bitch! I just knew I was screwed. I was willing to bet she was gonna snitch me out.

"I'm so sorry. I just started going there a few weeks ago."

"I know, baby. I greet all the visitors and new members."

Damn, that's just what I needed.

Before things got out of hand any further, I grabbed Carmen's free hand and began to walk *around* the roadblock named Mrs. Cleveland.

"It looks like you won't make the early morning service," Mrs. Cleveland said while grinning, as if to say, 'I know you two were up screwin' all night and now you're going to miss the service.'

"I know, but I wanted to compare the eleven o'clock service to the nine o'clock service and see which one I like best," Carmen responded to my surprise. She played it off smooth as hell.

Just when I thought we had gotten away from "Mrs. CNN", she dropped this bomb: "I've been trying to get Mr. Man here to come visit our church. Is he joining you today?"

I was stunned. Sensing the awkwardness of the situation, Carmen also cleaned that up.

"He can't today. He has to go help his sister get her car running so she can get to church on time."

Goddamn, Carmen was smooth…a little *too* smooth. She was either the coolest chick I'd ever been with or the slickest. Satisfied that she'd gotten on my nerves, "Mrs. Nosy Ass" stepped out the way and hummed a tune as she continued down the hall toward her domain.

"I'll see you at the eleven o'clock service, Carmen," she shouted back and then disappeared behind her door.

"That was interesting," Carmen said as we took the stairs. "She really likes to talk I see."

"You just don't know," I replied. "That woman has been my nemesis since day one. She stays in my business."

Carmen laughed. "I can imagine her with a glass to her ear, against the wall, listening to you and your company."

She was closer to being right than she knew.

Upon exiting my building, Carmen stretched and relished the feel of the late September sun on her face.

"I love September. It's my favorite time of the year," I commented.

"Mine, too. I love the fall. It kind of reminds me of home." Her mood changed for a moment as if she felt a sudden pain, then it was gone. I started to ask her if she was okay, but for some reason, I felt it best to let it go.

"How did you get the name Rio?" she asked, changing the subject.

"My father named me. He was supposed to go to Rio de Janeiro with his brothers on Christmas Eve, but I decided, two months prematurely, that it was time for me to make my entrance in to this world. Needless to say, Moms made him stay home. So, as a reminder, he named me Rio…Rio Romero Clark."

"That's a cute name. I like it," she said with a smile.

"Some of my friends call me R.C."

"I think I'll stick to Rio. I like how it sounds."

"Ohhhh, so I guess that means you're not my friend, huh?"

"Well, you still haven't filled out a friendship application yet."

I stopped her in the middle of the sidewalk, kissed her deeply in front of the world, and asked, "Do I still need to?"

"Maybe not."

Once at her building, I let her hand go so she could get her keys out of her bag. I noticed a set of car keys on her key chain, but I'd never seen her drive. I made a mental note to ask her about it later, and then followed her into the lobby. Her reflection stared at me in the polished brass doors of the elevator. I wondered what she was thinking.

Did she want me to leave?

Was that a one-night stand?

What the fuck?

Just when my wonder almost turned to anger, the elevator arrived with a soft chime instead of the old school *ding* the ancient elevator in my building issued.

"Damn! You live in a cool building," I said.

"Humph! It should be. It cost enough to live here."

Inside the elevator, she pushed the button for the sixth floor. I felt her hand reach for mine as we leaned back against the elevator wall.

Instead of merely giving her my hand, I turned and kissed her. Before we knew it, the familiar chime told us the short trip was over.

When the doors opened, a little girl stood there open mouthed. She was followed by someone who I assumed was her brother.

"Ohhhhhhh Carmen! You was kissin,'" she said with lips that formed a perfect letter "O".

"Be quiet, girl. Mind ya own business," her brother said. For some reason, his eyes lingered on me. He looked at me like I'd stolen something.

Carmen gave the girl a kiss on the cheek and said, "We were just talking."

"People don't talk with their lips together," the little girl responded.

"How are you, Ray?" Carmen asked the stone-faced boy.

"I'm cool," he said as he pushed the button marked "LOBBY".

As the door closed, he managed to mean mug me one more time.

"What the hell is wrong with homeboy?" I asked.

"I think he's a little jealous of you. He has a slight crush on me," Carmen said with a smile.

No wonder he was looking at me crazy. I had his chick.

"Well, he'll have to get over it." I grabbed Carmen's heart-shaped ass.

"What time do you have, sweetie?" she asked.

"It's about 8:48 a.m."

"I'll have to hurry before my ride gets here. I usually ride with my girlfriend, Zoe. Sometimes, we stop at the Country Kitchen for a quick breakfast before church if we attend the late service."

"Does she know you're running late?"

"No, but she knows if I don't call her, or if she calls me by eight o'clock, we'll be going to the late service."

"Ohhh, I see, just in case you playas are too played out from the night before, huh?"

"Ha-ha. Very funny," she said with her hands akimbo on those curvaceous hips. "You're the one, Mr. Rio! You even have a player name to prove it."

"Now ain't that some shit. You trippin', woman," I said with a laugh.

"You probably had to hide your girlfriend's stuff before I got to your house last night."

"Oh see, you're out of line for that." I wrapped my hands around her waist, pulling her close to me so we were crotch to crotch, and then kissed the tip of her nose.

"You know you is my baby," I said.

"Oh really? How can I tell?"

"If you weren't, I woulda kicked you out at three o'clock this morning."

"You mean you would've *tried* to kick me out."

"You think you bad, huh?"

"I know I'm bad."

"Show me how bad."

"If you're lucky, I just may do that," Carmen said. Her smile was like a warm jacket on a cold day.

"Well, let me get out of here so you can get ready. I'll look for you later, okay?"

"Yes, you do that," Carmen said as she unlocked her door.

"I should be back around two or three, depending on Zoe. We may go to lunch instead of breakfast. I'll tell your neighbor you said hi."

"Oh, you have jokes, I see."

"Sometimes," she said as she opened the door and stepped inside. Before closing the door on our first date, Carmen surprised me by saying, "Come here," and grabbed the back of my bald head. She pulled me to her mouth and kissed me.

"Don't forget about me."

"How can I?" I said and left.

Outside her building, I felt real damn good.

We had one hell of an erotic night.

I replayed the night's events over and over in my head, determined not to let that be the last one.

During the short walk home, I discovered I was hungry, as hell. Not being dressed, I decided to go cook me something to eat. Upon entering my spot, I was immediately hit by a sense of longing for a repeat of the previous night's sexual extravaganza.

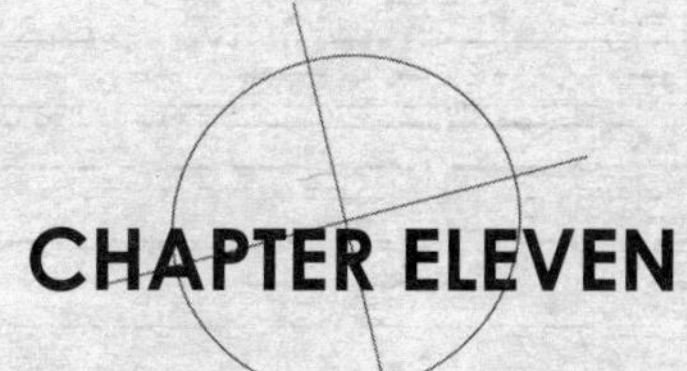

CHAPTER ELEVEN

The phone rang. It was my boy, Dominic.

"Wassup, Rio? I tried to call you last night. What you get into, dawg?"

"Not a whole lot. Just kicked it with this chick," I answered, not wanting to share too much with him.

"Who was it? She got a friend or sister? Holla at me!" Dee laughed his crazy laugh.

"She ain't got shit for you, fool! What the hell you doin' callin' me this early in the mornin'? You usually sleep in on the weekends."

"Brenda was trippin' last night, so I left and stayed at Renee's house. You know how we do it, playa. I was on my way home and called to see what you were gettin' into today."

"You mean to tell me you ain't been home yet?"

"Hell naw! Brenda told me to get the hell out last night, so I left."

"Nigga, tell me what you really did. I know you better than that. I bet you started some shit with Brenda just so you could have an excuse to stay out all night. You probably told her you were with me."

Dee laughed like a hyena and said, "Yeah, nigga! I was fuckin' with Renee earlier that day and she had me hard as hell. She was tellin' me shit like she was gonna suck my dick all night if I could get out the house. I wasn't about to pass that shit up!"

"Are you talkin' about 'big girl' Renee?"

Dee was the kind of dude who would screw anything with a hole. I'd seen him with some women that made me say OUCH! He's had a few cutie pies, but that wasn't always the case.

"Yeah, that's my girl. You don't know nothin' about that big girl lovin'," he said.

"You got that shit right. Where you at?"

"Coming down your block now. What you got to eat?"

"I ain't got nothin' for ya bummin' ass. Come on up. Later."

After I hung up the phone, I discovered I was in good enough of a mood to even deal with Dee's insanity.

It's amazing the power of the almighty pussy. It'll make a man leave the mother of his kid at home just to sneak out for a piece. I'm damn glad I didn't have any kids. I felt that I had at least a good six more years before I'd even consider havin' any squabs. Even though I hated condoms, those muthafuckas had kept me out of a *lot* of trouble. The threat of AIDS and babies made me wrap my monster. Well, most of the time it did.

In the fridge, I had one onion, two cans of Coca Cola, half a pitcher of water, three slices of Salami, an empty milk carton, and a pot with something in it that seemed to have spawned a few new life forms. Dee was gonna starve unless he wanted to go get something to eat.

I heard the familiar sound of Dee's voice outside my door shortly after buzzing him in. He was the most talkative dude I'd ever met. Dee was harassing the white girl who lived across from me, running the same lines of bullshit I'd heard him use many times before.

My neighbors name was Sabrina Rodgers. She was about 5'2", 115 pounds, red hair, green eyes, and no lips. She was decent looking for a white girl.

She was twenty-four years old, single with no kids, and as far as I knew, had no man. I had seen plenty of females going in and out of her door, white, black, Asian, the whole rainbow.

I think there was some hot lesbian action jumping off in Unit 3307. I watched as my neighbor, being as polite as possible, tried to let Dee know she wasn't interested. I decided to throw her a lifesaver.

"Dee, your son's on the phone."

"Okay, tell him I'll be right there. Well look, Sabrina, I have to go. Can I give you a call later?" Dee persistently asked.

"No, I'm sorry. My boyfriend wouldn't like that," she said and gave him the "if-I-was-single-I-would-but-you-know-how-it-is" look.

"Well, take my card just in case thangs change," Dee said and gave her a grin like the Big Bad Wolf.

Sabrina took his card—obviously just so she could get away—faked a smile, and headed to the elevator, seeking freedom from the Big Bad Wolf.

"Nigga, why you cock blockin'? You see I had that bitch!" Dee said as he followed me inside.

"The only thing I did was save ya ass from gettin' pepper sprayed by that dyke. I told you she's strictly clitly."

"That just means mo' pussy for me. If you wasn't player hatin' on me, I coulda hooked up with that hoe and probably got you some of that pussy, too."

"Boy, you a fool," I said and shook my head. Dee looked in my fridge and discovered the fine cuisine inside.

My mind was still on Carmen. The taste of her lips was still in my mouth.

"Hey man, is this all you got to eat? Damn, you sorry. You need to get you a bitch in here to cook for ya ass."

"If I wanted a broad here to cook for me, I would have one. I'm not the one who spent a night with a chick and couldn't get fed. You *must* not have hit it right," I said, leaving him speechless.

Dee gave me the finger. "Fuck you, nigga! At least I got my dick sucked."

"Hey, I'm about to hit the shower real quick. Then we can go get something to eat."

"Dude, what the hell are all these cotton balls on ya floor?" he asked, holding one between his thumb and forefinger. "What's this red shit? You been bleedin'?"

I'd forgotten all about the trail of cotton balls from the previous night.

"That's nail polish."

"What! You paintin' your toes now, nigga? You better hurry up and get some pussy."

"I had some company last night and I helped her paint her toes."

"I wouldn't do that for any broad. Real pimps don't do that kinda shit. I'm gonna have to pull your player card, homie."

Growing weary of Dee's bullshit, I flipped him half the peace sign, disposed of the cotton balls, grabbed some clothes, and headed for the shower.

After getting dressed, I tossed my dirty stuff in the hamper and went to see what Dee was up to.

"Hey, wake up!" He lay on my couch, sleeping like a dead man.

"I'm up. I was just waitin' for you. I'm hungry as hell," he said. We settled on going to a local spot on the east side called "Johnny's" where we could have some real home cooked grub. All the way there, I was forced to listen to the "Adventures of Dee". He finally ran out of tales from the previous night's freak show by the time the food arrived.

"How you gonna explain where you were last night to Brenda?"

"I'm gonna tell her you and me went out drinkin' and I spent the night at your house."

"And you think she's gonna buy that?"

"Hell, she better. She's the one who threw me out the house," he said with a mouth full of pancakes.

"You could've at least called me to let me know what you were up to, fool. I told you, you need to use more finesse."

"I tried to call you all night, but ya ass didn't answer the phone. You *need* to get a cell phone or a pager, nigga."

"Fuck that! I don't need to have folks trackin' me down. *I'm* in control of who I wanna see or hear from."

"Anyway, if you hear from Brenda, we hooked up about nine o'clock last night and went clubbin' at the French Quarters in Palo Alto. I spent the night and didn't leave until," he looked at his watch, "ten-thirty this morning."

As I figured, he was gonna use the old "I-spent-the-night-at-Rio's-house" excuse. That wasn't the first time I'd been his scapegoat.

I knew there were two sides to every story, but I didn't think I could stay someplace where I wasn't happy. Dee had crossed the unfaithful line so many times that Brenda would've been more than justified in going out and screwin' a gang of men.

He kept telling me he was planning on moving out, but I think he knew how good he had it at home. Brenda was the type of woman who took care of the house, bills, kid, put up with his bullshit, and didn't complain because she was raised old school.

Hell, I was willing to bet she was already out messing around. Women could be just as doggish as men. They're just smoother with their shit than most men are.

That was one reason why I hadn't gotten married yet. It was hard for me to trust a female. However, I was feeling Carmen for some reason. She was the first woman I liked enough to actually want to have sex with and *not* kick out when we were done.

I wanted something more.

What that something was, I had no idea.

I'd been through so many one-nighters, I was tempted to put a sign over my door that read, "Don't bring your toothbrush, 'cause you ain't stayin' that long."

♦♦♦♦♦♦♦♦♦♦♦

Dee dropped me off at my place and went home, satisfied with his alibi being airtight. The shit you had to go through being in a relationship was nuts.

I was tired as a bastard. My weekend activities had caught up with me. I kicked off my shoes while I simultaneously looked for my remote control and cordless phone. Those were two of the best inventions since the wheel.

It was 12:51 p.m., about ten minutes to kickoff. The Raiders were playing the Broncos in Denver, so the game wasn't blacked out. Before focusing on the game, I went to the bathroom. Once I was done, I went and sat on my *real* throne. I'd given that name to the black leather recliner I bought six years ago when I first moved into my apartment. It was comfortable as hell and knew the contours of my body well.

After sitting, something on the end table on the left side of my sofa caught my eye. When I realized what it was, I broke out in a big ass Kool-Aid grin. It was a bottle of Fire Engine Red nail polish. How the hell did I miss that? I could've sworn it wasn't there earlier. I held it in my hand and slumped down into my recliner, ignoring the announcers telling me which team had won the coin toss.

I was transfixed on the bottle of nail polish. The way Carmen closed her eyes with pleasure as I massaged those cute, size seven feet and the way the color came alive on her toenails played in my mind.

I had a burning desire to be with her. At 1:18 p.m., I paced the floor with the polish in one hand and the cordless phone in the other.

"Slow your roll, playboy," I told myself. "Sit ya ass down and relax."

After all, she was probably still in church or having lunch with Zoe. I sat in my chair still holding on to the bottle of polish. It turned over and over in my hand as I attempted to get into the football game.

I had dozed off by halftime and woke up at 2:21 p.m. I imagined Carmen had finished her lunch and may even be home.

I did my *damndest* not to pick up the phone and call. I even went as far as to move the phone to the coffee table across from me, like that would stop me from calling.

That was the part of the game I called "Make or Break". It's when after you first have sex with a new partner and you've both had time to reflect on what happened, you decide whether or not it's worth a second round.

"Make or Break" afforded you the opportunity to think of all the excuses in the world not to see the other person again. You could say stuff like "I haven't called because I lost your number", "I think we're moving too fast", or "I just want to be friends." On rare occasions, I felt anxious when I really wanted the second round—like I did with Carmen.

Since she lived right down the street, it made matters worse. That meant if there was no "round two", I'd still have to see her from time to time and be haunted by the memories of what once was. Like Uncle Lee always told me, "The game is cold, Youngblood."

CHAPTER TWELVE

I gathered myself and cleaned up a little during halftime to help get my mind off of Carmen. When I got done, I sat back in my recliner. I picked up the bottle of nail polish and continued rotating it in my hand as the game wound down to the two-minute warning. As soon as they broke away to a commercial, the phone rang. According to my Caller ID, it was from someone named Carmen Massey.

"Hello?" I answered as though I didn't know who it was.

"Hello, Rio, how are you?"

"I'm good, just here watching the last of the Raiders game. What you up to, princess?" I said in the coolest voice I could, trying not to let my giddiness show.

"Relaxing. I didn't get out of church 'til almost three o'clock. The preacher was on a roll. After that, Zoe and I came back to my place and ate some of my leftover spaghetti. I saw your car and was going to call earlier, but I knew you were into your game and I didn't want to disturb you. I know how you men are about your football. After all, I have five brothers."

I guess I passed the first round.

"Is that right? You have any sisters?"

"Yes, I have two older and one younger. Do you have any?"

"Yeah, I have an older sister and a younger brother. I'm the middle child."

"I'm kind of the middle child, too. I have three older brothers, two older sisters, one younger sister, and a set of younger twin brothers."

"I guess you are almost in the middle. Is your friend still there?"

"Yes, but she's getting ready to leave as we speak. Can you call me back in about ten minutes so I can see her out?"

"Okay, I can do that." After we hung up, I was pumped up as hell. Was it the classic case of the thrill of the chase, or was I really feeling her?

I wasn't sure yet, but I knew one thing, I wasn't gonna rush things. I liked how we got along. Our chemistry was cool, even though I didn't trust women much. My lack of trust stemmed from the way I was raised. My father, my uncles, and even my grandpa were all players from what I understand. All I heard growing up was "you can't trust a bitch" or "you have to always keep a spare woman."

I remember when I was about six years old riding with Pops on our way to his girlfriend's house. At the time, I didn't know what was up. I only knew her as Miss Pearl.

She lived in Richmond in a white house with red steps. Why I remember that I don't know. Maybe it's because that's as far as I was allowed to go with Pops. He used to always buy me a grape Fanta soda and a bag of Lay's potato chips. He would say to me, "Stay here, Rio. I'll be back in a few minutes. Blow the horn if you get scared or if you need me, okay?"

I'd nod my head like a good boy as I opened my chips and savored the taste of the purple soda. He never stayed too long, maybe about thirty minutes at the most.

Back then, you didn't have to worry much about kidnappings and shit. It seemed like as soon as I was drinking the last of my Fanta, Miss Pearl's door would open and there would be Pops fixing his clothes and straightening his hat as he said his goodbyes.

I never saw him hug or kiss her, but I'm sure there was a different goodbye scene which took place behind her front door.

Pops must have gotten a lot of blow jobs from Miss Pearl because he was always neat when he came back to the car. His hair was still cool as well as his clothes. He wore a big afro back then and kept it shaped up. He always had the latest fashions no matter how crazy they were at the time.

My father was a well educated man. He graduated from UCLA with a degree in Sociology in 1960. He moved to Oakland four years later and lives in the same house. He began teaching at UCSF in 1968 after a few stints teaching high school. He met my mother, Oleda Swanson, while working for UCSF. She was a student counselor and from what I was told, it was love at first sight. They met in a hallway one day, had dinner that night, and were married less than a year later, with my sister Yvette growing in my mother's belly.

They had what would be considered a good marriage: nice home, good kids, good jobs. The American dream.

As I got older, I started noticing things. My parents did a good job hiding their problems. As it turned out, my father had an addiction to the "Almighty Pussy".

I'm sure Yvette understood what was going on a lot better than me and my little brother Damon. Yvette would threaten us with great bodily harm if she caught us listening. I did occasionally hear stuff like "who was that hoe?" or "you ain't shit" when I did eavesdrop.

Maybe it was for the best that Yvette did try to prevent us from hearing. It was easier to keep up the false front that everything was peachy in the Clark household.

Pops and I still had our grape Fanta and chips days, and I often wondered if he ever took Yvette or Damon with him on his little visits to see his mistress.

In retrospect, I doubt that he did. I know Yvette would've not only snitched on him, but she would have been on the horn the entire time Pops was gettin' his freak on. And Damon would have insisted on coming in. After all, he was the baby and loved getting all the attention he could.

Therefore, I was left being the logical choice. He could leave the house with me and look completely innocent to Moms—a father taking his boy out for a ride in the Lincoln.

He once told me every man should own a Lincoln at least once in his lifetime and gave me a wink. The wink indicated to me a Lincoln was the kind of car a *real* player would drive.

Funny the things you remember from your childhood. I remember the clothes he wore, the smell of his cologne, and the air conditioning blowing in my face the day he gave me that wink as we were off on another "Miss Pearl" run.

♦♦♦♦♦♦♦♦♦♦♦

It had been about twenty minutes since I last talked to Carmen. She said to call her back in ten, but I made her wait a few extra minutes. After deciding she'd waited long enough, I picked up the phone and dialed the magic numbers. She picked up on the second ring.

"Hello?"

"May I speak to Carmen?"

"This is she. What you up to, Rio?"

"Not much. Did I give you enough time?"

"Yes, I was just watching some TV and wondering what I'm going to cook for dinner."

"Oh, did your TV get delivered?"

"No, I'm watching the one in my bedroom."

"Cool. You decide what you gonna have for dinner?"

"No, not yet. Since I had spaghetti earlier, I'm not very hungry right now, but I know I'll be later. What are you having, Mr. Rio Romero Clark?"

"I dunno. I have a taste for some good ol' soul food, though."

"That does sound good. What do you like?"

"I love smothered steak, rice and gravy, mixed vegetables, and red Kool-Aid."

Carmen laughed in my ear. "I know you did not say red Kool-Aid."

"Yes, I did. I got some ghetto in me, baby."

"Well, I don't have any *red* Kool-Aid, but I can help you with all the rest. That's if you're interested."

"Hell yeah, I'm interested! For a hook up like that, you can get your dishes washed, floor mopped, and the garbage taken out!"

"I want that in writing."

"Are you serious about cookin', Carmen?"

"Yes, I haven't had any smothered steak in a while."

"Well, in that case, you want me to bring anything?"

"Hmmmmm, let me check... No, I think I have everything. Just bring your appetite and your dishwashing gloves."

"Okay. I can do that, Ms. Got-Jokes. When's a good time for me to stop by?"

"If you like, you can come now and keep me company while I cook."

"A'ight. I'll be there in about twenty minutes."

"Okay, Rio, see you then. Bye."

Grinning like the Cheshire cat from "Alice in Wonderland", I changed into slacks, a dress shirt, and loafers. I went through my sweat pants pockets and found the Juicy Fruit wrapper with Angelina's phone number on it. I put it into my "box of stuff" I kept in the closet. The only way anybody could find it is if they were looking for it, and believe me, I had run into some nosy ass women who had gone through my shit before. Of course, they were no longer in the picture.

I took my time walking to her place. It gave me the chance to clear my head and get my cool together. A few minutes later, I was at the locked lobby door of her building. I buzzed "Unit #616" and heard the familiar vocal tone and well-pronounced words, laced with a hint of a southern drawl.

"Hello?"

"Hey! It's me, Rio."

"Okay, come on up."

Living there within a stone's throw of Lake Merritt, she had to be paying a grip for rent. Even though I lived only a few buildings down from her, her building was considerably more modern than the one I lived in.

While waiting for the elevator, I felt an unfamiliar feeling: Butterflies in my gut.

What the hell was going on? If Uncle Lee was there, he would have laughed his ass off.

He always told me *never* let a female give you butterflies. Always look at all of them the same way, as just another piece of ass. Ultimately, that's all they were. That was one of his favorite sayings. Most times, I could pull it off with no problem, but sometimes, the butterflies turned into vampire bats.

I was cool leaving the elevator. But before I knocked on the door, I decided to be an ass and put my finger over the peephole.

"Who is it?"

"Federal Express, ma'am. I have a delivery for you." After a moment's hesitation, she said, "Rio, is that you?"

She had one of those swiveling type peepholes, and I could feel her trying to move it around to see who the hell was on the other side of her door. "BOO!" I shouted as I removed my finger.

I stepped back and put on the most innocent face I could as she unlocked her deadbolt.

"Okay, smart-ass, you almost didn't get in." She tried to look hard, but the upturned corners of her mouth deceived her.

"Hi," I said as I kissed her growing smile.

"What was that kiss for, funny man?"

"Just because." I entered the doorway.

It was apparent she had been busy getting her place together. The boxes which once sat in the corner of the living room were gone. There was something else different, but I couldn't put my finger on it.

"Have a seat. Here, I'm sure you'd like this." She handed me a remote control.

That's what it was! Carmen had moved her TV from the bedroom to the living room.

"Go ahead and make yourself at home. I just started the steak."

After taking a good look around, I noticed nothing she owned came from the flea market or a secondhand store. She had some lavish shit. It looked like she was used to having only the finest in life.

"Would you like some wine? I have red and white."

"You have any Ripple?"

A look of disgust crossed her face. "Hell no! You have me mixed up with one of your tramps."

"Well, in that case, I'll have some white wine."

From the kitchen, I heard the pop of a cork followed by the sound of liquid leaving the confinements of one container only to enter another.

Her tan leather couch soaked me in. When she brought me my glass of wine, I saw she was wearing a purple Minnesota Vikings jersey, blue jean shorts, and white booties on her feet. The jersey was so long it fit her like a mini skirt. Her legs were flawless and smooth as a baby's ass.

"How long have you been dancing?" I asked as I examined her sexy legs.

"All my life it seems."

A bear trap-like comb held her hair up on the top of her head. She sat next to me on the couch after handing me my glass of wine and holding her own.

"Let's toast," I suggested as I raised my glass.

"Okay, how about to a new friendship?"

"And one that lasts," I added as our glasses clinked.

After a few sips of wine, she went to check on the steak. She sure knew how to make a brotha feel at home. I admit I did have chauvinistic tendencies, but there was something about a woman in the kitchen that turned me on something fierce.

I guess it's similar to a woman liking a man in a uniform. That was one thing she'd never see me in if I had it my way, though. I didn't work my ass off getting my Cisco certification to end up wearin' somebody's uniform. I landed a job at the phone company in the networking division and got to wear whatever I wanted.

Even though I had a 3.5 GPA in high school, three B's stopped me from going to college: Breast, Blunts, and Buddies. I was too caught up in the streets.

♦♦♦♦♦♦♦♦♦♦♦

After the toast, Carmen and I sat and talked for a while. The TV was on just for background noise. The conversation was so good we almost forgot about the food.

"Can I use your bathroom so I can wash my hands?"

"Yes. It's the room at the end of the hall with the sink in it."

"Ha-ha, you mucho funny."

Her bathroom was even plush. Everything in it was black and Lavender, along with some tight artwork on the walls.

The only other colors in there were from the many, many candles that encircled the room. It wasn't like she just cleaned it up because I was coming over. It looked as though that was the norm—and I liked that.

Outside the plush restroom, the smells that emanated from the kitchen made my stomach talk. Carmen had fixed me a plate which contained steaming smothered steak on a bed of pure white rice and its neighbors were fried cabbage and black-eyed peas.

"Oh, I see you got skills," I commented with a wide grin.

"How do you know? You haven't even tasted it yet."

"Well, if it tastes half as good as it looks, I'm gonna be buggin' you for the next hundred years or so for meals."

"Be careful what you say, Mr. Rio." Carmen sat down, closed her eyes, and said a silent blessing.

Looking at her with her eyes closed and head bowed, I imagined her sitting down to dinner as a kid with her other eight siblings, enjoying that very same meal.

After the first bite of steak, I was ready to reserve the next hundred years of my meals there.

Over dinner, I learned a lot more about my girl. I found out she moved to California two years ago, even though she hadn't been there since she was a kid. In her haste to escape Keith's punk-ass, Carmen settled for an apartment in a rough neighborhood in East Oakland. She rarely went outside because the area was so bad.

The cops even had a special name for that area. It was called the "Kill Zone". After living in Beirut, California—a.k.a. East Oakland—for almost a year, she moved down the street from me. Carmen had been living down the street from me for over a year and I'd rarely ever seen her. I also learned were her birthday was November 8th, she would be turning thirty-two—she was two years older than me. She was the proud owner of a 1998 Mustang, but left it in Alabama because she hated driving in the Bay Area.

From what I'd gathered so far, she came from family money. Her father was a dentist and her mother a real estate broker. Each of the kids, including Carmen, had their own homes back in Alabama.

For some reason, she didn't go too deep into her own personal past, just sharing the schools she attended, favorite things to do in Alvintown, being country and cooking.

After polishing off that good meal, I felt like King Tut with my Queen about three feet away from me.

"Would you like some dessert?"

"Oh no, baby, I'm about to burst."

"Are you sure? I have some of that sweet potato pie I was telling you about."

"Don't tell me you made some sweet potato pie, too."

"Yes, I did. I made it earlier this afternoon while the game was on. I had a taste for some."

"You're foul for that! Now you know I have to have at least one piece."

She cut me a slice that was almost one quarter of the pie. She cut herself a thin sliver and joined me at the table.

I had fun spending time with her. We had a real good meal, and the funny thing was my entire focus had been on her, not sex.

Watching her eat pie, however, did make me wonder how her lips would feel engulfing my penis. Before I let "little head" take over my thoughts, I asked her about her choice of artwork.

"My mother got me started collecting artwork two years ago when she came back from a trip to Africa. I fell in love with the sculptures and paintings she brought back with her."

Carmen pointed out a foot-high statue of an African warrior, spear upraised and shield at his side as though he was running toward battle. The likeness was right on the money.

"She gave me this for my thirtieth birthday. It was hand carved by an old African man from a single piece of wood."

"No shit?"

"She met him in a village while on safari. Through a translator, he told her to pick out a piece of wood from his wood pile, come back in a day, and she would have something special." Carmen held the statue out to me. I studied the finished product in my own hands. The artist did damn good work.

"Sometimes, I go to art shows and buy pieces."

I pointed to a painting on the wall. "Did you get this painting from your mother?"

It was an image of a topless African woman in a leopard-skin skirt with a matching head wrap. She stood at the edge of a watering hole as two kids splashed in the water. The scene was right out of National Geographic.

"No, I bought that one at an art festival in Sausalito last summer."

Carmen told me the painting was by a famous African artist—whose name I couldn't pronounce—and the last appraisal on it was about $7500.

Compared to the Oakland Raiders memorabilia on my walls, along with the picture of my parents on their twenty-fifth anniversary, I was a little art challenged.

A melodic chime from the grandfather clock in the far corner reminded us of the time: 6:30 p.m.

"Well, I guess it's time for me to do the dishes."

"No, I'll do them *this* time. You'll just owe me," Carmen said as she went to the kitchen and ran some dishwater. The kitchen was sparkling clean in no time at all. The food was put away in actual containers, not stuffed in the fridge while still in the pots like I'd been known to do on occasion.

She was one hell of a woman, at least so far. I hadn't known her long enough to make the final call, but so far, she displayed definite "wifey" material.

After she finished cleaning up the kitchen, she took her place next to me—under my right arm—on the couch.

I rubbed her shoulder as we watched Fox's Sunday night lineup. My hand worked its way into her hair. Up close, I saw she had what some folks called "good hair." I removed the comb that held her hair up. Her hair was set free and fell to its customary place a bit below her shoulders.

"Damn, your hair is soft. You must have Indian in your family," I joked.

It killed me when a nigga with decent hair would claim to have some "Indian" in their family.

"Actually, you're right. My grandmother was a full-blooded Blackfoot Indian." She got up and went into her room.

Carmen returned with a black and white, 8x10 picture in a silver frame of a chocolate, dark man in a black suit with a beautiful, full-blooded Indian woman. It looked like the picture had been taken back in the thirties.

"Her maiden name was Reyna Wild Deer. She met my grandfather in West Virginia back in 1921. He was twenty and she was fourteen when they got married."

"I see you got it honestly."

"Yeah, a few years ago, I let my hair grow until I was able to put it in two long braids that reached the middle of my back. I got tired of people calling me Pocahontas." She put the picture on the coffee table.

"When you gonna grow it like that so I can see?" I combed her soft hair with my fingers.

"It doesn't take long for my hair to grow. I usually cut it every other year. I'm due to cut it off this summer."

"No!" I poked my lip out like a little kid on the verge of a tantrum.

"I have to, sweetie. It gets in my way when it gets too long."

"How about I promise to help you wash and brush it?"

"Rio, you're silly."

"Pleeeeeeease?" I poked my lip out further.

"I'll think about it if you pull that lip back in. Do you always poke your lip out when you want something?"

"Depends on what I want." I put my lips on hers and kissed her.

At first, it was just a quick peck on the lips. But when she continued to look in my eyes as I backed away, I stopped my retreat and returned to her mouth, inserting tongue.

She put her hand behind my neck as I kissed her long and slow. We took a break for air, then resumed. I kissed her ear as she moved her head slowly to the rhythm of my kisses.

"Mmmmm, Carmen," I whispered in her ear as I continued to kiss her ear and neck.

"Yes, baby," was her soft reply. As we continued to kiss on the couch, I managed to kick off my loafers and lay back with her lying on top of me.

After we took a short break from our necking, she laid her head sideways on my chest. I brushed her hair back so I could see the side of her beautiful face.

Her eyes closed as she listened to my heartbeat talk to her. We lay like that for a while as I rubbed her back and head. I hugged her tight and she hugged me back as our feet rubbed together, getting acquainted with one another.

Her breathing took on a sleeper's rhythm. As she fell asleep on top of me, I was conscious of the ticking of the grandfather clock above the sound of the latest "Got Milk?" commercial in the background.

While listening to the steady "tick, tick, tick, tick" of Grandpa Clock, I reluctantly gave in to the Sandman.

The next thing I knew, the remote had fallen out of my hand to the floor. My arms encircled Carmen as we both fell asleep.

I stirred awake to the sound of the ten o'clock news. We had slept for about two and a half hours.

Carmen was still asleep. When I bent my head down and kissed the top of her head, her eyes fluttered a little as though she was disoriented.

"Oh my God! What time is it, honey?" Carmen asked.

"It's about ten after ten."

"What? Were you sleeping, too?"

I grinned at her. "Yeah, I was knocked out. I guess we did the black thing—ate and fell asleep."

"What time do you have to get up for work, Carmen?"

"I usually get up by five in the morning so I can make it to work by seven. By the time I get dressed, have breakfast, and grab the bus, I arrive at work about 6:40 and have time for tea before I start."

"Damn! Let me get out of here so you can get some rest."

"I'll be okay, Rio. I'm a night owl."

"Shhhhhhhh!" I put my finger to her lips. "You need to get ya rest."

When she got up, I noticed how warm she was on top of me. I'd have to remember that when the rainy season arrived. Her body heat could come in handy.

When I sat up to put my shoes back on, she went to the bathroom. When she returned, she walked over and rubbed my head.

Carmen watched as I flipped through the TV channels in silence, neither of us wanting to be the one to end the evening.

I took the role of the bad guy and began the ending of the night. I stood up, stretched, and looked down at the indentation I'd left in the couch. I made a mental note to work on making that my own personal spot.

"Well, Love, it's time for me to cut out." I took her hand and walked toward the door.

A yawn snuck up on her. Before she could get her hand up to cover her mouth, I caught a glimpse of her nearly perfect teeth.

"Oh, excuse me. I think church and Zoe driving me crazy all day has caught up with me."

"I know what you mean. Between the good meal you served and you making me so comfortable, I'm worn out, too."

"Thanks. That was nothing, though, just something thrown together."

"Well, if that's just something thrown together, you gonna have me sweatin' you hard for the real deal."

I held her face in both my hands and kissed her. Before my dick got any harder, I released her and turned the doorknob.

"Good night, princess. I'll look for you later, a'ight?"

"Okay, be careful going home. Call me tomorrow." Carmen closed her door softly.

On the way to the elevator, I heard the sound of her setting her door locks, then silence.

I couldn't remember the last time I didn't "get some" in a situation like that. Either I was slippin', or I *really* liked that woman. Any other time, I would've climbed inside her on that couch, hit it, and then looked for a reason to leave.

After all the broads I'd been through, it was hard for me to believe in love or commitment. I grew up watching folks fall in love just to get hurt. It happened to me once when I was a kid, and I promised myself I wouldn't let it happen again.

No fuckin' way.

Moms always told me love was gonna sneak up on me and I wasn't gonna know how to act. The way I saw it, my defenses were too strong for love to infiltrate. Besides, after witnessing Uncle Lee dodge love after all the women he'd went through, I *knew* I could get by without it.

Love could mess up a good thing, like it did when Amanda fell in love with me. She was damn near as fine as Carmen. Amanda was thirty years old, about Carmen's height and weight, half Jamaican, half Italian, butterscotch skin with green eyes, reddish brown hair, thick lips, ass, and breasts.

She worked as a buyer for an eCommerce company in San Rafael and lived in a plush condo near Hilltop Mall in Richmond. Everything was real cool when we first hooked up. We kicked it all the time, fucked, went clubbin', hung out and all that. But after almost a year of me just dropping by basically when I needed a sex fix or a place to lay my head, she started pressing me about where I expected our relationship to go.

Being content with things the way they were, I avoided the question for a few more months before she really started trippin'. She started wanting to just talk during the times we usually automatically had sex, wanted me to meet her family, go to her company events, shit like that. It was time for me to exit that situation. She was gettin' way too attached to a brotha.

So after about thirteen months, I told her we were moving in two different directions and that we needed to give each other a little space. I'd never forget the look of disappointment and rage in her eyes. I guess I could've chosen a better day to tell her than the day before Valentine's Day. Oh well, when it was time to go, it was time to go.

She knew from the beginning we were just fuck buddies. That was it. Why should I feel bad? She's the one who decided to take our relationship to another level without my consent.

That's what happens when you let feelings get involved. You get your fuckin' heart broken.

CHAPTER THIRTEEN

Each time I open my journal, I see Carmen's name mentioned more and more. I had better not be gettin' hooked on her! After all, she could be just as much of a player as me.

Hell, women were some of the biggest players on the planet. I'd watched my sister toy with many dudes' hearts over the years before she met her match. She got married to Mark five years ago and had two kids. She used to have one dude on the phone, another on the way over to take her out, and a phone book full of other suckas waitin' to be used.

This one guy named Norman was so sprung on her, he used to break himself every payday taking her out and buying her shit. He once sent her two dozen roses to the house and she just signed for them, put them on her dresser, and didn't even bother to open the gold-wrapped box full of flowers 'til they were dried up.

He used to take her to the mall, dinner, movies, concerts, anywhere she wanted to go. Yvette used to kiss him every now and then and hold his hand, but knowing Yvette, she wasn't givin' him any more than that.

I remember the look on Norman's face when Yvette told him she didn't want to see him any longer. I was on the side of the house taking out the garbage when I heard them on the porch talking.

Being nosey, I walked to the edge of the bushes just in time to see his heart shatter. They were about ten feet from my hideout behind the shrubs. She stood in front of him with a look on her face like that of a mother weary from telling her child, "No, you can't have your way."

The look on Norman's face was that of a drowning man looking for shore. I studied his face intently, determined *never* to be the drowning man.

He still called from time to time, and I was instructed to tell him, "Yvette's not here" or "She's busy. She'll call you back." After about a month or so, I guess he got the hint and finally let it go. Norman was one of many drowning men I'd seen in my day.

Yvette always got pissed off when I brought his name up. I think after she got older she realized how much she'd hurt him.

I had my heart broken once when I was about six years old. There was a girl that lived down the street from us named Kelly. She was the prettiest girl on the block and I was head over ass in love with her.

She was about three years older than me and we played together all the time. We played with my Hot Wheels cars, rode bikes together, played Twister, Hide and Go Get It, climbed trees, had all kinds of fun. She even used to let me see her panties. I loved her to death until the day she "drowned" me.

I'd never forget that day. I was on my way over to her house to show her my newest bug collection. I had a spider and a moth in a jar, hoping they would duel to the death and she would sit and watch the battle with me.

When I got to the end of the picket fence which opened to the walkway to her front door, I saw her sitting on the steps with Teddy.

Teddy was a ten-year-old boy who lived around the corner. He was tall for his age, and his bike was way cooler than my Huffy. He had a Schwinn Stingray, one of the baddest bikes made back in those days. I remember the way she looked at him as they sat there eating ice cream sandwiches on her porch.

She was so caught up in Teddy she didn't even notice me walking toward them. He saw me first and said, "What you want, little man?"

I looked at him and wanted to bust his head open to the white meat. Who the hell did he think he was, sitting next to *my* girlfriend?!

Ignoring him, I said, "You wanna come over my house, Kelly?"

"No, me and Teddy are going riding."

"Can I go ridin' with you?"

I must have sounded like Norman because Teddy laughed out loud.

"No. I don't wanna play with you, little Rio," Kelly said. Then she laughed at me, too. I was so hurt I dropped my jar of dueling bugs and heard it shatter like my heart did as I ran home.

I remember staying in my room for the rest of the day. When I finally left to go pee, my mother was coming out of the bathroom. She must've seen the look on my face and knew something was wrong.

At first I said nothing, but when she got down on her knees and looked me in the eye, I broke down right there in the hallway and told her I hated Kelly between sobs.

"Oh, my poor baby, you suffered your first heartbreak," she said, giving me a comforting "Mama" hug.

She took me downstairs and we shared a bowl of Rocky Road ice cream. By the time we were done, I felt a lot better, but I *never* forgot what happened to me that day.

♦♦♦♦♦♦♦♦♦♦♦♦

When I got home it was 10:22 p.m. I walked in and grabbed the cordless phone to check for messages as I went to the bathroom. When I clicked on the TALK button, I heard the stuttering dial tone informing me I was wanted. The robot voice told me I had two new messages.

The first one was from my brother Damon wanting to borrow some money. Typical call. I'd call his ass later. The second was from Yo-Yo. Like usual, she was calling to have her "sexscription" filled.

After I was done in the latrine, I found I was rather horny after lying with Carmen. Since I was dialing Yo-Yo's number, my decision had been made to take care of my craving.

"Hello?"

"What you up to, girl?"

"Not much, just wantin' some company."

"Then why you call me earlier? You know all I wanna do is fuck you."

"You are so damn nasty, Rio, and you know I like that, huh, baby?"

"Yeah, I know you do with ya freaky ass."

"Well, get over here and get this pussy."

"I'm on my way. Gimme fifteen minutes."

"Okay, I'll be waiting. Bye."

Yo-Yo lived a couple of exits down the freeway from me, so it wouldn't take long for me to get there.

After a quick ho bath, I was out the door with thoughts of new ways to give Yo-Yo my dick.

I arrived at her doorstep at 10:51 p.m. She lived in a nice house off of Fruitvale Avenue. From what I gathered, her old man bought the house with money from armored car robberies and dope dealing in L.A. years ago. I told Yo-Yo I didn't wanna know her business. I just wanted to bust a nut.

When she opened the door, she was dressed in a tee shirt and white panties with little red hearts all over them. To my surprise, when I stepped inside, she hugged me and gave me a kiss on the lips.

"Hey, ain't that against the rules?" I asked as I brushed her off me.

"What are you talking about?"

"Kissin'. Remember you said no kissin'?"

"Oh, that. Well, rules can be changed."

"Is that right? Well, I may change a couple of 'em myself."

Yo-Yo was a pure ghetto queen. She wore the fake nails, fake hair, different colored eye contacts, and had ghetto booty. She was one of them heffas that just knew she was fine.

I think she liked me because I wasn't scared to talk crazy to her. She was used to dudes she could run all over. Rio wasn't one of those guys, though.

Again, she kissed my lips and added some tongue. While kissing her, I grabbed two hands full of her big brown ass. She didn't kiss me like Carmen. Yo-Yo kissed me like a freak. Carmen kissed me with passion and I liked that.

"Sit down on the couch and suck my dick."

"Damn, you sound as horny as me," she said while stroking my dick.

As Yo-Yo sucked me, I thought about Carmen. I imagined her pretty mouth on me, not that hoochie broad Yo-Yo's lips.

Just the thought made my dick grow inside Yo-Yo's mouth. She moaned with pleasure, assuming my hardness was her own doing. Yo-Yo sucked me vigorously. I looked down and watched her do her thang.

I pulled out of her mouth and told her, "Go get a condom and come back."

"Don't you wanna come to the bedroom with me?"

"No, I want you right here."

Not questioning my motives, she went to her room and returned a minute later with a Magnum condom and no clothes on. After dropping my jeans and drawers to my ankles, I told her, "Get on ya knees and suck me some more."

I could tell she got turned on when I commanded her. After dominating all her other dudes, having the roles reversed got her hot as a blowtorch.

Thoughts of Carmen in my head had me hard as iron. I found myself pumping Yo-Yo's mouth as though it was her vagina.

"Bend over the arm of the couch and gimme that rubber."

"What you gonna do, Big Daddy?"

"Shut up and spread that ass," I demanded.

Doing what Daddy said, she bent her big ass over for me. I looked at her swollen pink lips that begged to be parted by my throbbing dick.

I rolled the condom over my black anaconda, slapped her ass, and watched it quiver.

"Mmmmmmm, slap that ass again for me, baby."

"Shut up! I got this."

She began breathing hard as hell and pulled her nipples as I took charge of the fucking. I rubbed my dick head up and down between those swollen, wet lips, wishing I was with Carmen.

"Fuck me, Rio! Gimme that dick!"

"Beg me for it, bitch. Let me know you want it."

She damn near cried for me to enter her. In one motion, I grabbed her hips and slammed my dick all the way inside her, giving her what she wanted.

I dug deep inside her. "Is this my pussy?"

"Yessssss, Rio, yessss. Mmmmmm, take it all, baby."

"You my bitch, Yo-Yo?"

"Yesssssssssss, I'm your bitch," she moaned in ecstasy.

Bent over the arm of her couch, her ass was in the perfect position for me to stand up and watch as I plowed in and out of her.

Yo-Yo was so wet it felt like I was screwin' a jar of warm grease. She usually tried to be quiet when we fucked, not wanting me to know how good it was, but that night, she let it all go.

As I pumped her coochie, I slapped her ass again and watched it shake. When I put my thumb on her asshole, she cried out, "Mmmmmm, yesss, I like that."

In no time, my entire thumb was in her ass, going in and out in sync with my dick entering her pussy. I made a decision to get that ass for real. I pulled out of her hot, wet hole, put my dick head on her asshole, and in one pump, I was deep inside it.

Yo-Yo let out a cry, grabbed a throw pillow off the couch, and bit down on it. Having her in that position of submission not only made my ego swell, but my meat, as well.

Her tight, hot ass made me wanna bust a nut. I grabbed her hips tighter and began to pump and grind deep inside her asshole.

Sensing I was about to cum, she pushed back on my dick in anticipation of me giving her my juices.

My entire body went rigid as I pumped my hot cum in her ass—albeit inside the condom—and imagined I was inside Carmen's ass instead.

Both of us were depleted after our mutual orgasms. I pulled my rubber-covered penis out of her and observed the volume of cum inside.

Yo-Yo laid on the couch on her stomach, hair matted to her face by sweat. As she lay there recovering, I went to the bathroom, washed up, wrapped the rubber in toilet paper, and dropped it in the trash.

When I came back into the living room, Yo-Yo was laying on her stomach asleep. I went to her bedroom, got a blanket, and tossed it on her before I left.

"Where you goin'?"

"Home. I gotta go to work in the morning."

"You have to leave already?"

"Yeah, I told you I have work in the mornin'."

I didn't even bother to look back at her as I left. She knew our rules.

After I opened the door to my car, I suddenly felt like shit. Yo-Yo was good for the times when I just needed to bust a nut, but sometimes I wanted something more meaningful. That was one of those times.

When I got home at 12:44 a.m., I was tired as hell. I took a shower, found my bed, and passed out on it.

CHAPTER FOURTEEN

Over the next two weeks, Carmen and I talked off and on, but we'd only seen each other a couple times. She'd been tied up the past two weekends, and our telephone conversations had been getting cut short by calls she had to take.

I began to think she didn't have time for a man in her life. At least that's how I justified my missing her.

Somehow I had to get the tables turned so she was looking for me versus me sitting there pining for her.

I had even screwed a couple of my usual "fuck buddies" in the meantime, but got no satisfaction from them other than an orgasm. Whatever the case was, I couldn't go on like that.

The third weekend since we'd kicked it was coming up. If we didn't hook up, I was gonna lay my cards on the table and tell her what I thought.

What was it I thought?

What the hell could I say? After all, Carmen wasn't my woman. She was just a friend.

That Thursday evening, I decided to take a walk to the corner store and get some toilet paper, zig zags, and a beer. On the way to the store, I paused to stretch and sneak a peek at Carmen's building.

I didn't know why I bothered. I couldn't see her place from that vantage point anyway. I shook off the urge to walk toward her place and continued in the opposite direction to the store.

After I got my goods and headed back home, a black Honda passed me with a familiar face on the passenger side.

It was Carmen.

I wasn't able to see the driver, but I bet the person driving was the reason she'd been avoiding me. It probably was Bernard's punk ass. When I got to my walkway, I saw her get out of the car, smile, and wave goodbye to whoever the hell the driver was.

A feeling of jealousy burned in my gut. I didn't recognize it at first, but when I did, I turned and entered my building, hopefully, before she saw me. When I got to my door, I heard the phone ringing. By the time I got inside, I'd missed the call. Before I picked up the phone to see if they had left a message, I opened my Corona and took a long swig. I needed to take the edge off.

After finishing off the bottle, I had a seat on the couch, laid my head back, and chilled. My emotions ranged from anger to sadness to utter confusion.

How the hell did I get to that point? Me, Rio. I was one of the biggest players in Oakland, hands down.

While sitting on my couch, I grabbed the phone to see if I had any messages. I did. Now the question was how would I handle it if it was her? Well, I wasn't gonna worry about it.

After all, the worst she could say was she didn't wanna see me anymore.

I wouldn't like that, though.

I finally decided to check and see who the message was from. My heart fluttered when I heard a voice say, "Hey stranger, why'd you rush inside? Didn't you see me waving to you? Well, call me when you get this message, okay? Bye."

Feeling like "The Man" again, I found myself pacing the floor with a fat grin on my face, happy as hell she'd called. I needed to calm down, so I walked to my balcony and got some fresh air. Since I was still holding the phone, I dialed the magic number.

"Hello?" her sweet voice said.

"Wassup, stranger?"

"Stranger? You're the one, Mr. Rio, Mr. Never at Home."

My coolness kicked in. "I'm always home. You must've been callin' one of your other fellas."

"What? You have your nerve. You're the one with the Bible-sized black book."

"Yeah, but it has your name and number written in it from cover to cover."

"Okay, crazy man, whatever. What are you up to this evening?"

"Not much, just loungin' around. What about you?"

"Same as you. I didn't have to teach my dance class tonight, so Zoe and I went to dinner at Mexicali Rose. I love that place. Have you had dinner yet, Rio?"

"Yeah, I went to Mickey D's"

"Oh no! Do you really eat there? I haven't eaten there since I was about fourteen. I worked at the one near my house, and after three months of cooking that crap, I can't stand it to this day."

"I don't eat there often, but nights like this, when I don't feel like cookin', they get me."

As I glanced at my watch, I noticed it was only 6:20 p.m., and the sun was just starting to set.

"Hey, you wanna take a walk with me?" I asked.

"When?"

"Now."

"Where are we going to go?"

"To the lake. Get a jacket and meet me in your lobby in ten minutes."

"Okay, see you there."

After we hung up, I brushed my teeth and swigged some Scope. After all, I couldn't kiss my girl with beer breath.

My girl...ain't that a bitch. I couldn't remember the last time I'd referred to *any* female as "my girl".

As a precaution, I went to the nightstand where I kept a couple rolls of wintergreen Certs, tossed one in my mouth, and placed the rest in my pocket.

My FUBU jeans and gray Ecko sweater would suffice for a cool evening stroll. I exited the lobby doors, took a breath of late September air, and headed to Carmen's place.

When I hit the sidewalk, I saw her standing outside her building. She was dressed in a pair of faded jeans, a navy blue Zeta Phi Beta sweatshirt, and a pair of white K-Swiss tennis shoes. Her hair was braided straight back, no extensions, all her own.

As I got closer, I noticed we had matching grins on our faces.

"Hey, sexy," I said as I grabbed both of her hands.

"Hi, handsome," she replied. The hand holding turned into a hug. It was the kind of hug that said, "I missed you."

"So where are we off to, Mr. Rio?"

"Come on and I'll show you." I took her hand and walked her towards Lake Merritt.

Shifting the Certs around in my mouth so I didn't sound like I had a mouth full of gravel, I asked, "Are you sure you have time for a new friend?"

"Only if it's a good friend," she answered with a crafty smile.

"Well, you must hate me since you left me hangin' for so long."

Carmen stopped in the middle of the sidewalk, put her hands on her hips, and said, "Rio Romero Clark, you have a hell of a lot of nerve saying that to me. If you'd stay your butt home sometimes, maybe *somebody* would be able to see you when *somebody* was thinking about you."

That admission, whether joking or not, sent a charge through me.

"Well, what do you have to say for yourself?"

"How can you tell when I'm home or not?"

She brushed her braids off her shoulder. "I know your car when I see it. Usually if it's not there, you're not there. That is, unless one of your girls picks you up."

"Time out, time out! That was a low blow. I'm here now. Let's walk and talk so you can tell me how much *somebody* thought about me."

As we continued our walk to Lake Merritt, our conversation went all over the place. It was like we were two old friends who hadn't seen each other in years and were trying to play catch up.

We casually strolled around the lake, stopping every now and then to look at the ducks or so she could smell the roses and examine the other flowers.

Then, we stopped at the playground and had a seat on one of the many picnic tables. The playground was empty except for us, a few seagulls and pigeons, and several people with Pooper Scoopers in hand, walking their dogs for the evening.

"I love this place. I've been coming here since I came to Oakland, to jog or sometimes just to sit and look at the birds and relax," Carmen said.

"Yeah, I like it, too, but it's a lot more interesting with you here."

"I missed you, Rio."

The way she said it was more like a confession than a statement. I was caught completely off guard.

"I missed you, too, princess."

Hearing myself say those words, it sounded like I was out of my body listening to a stranger's conversation. Maybe the hard shell I'd cocooned around myself over the years was fracturing. Whatever was happening, I felt powerless to stop it.

I turned to face her as she met me halfway for a kiss. Not a kiss of lust, but a kiss which justified what we had just said to one another. It was a kiss that proved we had indeed missed each other.

After the kiss, I had her sit on my lap. Carmen sat down, put her arm around me, laid her head on my shoulder, and played with my ear.

God, I had missed that woman.

She had awakened feelings in me that would have been considered blasphemy in the "Player Religion".

We sat in that position, intermittently kissing, until the first stars began to twinkle above us. I felt her shudder from a slight breeze.

"You gettin' cold?"

"No."

"Liar. Let me get you home. I felt you shiverin'," I said, although I didn't really want her to leave my lap.

We stood up and stretched. As we did, I popped a Cert in my mouth. I offered Carmen one, too.

When she reached for the roll, I pulled her to me and kissed her as I transferred the Cert I had put in my mouth into hers.

Carmen sucked on the wintergreen mint and said, "I like how you share."

As we stood at the curb waiting for the light to change, I heard a car horn blowing.

I looked at the cars stopped at the light and saw Yvette in her silver Expedition, honking and waving.

"Is that one of your many fans?" Carmen asked.

"No, that's my sister, Ms. Jump-to-Conclusions. Come on so I can introduce you."

Yvette turned down her music as she pulled to the curb. I discovered she had my niece and nephew with her.

"What are you doing out here, Re-Re?" Yvette asked.

Oh no! I hated when she called me Re-Re. That was a nickname my mother called me when we were kids.

"Aren't you going to introduce me to your friend? I know you were raised with better manners than that."

"I am, I am, gimme a chance. Carmen, this is my sister Yvette. Yvette, this is Carmen."

They exchanged the usual "hi, how are you's" and the "pleased to meet you's".

From the back of the vehicle, I heard some younger voices say, "Hey, Uncle Rio! Can we have a dollar?"

That was our usual greeting. Ever since they could remember, I'd always given them a buck or two whenever I saw them.

"What are you guys up to? Y'all need a ride?" Yvette asked.

"Nah, we were just takin' a walk. We're on our way back."

Yvette gave me a look that asked, "Is she your latest victim?" She'd always hated the fact I'd never really settled down with one woman, which was part of the reason I didn't see her very often. We always ended up arguing about my "playerisms". Usually one of us would leave before something was said we'd both regret. I did love her, but sometimes she just rode a nigga *too* much.

♦♦♦♦♦♦♦♦♦♦♦

After I said goodbye to my niece and nephew, I took Carmen's hand and told Yvette I'd see her later. I knew Carmen could feel the tension between Yvette and me, but she didn't ask any questions.

Carmen let go of my hand and put her hand around my waist, rubbing the small of my back. As I placed my arm around her shoulders, we continued our slow stroll.

I suddenly realized that by walking all hugged up with Carmen, there was a high risk of me being busted by one of my other associates.

With that thought in mind, I picked up the pace and asked, "You wanna go to the movies?"

"Sure, what are we going to go see?"

"Let's go see somethin' scary."

"Okay, sounds good to me," Carmen said.

I felt a lot better once we were in my car. Even though my car was well known, the limo tint helped to conceal the contents. It wouldn't look good to have a couple of my females scrapping in the street on my behalf. I knew Carmen had enough class to not get into that kind of drama, but a few of my other associates weren't quite as refined as my new "Queen of the Hill".

Carmen's mannerisms were very sexy. She was one hundred percent ladylike on the streets and a freak in the sheets. The fact that she had her own money and other things going on in her life besides me was intriguing. She wasn't like a lot of broke hoes out there who counted on a nigga to be their whole world just because they were giving up the coochie.

"Hey, Carmen, call up 777-FILM and find out what time the movie is playin' in Emeryville."

"The next show starts in twenty-five minutes," she answered after placing the call. Since the theatre was only about fifteen minutes away, I eased up off the accelerator and moved out of the fast lane.

"Why don't you like driving, Carmen?"

"It's not that I don't like driving. It's more the case I don't like driving here in California. The people here drive too crazy and the traffic's terrible. I've been thinking about having my car shipped out here, though. I'm not really looking forward to spending another winter here on public transportation and expensive cab rides."

"Why don't you just fly down and drive it back?"

"I'm not going to try and drive all the way back here from Alabama to California by myself! There are *way* too many nuts out there. I priced this one company who said they would pick it up and deliver it for about twelve hundred dollars."

"Hell, for half that amount you can get a plane ticket and have enough leftover to pay for gas, room, and food."

"I know, but I'd rather ride back with someone who could help with the driving and keep me company. Some of the highway between there and here is very boring."

"What about ya girl, Zoe? Y'all seem to be tight and get along well. Have you asked her?"

"Yeah, we talked about it, but it's hard for her to get away. She has to help take care of her grandfather who has Alzheimers and requires lots of care."

"I'm sorry to hear that. I know that's hard to deal with."

"Yeah, she's been living with him for the past two years. Most of her family is in L.A., except for a few in Sacramento, and they are rarely ever up this way."

After all the information she provided, I sensed an opportunity. If I was to offer to help her bring her car back, I could be a hero and enjoy doing her across the country.

On the other hand, I'm sure she'd want to stop by and visit her family, which probably meant I would be meeting her parents. I did like her a lot, but I sure wasn't ready for that.

Why did the quest for new pussy have to be so complicated sometimes? After all, I've had lots of fine women and women with money, but Carmen was something different. If she was running a game on me, she was doing a damn good job. I was gonna have to keep my head clear so I wouldn't slip and let my heart get caught up in her game. I let the subject of picking up her car die and pulled into the nearly empty theatre parking lot.

"It looks like we're the only ones here tonight."

Carmen checked her face in my visor's vanity mirror.

"Well, this *is* a weeknight. Maybe we are."

I was able to find a parking space close to the ticket window. There were only a few people ahead of us. As we stood in line, Carmen standing in front of me, I wrapped my arms around her. We managed to blend in with the other couples well.

After purchasing the tickets and entering the doors, the smell of fresh, hot popcorn permeated the air. Judging by the way Carmen inhaled through her nose and looked in the direction of the snack bar, I sensed she had a taste for some.

"That popcorn smells good. You want some?"

"Not a whole one, but if you get some, I'll eat some of yours," she responded with a grin.

It cracked me up how some women could be starving like hell but didn't want to appear greedy, so instead, they would order the "small portion" or just share yours.

When we reached the counter, I ordered a large popcorn and asked, "Do you want butter on it?"

"Yes, I like lots of butter on my popcorn."

Popcorn in hand and a fistful of napkins later, we were directed to theatre number eleven. I loved that theatre. They had stadium seating and chairs you could lean back and rock in if you liked. I could almost count the number of people in the theatre on one hand.

"Where you wanna sit, Carmen?"

"It doesn't matter."

I took her to the top seats and sat beneath the projector with our backs against the wall of the projection booth. While watching the previews of upcoming movies—and the commercials that they were starting to sneak into the movies—I was comfortable as hell throwing buttered popcorn in my mouth and being with my chick.

Twenty minutes into the movie, we were halfway through the popcorn. The further down we went into the bucket, the more butter we found. It seemed as if homeboy went overboard when Carmen told him she liked lots of butter.

"You want any more popcorn, baby?" I asked.

She wiped her hands. "No, thank you. I'm getting full. Besides, he put *too* much butter on it, even for me."

Normally, I would've just dropped the bucket on the floor and been through with it, but since I was there with my date, I had to show I had *some* home training. Therefore, I put it in the seat next to me instead.

While laying her head on my shoulder, Carmen rubbed my chest with her left hand, moving in little circles. A short time later, I found the circle expanding. The next thing I knew, she had her hand under my sweater feeling the washboard abs I'd been working on. I could feel her fingertips tracing them, working her way up and rubbing on my chest.

She repositioned her head so her lips were aligned with my ear. Soon, I felt her lips kiss my earlobe, then the side of my neck as she rubbed on my chest. She had totally tuned out the movie and tuned into the Rio Show.

It seemed as though Carmen was using some of my own moves on me. Either our chemistry was perfect, or she was smooth as silk. *The hell with it*, I thought. I just relaxed and enjoyed the attention. As Carmen kissed my neck with growing intensity, I felt some growing of my own down below. She was almost sitting sideways in her seat while kissing my neck and rubbing on my navel.

She worked her way down and her hand found the creature stirring under the fabric of my jeans. I continued to try and watch the movie while Carmen had her way with me.

Her massaging of my crotch had turned into a quest to unzip my pants. Looking around, I saw the nearest people were about four rows in front of us, and we had our entire row to ourselves.

I soon discovered Carmen wasn't as innocent as she looked. As she successfully unzipped and unleashed my "beast", I also tuned out the movie and resigned myself to be her sex toy.

I settled back in my seat and felt the warmth of her soft hand wrap around my pulsating dick. She continued to kiss and bite my neck as she stroked my fat, mushroom-like dickhead.

"Pass me the popcorn, baby," Carmen whispered in my ear.

"Hmmm?"

"Pass me the bucket of popcorn," she repeated.

Being a good little sex toy, I obliged. She reached into the bucket and to my surprise, grabbed a handful of popcorn, squeezed it, and then let it fall back into the bucket.

In the dim light emanating from the projector overhead, I saw her left hand was glistening from the gobs of butter that saturated the popcorn.

Before I knew it, she'd wrapped her warm, butter-coated hand around the hard, smooth, swollen head of my dick. She slowly stroked me from the tip of the head down to my pubic hair.

I'd gotten plenty of hand jobs, with a variety of lubricants, but *never* with artificial popcorn butter.

I could tell by the devilish look in Carmen's sexy eyes that she enjoyed having control of me like she did.

After she caught me looking in her eyes, she moved in and put her tongue in my mouth as if to say, "Sit back and enjoy, baby. I'm running this."

Conscious of the fact there were people only four rows ahead of us, I tried to keep my sounds of pleasure down to a minimum as she continued to jack me off.

Her hand slid up and down my shaft effortlessly thanks to the butter lube. Between the heat friction from the motion of her strokes and the slick smoothness the butter provided, I found myself squirming in my seat. I fucked her hand as if I was inside her.

"You're gonna make me cum, baby," I managed to whisper as the kissing and stroking continued.

She whispered back, "I know. I want you to shoot it for me."

Her answer made me pump harder. I felt my ass lift out the seat and heard myself grunt as I got closer to releasing my buildup.

"Shhhhhh! Keep it down," Carmen said in my ear.

If any of the people in the rows ahead of us would've turned around, they would've known something was up.

My head was leaned back against the wall and my eyes were shut as Carmen jacked me faster, bringing me to the point of eruption. At that point, both my arms were splayed out, hands gripping the vacant seats, and nails digging in as I approached the land of Climax.

When the first drops of pre-cum dribbled down my shaft, I heard Carmen utter a low moan as the warm liquid dripped on the webbing between her thumb and forefinger.

"Mmmmmmmm, yesssssssss, let it go for me, Rio. I want it all."

No longer able to hold it—and not wanting to anymore—I busted a vicious nut. I felt my sperm pump, shoot, and squirt out of my one-eyed soldier.

While it was shooting and running down my shaft onto Carmen's hand, she moaned lowly as if she was cumming, too.

She continued to stroke me with the mixture of artificial butter flavoring and sperm until I grabbed her hand gently and almost begged her to stop. My dick was *way* too sensitive at that point.

"Did you like that, baby?"

"Mmmmmm. I think you can tell how much I liked it by how much sticky juice is on your hand," I replied with pleasure.

Carmen reached between her legs and pulled out the wad of napkins I had given her earlier to hold while we were eating the popcorn. She proceeded to clean me off, careful to touch the sensitive head lightly. Each touch made me twitch.

It took a gang of napkins to clean up my spill. In the faint light, I couldn't see if any had landed on my pants.

After she was done, all the jizz-stained napkins were deposited into the half-full tub of popcorn. I lay back spent, as my man Austin Powers would say.

Since we'd missed the first portion of the movie, we mutually decided to catch it again some other time and headed out.

I wrapped my arm around her shoulder. "Damn, that was good, Carmen! You are one hell of a woman."

"Thank you, Mr. Rio. I'm glad you enjoyed it."

As we approached the restrooms, I gave her a kiss and told her I'd be right back. She did likewise and disappeared into the women's powder room.

At the piss trough, I performed a quick visual inspection and spotted a dime-sized wet spot on the left side of my zipper. Luckily, my jeans were dark blue and the stain was only noticeable if you were up close and looking for it.

I emptied my bladder, purging the remaining sperm from my satisfied penis, then washed my hands and hurried to rejoin my lover.

When Carmen emerged from the powder room, I was struck again by her beauty. The way she walked with those bowlegs and that winning smile made my heart swell. I greeted her with a hug as we prepared to leave.

"Hey, Rio! What's up?" I knew that voice, but I couldn't quite make the connection. It was a female, and I hadn't heard it in a long time.

When I turned to see who it was, I was greeted by a face from my past: Amanda.

"How are you doing? I haven't seen or heard from you in a while." Amanda kissed my lips and gave me a more than friendly hug. I couldn't believe that green-eyed bitch did that in front of Carmen.

"I'm good."

"That's good to hear. I'm sorry; I didn't mean to intrude on you guys. I'm Amanda, and you?" Amanda asked as she held her hand out to Carmen.

I felt Carmen's grip on my hand tighten as I introduced her.

"Amanda, this is Carmen. Carmen, Amanda."

The tension in the air was thick as pound cake.

Amanda looked Carmen up and down as if to say, "Who is this hoe?"

"I'm glad to meet you, Amanda," Carmen said, clearly not pleased at all.

The body language between the two of them was deafening. Carmen's body language said, "Let's get out of here before I have to stomp a mud hole in this hatin' bitch."

Sensing that, I took Carmen's hand and began to walk toward the exit again.

"Are you two on your way out? How did you guys like the movie?"

"It was all right, Amanda. I'm sure you'll like it," I said, irritation lacing my tone.

During our hasty exit, I felt Amanda's eyes burning a hole in my back, and I'm sure Carmen felt the same heat. Even though we had been split for over seven months, Amanda was still jealous. She'd always been the jealous type.

"Let me guess, that was your ex-girlfriend?" Carmen asked.

"How could you tell?"

"Oh, a woman knows. She had the look of a woman who still had feelings for her ex-man."

"Well, if that's true, she'll have to get over it. We've been over for a long time."

Carmen looked at me out the corner of her eye. "Yeah, that's what *you* say."

During the ride home, we were both quiet since the last five minutes in the theatre. Finally, Carmen broke the ice.

"Why did you two break up, Rio?"

"Amanda decided we were moving too fast and she needed some space to find out what she really wanted," I responded, lying my ass off.

"That's too bad. It's hard when both people in a relationship aren't on the same page. Were you in love with her?"

That was a question I wasn't prepared for. If I said yes, she might have assumed I still had feelings for Amanda. If I said no, she'd think I was lying.

Opting for the yes option, I told her, "Yeah, I think I was, but it's over now. I don't even remember the last time I saw her."

"What's the longest relationship you've been in?" I asked, changing the subject.

"Nine years."

"Nine years! That's a long time. What happened?" I felt, rather than saw, her flinch after I asked her that last question.

"We were engaged to be married three years ago, but things didn't work out. I found out he was sleeping with his son's mother."

"No shit? How'd you find out he was messin' around?"

"We were at his sister's wedding reception at his mother's house. His son's mother was invited because she was one of his sister's bridesmaids. I told him I wasn't comfortable going if she was going to be there, but he insisted."

"Damn! He really wanted you to be there knowin' his baby's Momma was gonna be there, too?"

"Yes, he was that kind of an asshole. Anyway, I gave in and went. Near the end of the reception and after several glasses of champagne, he and his ex danced a few times and seemed to be getting very chummy."

"What? Are you bullshittin'?"

"I wish. Apparently, he had forgotten he came with me. Already feeling humiliated, I went outside to sit on the porch swing to get some air. It was kind of chilly that night, so I went upstairs to get my coat out of what I thought was the guestroom. You can guess what I found."

"Oh no! You caught 'em kissin'?"

"No....she was bent over in her bridesmaid's gown and he was screwing her."

"I'm so sorry, honey. Damn."

"It's okay. He actually gave me that clichéd line, 'It's not what you think.' I just stood there for a minute in shock and then I turned, closed the door quietly, and left."

"What a punk ass nigga."

"What's even funnier is that he didn't even come after me right away. I think he actually kept screwing her until he got his nut. He always was a selfish bastard." Carmen stared out my sunroof at the stars and rubbed her hands together.

I could tell it was a very sensitive subject by the way she kept blinking her eyes as though fighting back tears. I took her hand and squeezed it, letting her know it was okay.

We didn't talk the last ten minutes of the ride. We just listened to Teena Marie singing "Portuguese Love" as we left the freeway.

CHAPTER FIFTEEN

At 9:48 p.m., we pulled up in front of Carmen's building. I didn't want her to be alone after her revelation to me. After opening the passenger's side door, I asked, "Do you have to go home right now?"

"What do you mean, Rio?"

"Can you come up for a minute?"

"Okay, why not? It's still kind of early. Do you have any tea?"

"No, but I have some hot chocolate. Is that cool?"

"That's fine. I just want something warm to drink."

I had to replay in my head how I'd left my place. I hoped like hell I didn't leave anything out that I shouldn't have.

Right when we were getting ready to enter the lobby to my building, she said, "I forgot, I need to go back to my place. I left some fish out on my counter. It's been out all day."

Just when I thought she was going to cancel me for the night, she asked, "Would you mind going to my place instead?"

"Okay. That's cool as long as I'm with you," I responded with a smile. After that, she stopped and gave me a hug.

"Rio, I really appreciate you being so nice to me. It's been a long time since I've had a chance to talk about what happened between Keith and me."

"Not a problem. That's what friends are for, right?" I held her chin in my hand and looked into her eyes.

"My family really likes him, but they don't know the truth about him. The only reason I think I stayed with him as long as I did was because there weren't a lot of guys to choose from in our town."

"It sounds like they had you guys married from birth."

"Pretty much. Everybody there expected us to get married. I caught him messing around on me more than once and just turned a blind eye to it, but that time at the wedding reception was it. I packed up everything I had, quit my job, found a place here, and two months later, I was on a plane to Oakland."

All I could think was, "What kind of crazy son of a bitch would treat a woman that fine, successful, and smart so bad?"

After I thought about it, I knew why. It was because of what I called the Mountain Climber Syndrome. It's like when you look at a big ass mountain for years and years, then you finally decide to try and climb it. You slip, sometimes fall, run into bad weather, low oxygen, but you want to reach the top of the mountain so bad you won't let anything stop you from obtaining your goal of conquering that big, bad rock. Then one day, you look up and you see the summit ahead of you. You're happy as hell you've done it. You unfurl your flag that says, "I climbed this bad son of a bitch!" You dance, celebrate, and are congratulated by your peers. You are The Man!

That goes on for a while. Some climbers are content longer than others with their accomplishment. You've reached the peak of the mountain so many others had wanted to climb but had failed. As you look around from your perch atop that mountain, you begin to notice other mountains; some bigger, some smaller. Even though the mountain you were currently on top of was the envy of many, and still a damn good mountain, you get an urge to feel the thrill of reaching the peak of the mountain across the way.

Finally, your urge gets the best of you, and the next thing you know, you have on your mountain climbing gear and are headed out to plant your flag on another peak. Strange thing about the "Mountain Climber", he wants his flag to be the only one planted on his mountain even while he's busy climbing another one. Shit doesn't always work that way, though.

♦♦♦♦♦♦♦♦♦♦♦

We walked to Carmen's place in relative silence, both of us reflecting on the events of the evening. Once we got to her place and crossed the threshold, we were greeted by the smell of ripe filet of sole.

"Dammit! I knew I shouldn't have left it out this long!" she shouted as she slammed her keys on the countertop, causing them to skid across the surface and fall to the floor. I'd never heard her cuss as much as she had that night.

I picked her keys up and placed them on the counter. "Don't worry 'bout it, baby. I'll take it out to the trash for you and take you out for a nice fish dinner tomorrow. Will that put a pretty smile back on your face?"

"That's okay. You don't have to. I guess I'm just on edge because of the opening of old wounds and the fact that I'm suffering from my monthly."

That explained a lot. Her "Aunt Flow" had come to visit. Damn! I really wanted to climb inside her, too. After that great hand job, I couldn't wait to feel her inner heat.

"Where's your trash bin?"

"It's downstairs in the underground parking garage."

I gave her a kiss, picked up the fish, and went downstairs to dispose of the olfactory nuisance.

When I returned, I smelled the scent of Egyptian Musk incense burning as her kitchen curtains danced in the mild breeze, dissipating the fish stench. Carmen, meanwhile, was flipping through the channels on her brand new plasma screen TV.

Sitting next to Carmen, I'd almost forgotten we both had to go to work in the morning.

"I'm sorry for being so bitchy, Rio. Unfortunately, I'm one of those women that get extreme PMS."

I kissed her nose. "That's okay, love. I'll make sure to keep all sharp objects away from you."

"You're a wise man. Damn, these cramps are killing me." She rubbed her lower stomach.

"I tell you what. Lay down here in my lap and I'll rub your tummy for you. Will that help?"

"It just might. I'll be right back, okay?" She went to the bathroom.

After popping a couple of Motrin, she laid her head in my lap and I rubbed her sore belly. If Dee would've seen me, that nigga would've passed out with laughter. If Uncle Lee saw me, he would probably have kicked my ass and asked me what the fuck I was doing. Right then, as good as it felt being with Carmen, I might've taken the ass kicking he would've dished out with pleasure.

"You don't have to worry about Amanda," I said out of the blue. "She's past history and I can promise you that."

"You don't owe me any explanations, Rio. Our pasts are our own business. Let's just forget about it, okay?"

"I'd rather get this out in the open, Carmen," I continued while rubbing around her belly ring. "Especially if we're gonna get as close as I hope."

"Oh? And just how close is that, Mr. Rio?" She looked up at me with a serious face.

"Well, back in the day, we used to call it 'asking you to go with me'. Now-a-days, I guess it's called 'I want you to be my chick'.

Carmen laughed so loud she scared the shit out of me.

"I haven't heard the term 'go with me' since I was a kid!" Her laughter kicked in again.

Maybe it was the Motrin or maybe it was nervous laughter. I wasn't sure. I just watched her laugh until a tear ran down her cheek.

"I'm so sorry. I'm not laughing at you, Rio. It's just you looked so serious when you said it that it caught me by surprise."

"And what if I was serious?"

"To be honest with you, I didn't think a single, handsome playboy like you could ever say those words. I know you have many women in your world, and I'm just flattered you have chosen to give *me* some attention."

"There's no need to prai---."

"Shhh, let me get this out." She put her hand over my mouth.

"Rio, I've been single since I arrived here. I've dated occasionally over the past couple of years and can count on two fingers how many men have been here in my place.

I promised myself I wouldn't get involved with *any* man I felt I couldn't totally trust. I must admit that I do like you—

maybe more than a little bit—but I can't risk another heartbreaking situation."

"You don't have to wo---."

"Hush. I'm at a point in my life where I'd like to have a man, not just a lover. A penis is as easy to get as a breath of air. Finding a *real* man who'll want to be around even after the sex has become less of a priority in the relationship is a lot more challenging."

"Carmen, I know what you're trying to sa---." She cut me off again.

"There are a lot of things I plan on doing with my life, and things I plan on having that would be much more enjoyable if I could share it with that special someone. Sex and money are two things I can get whenever I need, but the person I'm with has to mean something to me. For instance, remember that wonderful night when you gave me my pedicure? The only reason I decided to come over was because you're the first man I've met since coming here who didn't give me the vibe that all you wanted was a quick screw."

"Nah, your friendship means more to me than that, baby." I kissed the top of her head.

"Most men would have tried to find a reason to stay after helping me bring my groceries in. You were very much a gentleman, and for that I'm grateful." She put her hand on mine.

"I really didn't plan on having sex with you that night, Carmen. I wa---." She shushed me again.

"The night I came over, I fully intended on sleeping with you, but what we did was so intense I can't put it into words. I've *never* had a man turn me on as much as you did during foreplay. That was the most erotic night I can remember."

When she paused, I sat there dumbfounded. She had just broke it down to me, laying all of her cards on the table before I could even decide if I wanted to play my hand or not.

"I'm going to go change. I'll be right back, okay?" She stood up and kissed me on the forehead.

At that moment, I realized I had asked her to be my woman. Was I really ready for that? Well, it was too late now. The words had already flown out my mouth and landed on the runway of her heart. I just needed to know if I'd be able to make her heart a permanent stop on my flight plan.

When Carmen returned, she had changed into some comfortable looking pink flannel pajamas. She had also tied a red silk scarf around her head in hopes of keeping her braids intact for another day.

"I think I'm going to call in sick tomorrow. These cramps are really killing me. I've had them so bad in the past I've had to go to the emergency room." She lay back down in my lap.

"I'm sorry to hear that, baby. Did the belly rub help any?"

"Yes, it did. Thank you." She closed her eyes and relaxed.

Since it was getting late and she was nodding off from the combination of my belly rub and the Motrin, I decided it was time for me to leave. I really did want her that night, especially after that buttery hand job, but since she was on "the rag", it wasn't even gonna happen. I knew a few guys who would have gotten that period coochie, but Rio wasn't among that group.

"Baby, go to bed. I'm gonna go home so you can sleep."

"I'm sorry I'm not very good company tonight. Can I get a rain check for another visit?"

"Yeah, I think that can be arranged. I'll call you when I get off work tomorrow and check on you, okay?"

"Okay. I don't usually do anything when I feel this bad, except stay in bed," Carmen said as she got up.

As we unlocked from a deep goodnight kiss at the door, she told me to be safe and to call her when I got in. With that, I was out the door, down the hall, in the elevator, and on my way home.

When I got home, I checked the phone and found I had five new messages. I replayed my conversation with Carmen and recalled she never answered if she was going to "go with me" or not. In a way, I was relieved because I didn't wanna rush into anything too serious, too fast. On the other hand, I was a little concerned because she didn't jump at the chance to be with me.

Not that I was conceited, but I was one hell of a catch. I knew that for a fact. Many hearts had been broken because I didn't want any commitment.

I hoped Carmen realized that.

My phone messages were as follows: Dee wanted to know what was up and where I'd been; Yvette wanted to know if I could watch her kids on Friday night so her and hubby could go to some function; Angelina wanted to know why I hadn't called; some telemarketing scumbag asked me if I would like to buy something; and I had a call from my college girl, Tracy.

I'd forgotten all about her birthday.

I listened to her message again: "Hey Faker, wassup? I knew you was gonna forget about me, but that's cool. I know how you players are. Well, I still want my gift, so you better call me. You know I've moved in with my friend and it is hella cool! I'll be expecting your call. Bye."

The time stamp on the message was 10:30 p.m., fifteen minutes ago. She was gonna have to wait, though. I was way too tired to talk to her. Besides, if she had talked right, she might've ended up gettin' fucked. I wanted to be at my best when I did hit that young snatch.

Temptation was a bitch. I'd just left a woman I've wanted to get with for months and I was already plotting on getting some new pussy. I guess it was the "Mountain Climber" in me coming out. I went to bed before I ended up calling Tracy's ass and found myself driving to Benicia to get that coochie.

Angelina could wait until whenever. That was some on-demand pussy, so there was no need to worry about her. Dee,

I'd catch that fool whenever (most likely he'd find me first), and I'd call Yvette back after work.

I liked to think I was ready to really settle down and become a one-woman man, but it seemed like every time I tried, something happened and fucked it up.

I don't know how Moms and Pops made it so long. They'd been married for thirty-three years and counting. I think a lot of it had to do with my mother's upbringing. Very few people on her side of the family ever divorced. She was raised to believe marriage really was "'til death do you part".

Her parents had been married for forty-eight years. The Swanson women were serious about marriage. From what Uncle Lee told me about Grandpa, I knew he was a serious playa. I heard Grandpa even had two kids by another woman while married to Grandma, and somehow, she stayed with him. That was commitment for ya ass.

Even though Moms caught Pops—I don't know how many times—with evidence he'd been with another woman many times, she still hung right in there. As Pops got older, I'm sure he was grateful to have her. It had to be hell to stay with only one woman, though. Just the thought scared the commitment out of me.

CHAPTER SIXTEEN

During my lunch hour the next day, I called Carmen.

"How you feelin', boo?"

"Terrible. I'm still cramping."

"If you want, I'll stop and get you some dinner so you can relax."

"I'd really appreciate that, Rio. I'm not in the mood to cook anything. Are you going to eat with me?"

"Fuck no."

"What? Why did you say that?"

"I was just kiddin', baby. I gotta take care of my cook."

"So, you've made me your cook already? I suppose next you're going to start dropping your laundry off for me to do."

"As a matter of fa--."

"Don't even go there. I hurt too much right now to kick your butt."

"Well, I'll be there after work. I'm gonna stop and pick us up some fish. What kind you want?"

"Can you get me some filet of sole?"

"Yeah, I can do that."

"Thank you. I'll see you when you get here. Bye."

On the way home from work, I stopped at Big Momma's Seafood and ordered a snapper dinner and a filet of sole dinner to go.

On my way to Carmen's house, I thought about Uncle Lee. I remember I would beg my mother to let me go and spend the weekends with him when I was around thirteen or fourteen years old. He taught me how to drive, roll a joint, shoot, load and unload his .38 special, put on a rubber, shoot dice, box, drink, dress, and talk a broad out of her drawers.

Uncle Lee was my mentor, and my mother could not stand it. I remember she cussed him out one night when I was supposed to spend the night at his place. Moms happened to stop by to bring me some clean clothes, and when she came in, she was greeted by Uncle Lee sitting in the living room with two of his female friends.

At the time, I didn't see what Moms was so mad about. I was used to Uncle Lee and his women. I guess she didn't approve of the fifth of Hennessey and half ounce bag of weed on the coffee table. She told me to get my shit and made me come home. I was so mad at her I wanted to run away.

Sensing I didn't fully understand why she made me come home, Moms called me to the kitchen to explain. My lip was poked out so far, I damn near tripped over it. I played the role of the "mad kid".

"Rio, I know you're disappointed, but some of the things your uncle does are not good for you to be a part of. You'll understand when you're a little older. It's okay for you to be mad, but just make sure you remain respectful under my roof. Maybe after I have a talk with your uncle, you can go visit him again. Until then, I don't need to see you walking around here with an attitude."

I'll never forget how hurt I was. Uncle Lee could do no wrong in my eyes.

CHAPTER SEVENTEEN

As I approached Carmen's place, I saw Zoe's black Honda parked in front of Carmen's building. I'd finally get to meet the mysterious Madam Zoe.

As I approached her door, I heard the sound of feminine laughter. It sounded like my girl was feeling a little better. After I knocked on the door, I was greeted by my goddess dressed in jeans, a gray CK tee shirt, blue and white Nike women's cross trainers, and a kiss.

"Hi, baby! How are you? Come here, I want you to meet my friend, Zoe."

Sitting there in *my* spot on the couch was Zoe. That old saying about birds of a feather flocking together was true.

Zoe was about 5'10", 145 pounds, "light, bright, damn near white" complexion, had natural gray eyes, dimples, very long hair, a huge ass, voluptuous breasts, and a squeaky voice.

I hoped like hell Carmen didn't notice the way I gave Zoe the once over. I'm sure that Zoe did, though.

"Hello, Rio. So you're the one I've heard so much about," she said as I shook her hand.

"Well, I hope you don't hold it against me."

She smiled. "I've only heard the good stuff."

Damn! That voice would drive me crazy if I had to hear it everyday, but it wouldn't stop me from fuckin' the shit out of her long-legged ass.

"Here you go, Carmen. I got you a filet of sole dinner and me the red snapper."

"Oh, thank you!" She rewarded me with another lip smack.

Meanwhile, Zoe watched as though we were there for her amusement. "You two are so cute," she commented.

Blushing, Carmen took both bags of food and placed them on the counter. I did my best to keep my focus on Carmen, but Zoe's long legs—that protruded from the hem of her navy blue business suit—drew involuntary gazes from me.

"You want some fish, Zoe? We have filet of sole and some snapper," Carmen asked.

"Yeah, girl, I haven't had anything to eat since lunch time."

I could tell Ms. Zoe had a little ghetto in her from that statement. My eyes followed those legs when she got up and walked to the kitchen. She opened the fridge and asked Carmen what she had to drink.

As she bent over to take a better look inside the icebox, I saw the material of her skirt cling tightly to her big ol' ass.

After excusing myself to go to the restroom, I found my dick hard as hell. I felt like rubbing one out real quick, but decided against it. Instead, I washed my hands and then wrapped a wash rag rinsed in cold water around my pulsating crotch monster to calm it down.

Returning to the kitchen, I noticed the table had three plates with equal portions of fish and fries, and my side of potato salad.

Of the four chairs surrounding her solid oak table, the plate with the additional side of potato salad sat between the two of them.

Zoe had kicked off her navy blue and cream pumps and sat there chewing on a French fry in her stocking feet.

Carmen waited for me before she began eating. After I sat down, she said a silent blessing and then began enjoying her filet of sole.

"Do you want something to drink, Rio? I have Pepsi, milk, water, apple juice, and orange juice."

"Pepsi'll be fine, baby."

Over our meal, I found out Zoe worked for Clorox as some kind of executive administrator, which translated to her being a high-paid secretary.

My imagination ran rampant as I sat between them. Visions of a three-way Rio sandwich dominated my thoughts.

The more I tried not to look at Zoe, the more I was drawn to her. Her light gray eyes were hypnotic. My glances were split between those exotic eyes and her robust tits.

I'd encountered her kind before. She was the type of woman who got everything she wanted because of her looks. I could tell by the first paragraph that came out of her mouth that she had never been on any Dean's list.

She was more likely to have blown her way to a passing grade than she was to have opened a single book. Her "Ghettoisms" were plain as day.

I'd more than once caught her sitting with her legs uncrossed as if she had on pants. On those occasions, I was tempted to drop my fork so I could've bent over and seen what color drawers she had on.

The capper was when she finished eating and muffled a burp with the back of her hand. She was the type of person who could make herself at home no matter where she was. That bitch even smoked. I watched her open her cream and navy blue purse and pull out a pack of Kool Lights.

"You know you're not going to smoke that death stick in here!" Carmen said.

"I know, I know. I'm going to the balcony. Damn!"

When she stood up to go suck on her lung dart, her skirt hitched up high enough for me to see a small tattoo on her upper thigh. It looked like a little bull, maybe the Taurus zodiac sign. I had a sudden urge to investigate it up close and personal.

To get my mind off lusting for Zoe, I assisted Carmen with cleaning up. I went with Carmen as she washed the dishes and decided to tongue her good.

"What was that for?"

"I wanted to taste you."

"Is that right? Well, if you wait a few more days, I'll have something else you can taste."

"Oh really? Does your Momma know you talk like that, young lady?"

"How you think I got here?"

Damn, I was horny as hell. I wanted to do her right then, period or no period.

"What do you think of my buddy?" Carmen asked.

"She seems like good people," I said, acting like I hadn't paid Zoe much attention.

"Yeah, we met the first day I started working for PG&E. We were standing in line waiting for our food at Sam's.

I guess the lady was taking too long to get the orders ready, so Zoe's loud butt blurted out, 'Why don't y'all hire some damn help?' It was so funny hearing a well-dressed woman talking crap. We ended up sitting at the same table, laughing and talking our whole lunch hour. Since then, we've been the best of friends."

"That's cool. It's good to have friends like that. What y'all doin' tonight?"

"She wants me to go out with her. We haven't had a girl's night out in a while."

I felt a twinge of jealousy at that moment. How dare she even consider going out when she knew I was coming over!

"What did you have planned, baby?"

"I was hopin' to be with you, but I see I've been shot to the curb."

She stopped in the middle of washing the last plate. "Rio, don't do that, please. I know I invited you over, but to be honest with you, Zoe just broke up with her boyfriend a few days ago and needs to have her spirits lifted. Please understand. I promise I'll make it up to you, okay?"

I gave her my "sad face" and said, "That's okay. I know she comes first."

"You're so mean, Rio. Stop, you know you're my baby." She took her wet hand, placed it on my cheek, and gave me a long, hot kiss.

Zoe cleared her throat behind us. I had no idea how long she'd been standing there, but I would guess long enough to have witnessed our lip lock.

"I thought y'all would never break it up!" she said with a grin. "After a kiss like that, girl, maybe I should go out by myself so you two can handle ya business!"

"Shut up! Your mind is forever in the gutter," Carmen said.

"Oh, my mind is in the gutter? You're the one over there takin' advantage of the poor man."

"Hey, my dog's not in that fight!" I said.

"Don't pay any attention to her, Rio. She's always talking crazy."

Damn, Zoe had some big tits. The kind I would've loved putting my penis right between.

Feeling my temperature rise, I went and sat on the couch until Carmen finished in the kitchen. That ghetto bitch Zoe had me hot as the devil's bathwater. Something about a woman with a little slut in her was a major turn on to me. I sure hoped Carmen didn't notice me drooling for Zoe.

Not wanting to hold them up, and growing tired of avoiding Zoe, I decided to leave. Before I could make my announcement, Zoe sat down next to me and picked up the TV remote, flipping through the channels like a pro. Carmen went to the restroom, leaving Zoe and me alone. Zoe caught me watching her crossing and uncrossing her legs.

"Looking for this?"

Startled, I looked up and saw she held the remote control limply in her hand, grinning like a fox. Playing it off, I replied, "Yeah. I wanted to see if the Warriors game was on yet."

"You sure that's what you were looking for? I thought maybe you were tryin' to read my tattoo."

"What you mean?"

"Don't try to play it off, Rio. I've caught you a few times tryin' to sneak a peek."

Before I could try and defend myself, the sound of the toilet flushing and the bathroom door opening ended our little game. I tensed up and hoped she wouldn't snitch on me for looking at her thighs.

But she was cool. She acted like nothing happened. The girl had game.

Deciding it was the perfect time for me to make my exit, I stood up to leave. "Well, I think I'll head to the house so you two can get ya party on. I'll catch up with you later, hon."

"Okay, maybe we can hang out tomorrow if you aren't busy."

"We'll see. I'm not sure what I have to do yet, but I'll keep you posted."

As I was about to leave, I stole one last look at Zoe. To my surprise, she returned my glance while twisting a piece of her long, black hair around her finger. I'd seen that look many times before, usually right before the fuckin' started.

"I hope you feel better, baby. You go have some fun for me, a'ight?"

"Okay, Rio. I do feel a lot better now. It's almost over."

"Gimme a kiss so I can go." I drew closer to her.

She wrapped her arms around my neck and tongued me to death. While our tongues were busy, my mind was on that long-legged Amazon sitting on the couch. How I would've loved to taste her tongue. After the kiss, I waved bye to Zoe. She reciprocated with a smile.

"Oh, Rio, I meant to ask; would you like to go with me to our office Halloween party?"

"Yeah, when is it?"

"Next week."

"Okay. You have a costume in mind?"

"Yes. I'm going to go as a flapper dancer from the twenties. I found a purple flapper style skirt and matching headpiece."

"Damn, that sounds sexy as hell!"

"Thank you. I envisioned you as a depression-era gangster in a pin-stripped suit and fedora."

"I'm down with that."

"Good, 'cause I found both costumes at this costume shop in Alameda. If you give me your clothes sizes and a ride over there, I'll pick them up."

"You should already know I'd do that for you in a minute."

"Well, I'm not one to overstep my boundaries, Mr. Rio, so I thought I'd ask."

"It's gonna cost you, though."

"Here we go again. What's the going rate these days for a ride to Alameda?"

"It's gonna cost you a night of passion and freakery."

"Is that all? I see you come cheap. I was gonna give you that free of charge, but that's okay now," she said in her slightly southern drawl.

"How could someone as fine as you are be so nasty?"

"That's for me to know and you to find out."

"Well, I fully intend to find out soon." I broke our embrace and left.

CHAPTER EIGHTEEN

The following week I sat on my bed after showering and prepared for the Halloween party. After drying off and applying lotion, I went through my underwear drawer and found a pair of my "special drawers". They were some nut hugging, tight black briefs I bought while shopping with Uncle Lee in L.A. They had a glow in the dark yellow arrow pointing to my dick with a caption that said, "You are here."

At 3:20 p.m., I took my costume out of the closet and spread it out on my bed. After putting on my pants and socks, I got my Stacy Adams shoes and buffed them off. I buttoned up my black shirt, tied my white tie, tucked my white handkerchief into my breast pocket, put on my jacket, attached my faux pocket watch and chain, and last but not least, put on the Fedora.

Standing in the mirror, I looked like a genuine old school gangster. All I needed was a Tommy gun.

Oh shit! It was 3:39 p.m. I got my phone and called Carmen.

"Hey baby, I'm on my way out the door now. I'll be there in about ten minutes."

"All right. I'm running late, too. Zoe had me on the phone wanting to know when she should get there. I told her to meet us there at about six o'clock. Anyway, I'm on my way out the door. See you in a minute."

It stopped raining as I stood in her doorway and waited for her. A couple minutes later, she opened the lobby doors and greeted me wearing a purple and silver sequined headpiece that fitted her head like a shower cap. She wore matching purple lipstick and she looked like something right out the old Cotton Club movie.

Carmen's full-length wool coat was buttoned all the way down, so I couldn't see the rest of the costume. The only thing I saw was her purple shoes and her purple and silver painted fingernails.

"Wassup with you hidin' the rest of your costume from me? Lemme see, baby!"

She smiled and replied, "No, Tiger, you have to wait until we get there."

"Damn, you need to quit holdin' out on a brotha!"

"Patience, baby. You look good in that suit, Rio! It looks like it was made for you," she said as she straightened my tie.

"Thanks. I can't wait to see what's under your jacket."

After I let Carmen in and was about to close her door, I looked down and caught a glimpse of the top of the thigh-high stockings she wore. My dick stiffened.

After putting her umbrella and purse in the trunk, we were off to the party.

CHAPTER NINETEEN

Since we were among the first people to arrive, we were able to park close to the entrance. As we approached the door, we were greeted by a few of Carmen's colleagues.

"Hello, Carmen! Glad to see you made it!"

"Hey, how are you, Glenda?" They gave each other a hello hug. Glenda, as it turned out, was Carmen's department manager.

Glenda was a fifty-something white woman with blue eyes, long black hair (which I'm sure had been touched up to hide some gray), average build, and way too many teeth in her smile. She was dressed up as a witch, pointy hat and all.

"And who's this handsome gentleman?"

"This is my boyfriend, Rio. Rio, meet Glenda. She's the *boss*," Carmen said with a grin.

"Pleased to meet you, Rio. Don't call me "boss". The name's Glenda, the Bad Witch."

"Boy, don't I know that," Carmen replied.

"Hey, watch it! Don't make me turn your handsome prince into a toadstool!" Glenda said with false anger.

"Okay, I'll quit while I'm ahead. I don't wanna have to dance with a toadstool."

After their exchange, I was both elated and a little shaken. Carmen had introduced me as her "boyfriend".

On one hand, I was glad Carmen considered me her "boyfriend". On the other hand, since we hadn't actually gone "all the way", I wasn't sure how I was gonna feel after we finally did. What we'd done so far had been enjoyable as hell, but I wouldn't feel totally into Carmen until we had real sex.

What if we didn't click afterwards?

What if I didn't like her pussy?

What if she didn't give head?

What if I meet another woman finer and with more goin' on than Carmen had?

What? What? What?

I hadn't been that paranoid since I smoked my first joint.

I took a deep breath and tried to shake those thoughts and just enjoy myself.

"Honey, I have to go help set up. You don't have to come with me if you don't want to. You can go have a drink if you like."

"No, it's cool. I wanna stay with my 'girlfriend'."

The way she smiled at me let me know I made the right choice. The little "girlfriend" remark also got me an extra tight hug.

We walked to the coat-check room and I waited for the unveiling. Carmen, with her back to me, slowly gave me an unintentional striptease as she took off her jacket.

Judging by the way the coat-check girl's eyes lit up, I was in for a pleasant surprise.

"Your costume is so cute!" she said, as though she wanted to take a bite out of Carmen.

The back was low cut and the hem was a few inches below the top of her thigh-high stockings. The skirt matched her headpiece, purple with silver sequins and small silver fringes that shimmied and shook with each movement of her hips. Carmen's skirt showed off her Coke bottle shape. When she turned around, I felt like the sun had risen in my face.

The neckline was low cut, just enough to show off her generous cleavage. Looking at her dressed in the entire costume, I felt like I did when I saw her in the washhouse for the first time.

Goddamn, she was fine!

"Are you okay, Rio?"

"Hmm? Oh yeah...damn, baby...you make that costume look *good*! I'm proud as hell to have you as my chick."

Modestly, she said, "It's just a skirt and headpiece."

The way all the eyes followed my purple-covered goddess, I was a man to be envied that night.

Carmen met and greeted various co-workers on the way to the judges' table they'd set up on the stage for the upcoming costume contest.

"I can already tell you're gonna win the costume contest, sweetheart."

"I wish, but I can't because I'm one of the judges."

"What? You're kiddin'! You're the finest woman in here, bar none."

"Thank you, honey." She rewarded me with a kiss on the cheek.

It looked like they were gonna have a packed house. Many people were there early.

At 5:50 p.m., we were greeted by a squeaky voice that could only belong to one person, Zoe.

"Hey girl, love the dress! Wassup, Rio? Damn, that suit is fly!"

Zoe was dressed in a catsuit which left nothing to the imagination. It was all black, with a cat tail sewn on to her huge tail. She also wore a cat nose with whiskers, a black Zorro type mask, and a pair of black cat ears which sat atop her head.

That Amazon chick had body like a muthafucka.

Some buster in a Dracula costume escorted her. He wore fake fangs, fake blood, and make-up that made his coffee-colored skin appear to be pale.

"This is my friend, Larry. Larry, this is Carmen and her man, Rio."

"Hello, you two. How are you?"

I could tell right away the dude was *way* too square to be Zoe's man.

"When do we get our drink tickets? I'm ready to get my drink on! Heyyyy!" Zoe shouted. She was truly ghetto fabulous.

Carmen went over to Glenda, and after a short conversation and a laugh, Glenda handed her four envelopes containing the drink tickets.

"Here you go, Alky. You can go get your drink on now," Carmen said with a laugh. Our envelopes contained three free drink tickets along with a raffle ticket.

"What's the raffle prize, baby?"

"It's a dinner for two at the House of Prime Rib in San Francisco."

I studied the contents of my envelope and said, "Hell, I'd rather have that than the prize for best costume."

At the bar, I ordered my favorite, Long Island Iced Tea. Carmen ordered a Cosmopolitan, Larry a Kaluha and Cream, and Zoe a Screaming Orgasm.

It was the first time I'd seen Carmen drink anything stronger than wine. I wondered how she would act after she had a few drinks in her.

Larry and the "girlie drink" he ordered only confirmed my suspicions: He was no more than Zoe's chauffer for the night.

We staked a claim at a table near the stage. I couldn't keep my eyes off of Carmen. She was by far the sexiest woman in the building.

By the time we finished our second round of drinks, dinner was served. It was the same old choice of either baked chicken or a shoe heel sized steak, along with the side dishes of steamed veggies, rice pilaf, and dinner rolls I'd been served at mostly all the company functions I'd attended.

All during dinner, my right hand constantly found Carmen's thigh under the table. Her skin was butter smooth and baby soft.

I could tell she enjoyed my touch by the way she positioned her leg right against mine for easy access. I fought the enticement to reach under her skirt in fear I may have nutted on myself.

Having Zoe sit right across from me didn't help either. We'd exchanged glances more than once across the table. I felt a foot brush against my shin, but I declined to return the favor in fear it may have been Larry's foot instead of Zoe's.

The dessert cart was a lot more impressive than the dinner was. It contained an assortment of sweet, sinful treats in the forms of black cats, ghosts, witches, and pumpkin-shaped cookies.

As the dinner wrapped up—along with a few short speeches—the hip looking, Vietnamese DJ thumbed through his record crates.

Just like clockwork, he began playing music at eight o'clock sharp. He announced the music theme for the night was Jams from the Past.

He started it off with "Monster Mash", and all the inebriated guest—mostly white folks—rushed to the floor to get their groove on.

Seeing as the line was short, we all agreed to go get another drink instead of dancing. Since I was already feeling nice, I got a gin and tonic instead of another Long Island Iced Tea.

Carmen, however, had her third Cosmo, and judging from her giddiness, she was feeling nice as well.

I stood behind Carmen in the drink line, holding her around her waist and close to me. When the DJ played Michael Jackson's "Thriller", she gently swayed to the music and rubbed her body against mine. It was a good thing my suit had plenty of ball room or else my erection would have been seen for miles.

The four of us got our drinks, went back to our seats, and enjoyed the show being put on by the wild dancing drunks.

After thirty minutes of playing Halloween music, the DJ finally threw on "Let's Get It Started" by M.C. Hammer.

"Oh shit! That's my song! Come on, y'all, let's dance!" Zoe yelled.

We all followed Zoe and worked our way into the middle of the crowded dance floor. That was the first time I'd danced with Carmen since the night of the pedicure. And man, was I in for a treat. She danced in sync with every beat of the music. I was awestruck by the way she moved. I watched the fringes on her skirt move as though they were in a chorus line and her hips were leading them on.

She moved in close and began to grind on me. I put my right hand around her waist and gyrated in rhythm with her as the bass pounded.

Poor Larry tried to imitate me, but Zoe cut him off by spinning away and turning her tail to him. I knew he was gonna have blue balls that night.

We danced for three more records before taking a break to cool off. I took off my "gangsta" jacket and placed it on the back of my chair, then took off my hat and wiped my head with my handkerchief.

"Whew! I see you know how to work it on the dance floor, Mr. Rio."

"No, you're the one! I just tried to keep up with you."

"I'm going to the bathroom. I'll be right back, okay?"

"A'ight, just hurry and bring all *that* back to me."

"Silly, I'll be right back."

Zoe accompanied Carmen to the restroom. Many eyes followed those asses as they strolled to the bathroom.

I gave the other fellas a look that said, "Yup, I'm gonna do all the things to Carmen you're fantasizing about."

Minutes later, the chicks returned a bit revitalized. Meanwhile, Larry had been boring the shit out of me by telling me about his job at Clorox. He was a Data Analyst and he told me Zoe had been jockin' him to come to the party with her. I was tempted to tell him the only reason she chose him to come with her was because she needed a designated driver.

In order to mellow everyone out, the DJ played "Groove with You" by the Isley Brothers. I took Carmen's hand and led her to the dance floor.

After constantly begging her, Larry convinced Zoe to give him a slow dance. He looked as happy as a fag with a bag of dicks.

"It looks like ya girl has her hands full."

"Yeah I know," Carmen said with a laugh.

While the Isleys sung for us, I moved with Carmen, inhaling the light scent of her expensive perfume.

"I love your eyes, Rio." Hearing her say that almost made me piss on myself. I thought for a second she said she loved *me.*

"They love looking at you, too," I replied in my best Don Juan voice.

She smiled, laid her head on my shoulder, and rubbed the back of my neck. Watching Zoe struggle with Larry as he took full advantage of the dance to feel her up was comical. I watched as his hand slowly dropped to the top of her costume tail, and her hand lifted it back up to her waistline.

Zoe caught me looking when Larry had his back turned to me. She gave me a look like a fly caught in a spider's web.

I don't know if it was Zoe's grin or Carmen's body heat that made my dick pulsate.

"Feels like something woke up," Carmen said to my surprise.

"It's been wide awake since you took your coat off."

"Is that right? Well, I hope it has insomnia tonight."

"I want you, Carmen," I whispered in her ear as the song ended. She didn't answer with words. Instead, she bent my head over, inserted the tip of her tongue into my ear, and nibbled my earlobe before letting me go.

It was time for the costume contest to begin. Carmen took my hand and led me to the stage where she'd be joining the other four judges.

"This shouldn't take long, okay?"

"No problem. I'll just hang backstage."

The judges' tables were onstage in front of the curtains. I'd taken a seat to the far right of the stage, out of the crowd's view.

As the finalist began to parade across the stage, I felt the need to go pee. Instead of walking through the crowd, I decided to see if there was a bathroom backstage.

While the judges were busy scrutinizing for costume originality, I crept behind the curtain in search of a restroom. I noticed an office backstage I assumed the stagehands used as a breakroom. It contained a humming Coke machine, two snack vending machines, a couch, a table, and a countertop microwave.

Continuing my search for a bathroom, I was relived to see a blue triangle sign with a tiny wheelchair symbol and the word MEN across the top.

I rushed inside, tripping a motion sensor, and the lights blazed, making me squint.

After losing about a quart of urine, I washed my hands and worked my way back to the stage. On the way, I noticed an area of about twenty square feet in the corner. It was filled with crates, props, extra lighting, and two pallets stacked about three feet high with blankets movers used to wrap furniture in to protect it during transit.

I returned to my seat just in time to see the winner claim his prize. He was dressed up as Data, the android on "Star Trek, the Next Generation". He looked exactly like him, from the uniform all the way to the fake eye contacts.

He left the stage waving his gift certificate, while his girlfriend—who was dressed like Seven of Nine from another Star Trek spin-off—grinned at the certificate she'd probably end up spending.

Carmen spotted me and walked over to me.

"Where'd you go? I looked up and you were gone."

"I went back there to use the bathroom." I pointed behind the curtains.

"That's just what I need to do."

"Come on, I'll show you where it is."

"I don't know if we're supposed to go back there, Rio."

"Aw come on, those folks are way too drunk to notice."

"I guess you're right. Okay, where is it?"

Since the contest was over, they turned down the overhead lights so the party could continue. It was almost pitch black backstage where we were.

"I can't see a thing. Can you, Rio?"

"Yeah, here it is right here." I pushed the door to the women's bathroom open.

She, too, was momentarily blinded by the bright light in the women's restroom. A couple minutes later, I heard the sound of the toilet flush followed by the sound of water running as she washed those pretty hands.

"Whew, I thought I was gonna pee on myself waiting for that contest to be over."

My horniness took over. As the bathroom door closed behind her, I placed both my hands on her soft titties and gently massaged them.

"Careful, that may get you in trouble."

"That's good. I'm overdue for some trouble."

The softness of her breast under her clothes was maddening. I dropped my hands to her ass and followed with a deep tongue kiss.

It seemed she was as horny as I was by the way her tongue rushed to meet my own. Our hands moved, touched, and caressed as we stood there in the dark letting our cravings loose.

"I want you, Rio," Carmen moaned more than said. I picked her up as though she were weightless and carried her as we continued kissing.

The sound of the song "Atomic Dog" blared as I dodged props and crates on my way to a special place. Once my eyes had become accustomed to the dark, I got to where I wanted to be without a hitch.

"Where are we?" she whispered.

"Just relax. We're right where we need to be."

With that, I sat her down on the pallet of furniture blankets and resumed kissing and feeling.

Not even questioning me about how I found the spot, she relaxed and went with the flow. I was so hot and hard I could have fucked an elephant raw.

I began grinding between her wide spread legs. She met my every bump and grind with her own. Her skirt was bunched up above her hips, allowing me full access to everything underneath.

I felt her hand desperately search for my zipper.

"You ready for this, baby?"

"Oh yessss…Rio, I want you…now."

I was so fuckin' turned on, I couldn't wait for her to unzip me, and so I gave her a hand.

When she felt my hard, warm member in her hand, she let out a hungry sigh which told me it was feeding time.

I stood up and looked down at her silver lame thong and took it off.

Without hesitation, I entered her wet, steamy rainforest. We simultaneously let out moans of pleasure as we finally felt each other.

Our fucking was hard, fast, and furious. Her warm thighs were spread one on each side of our makeshift bed.

I remembered trying to consciously not mess her clothes up, but the thought was soon lost when she pulled my head down to her and sucked my tongue in rhythm with the strokes of my dick going in and out of her.

I heard the DJ announce he was about to play the last song of the night, which appropriately turned out to be "Fire and Desire" by Rick James and Teena Marie.

Carmen didn't hold anything back. She moaned with pleasure as I gave her the long stroke, pulling all the way out until the tip of my head was touching her wet lips, then slamming all the way back into the bottom.

I felt her claw into my back with her silver and purple nails, and in the dim light, the pleasure on her face let me know she was close to climaxing.

She drew in a deep breath, and at the same time, wrapped those strong legs around me, pulling me deeper inside of her. The action sent a signal to my ball sac which told my sperm it was time to surface.

Funny, I didn't once think about a condom, and neither had she. Right then, it would have been too late anyway. There was no way in hell I was pullin' out of that hot, wet place.

Faster, deeper, faster, harder.

We fucked each other out of control. I vaguely remembered hearing one of her pumps hit the floor as I wrapped my arms around her, letting her know I was as close as she was to cumming. She quivered and tightened her leg lock around my waist. I felt her pussy throb and grip my dick, causing my eyes to roll to the back of my head. I was about to explode.

"Ohhhhhhhhhhhhhhh Carmennn…gonnacummmmm!" I shouted, speaking in tongues.

"Give it… all…to meeeeeeee. Let…it goooo…mmmmm…" she whispered.

Carmen came violently, causing me to fill her insides with my warm liquid love.

We lie there out of breath and clutching each other for what seemed to be an eternity as I lingered inside of her.

Without warning, the overhead lights came on and the DJ thanked everyone for coming. Next, we heard the sounds of muffled voices and chairs scooting underneath tables.

I looked into her angelic face. "I guess this means the party's over, huh?"

Her headpiece was all but off her head, showing her hair which luckily was still pinned up underneath.

As I slowly and reluctantly pulled out of her, I saw a huge wet spot on the gray blanket we had used as a bedspread. *That's gonna need a good scrubbin'*, I thought.

I took her soft hand and helped her sit up. Her skirt was up around her belly button, but didn't appear to be in too bad a shape. A few of the sequins had been dislodged and decorated the gray blanket.

My hat was upside down on the floor lying next to one of her shoes. I looked at her feet and saw the other shoe was off as well. On the other side of the pallet, I spotted the other shoe on its side, as though it were sleeping.

"I can't find my thong," Carmen said.

I helped her look for it and saw it had slipped down between the pallets.

"I see it, but I can't reach it."

She tried, but even her arms were too wide for the narrow space.

"Damn, I just bought those, too. I guess I'll have to leave 'em."

"I bet it's gonna make some stagehand's day!" We both laughed at my observation.

"I have to hurry and go to the bathroom before we leave." Carmen slipped into her shoes, pulled down her skirt, and walked with her legs squeezed together. I guess with all the sperm I had just pumped into her that was to be expected.

I went to the men's room and washed up the best I could. We were in such a rush I wasn't able to show her my glow in the dark draws. It would have to wait until next time. I came out before she did and realized if we left via the stage, we'd be cold busted. I looked around and noticed a green glowing EXIT sign on the other side of the break room. I breathed a sigh of relief when I found it wasn't alarmed.

"Sorry it took me so long. I had a lot of cleaning up to do," Carmen said with a smile.

"Come on, we can go out this door to get back to the front and get our stuff."

She gave me a simulated accusatory look. "Hmmm, sounds like you've done this before, Slick."

I grinned and took her hand. "Only in my dreams."

When I opened the EXIT door, a blustery wind greeted us, but no rain.

Carmen did a damn good job straightening herself up, considering she had no comb or any of her other womanly things.

"Damn, that was good," I said to her and myself.

"Yes, it was. Real good," she agreed.

I removed my hand from hers and put it around her shoulders as hers went around my waist.

CHAPTER TWENTY

As we turned the corner heading back toward the entrance, we saw there was still a crowd of people milling about. Most of them were black folks talking about going to The Spot to keep the party going.

We managed to slip by mostly unnoticed and got back to our table. My coat was still on the back of my chair, but there was no sign of Zoe and Larry.

"I wonder where your girl and Prince Charmin' went."

"If I know Zoe, they're probably pulling up to her doorstep and she's sending him home disappointed."

We went to coat-check and got her jacket. From behind us we heard, "Uh huh! Where the hell y'all been?" in a high-pitched, squeaky, slightly slurred voice.

When we turned around, it was like Zoe and Larry knew what we had been up to.

"We were dancing," Carmen said, trying to keep a straight face.

"Bullshit! The last thing I saw was you disappear behind the curtain with 'Smiley Jack' there and I haven't seen you since."

Larry looked at me with eyes that said, "Damn, you're lucky!"

"We had to go out the back door and go to my car. I thought I had left my window open and I didn't want any rain to get in."

My lie even sounded weak to me.

"Yeah, right! Well, your shirt sure did get wrinkled a lot from 'dancing' as you call it," Zoe said, knowing damn well something went down. The way Carmen and I glowed, it was a losing battle trying to come up with a decent alibi, so I changed the subject.

"You guys goin' to The Spot? I heard some of the folks in front talkin' about goin' there."

Zoe took a step back behind Larry and put a finger to her lips, signaling me to be quiet. I guess their night was over.

"Nah, I'm too tired. Besides, I have to be at church early," she responded, playing it off. She even threw in a fake yawn.

"I guess I'd better get you home then," Larry said with hope that he was gonna get some.

Zoe said to Carmen, "You better call me when you get home. We need to talk."

"Okay, okay. Yes, *Mother*, I'll call you."

They hugged and said goodbye. Zoe hugged me and whispered in my ear, "Next time, zip your pants up when you're done," and gave me a smile.

I let my hands fall to my zipper and found it was halfway down. I turned around as nonchalantly as I could and zipped it all the way up.

I'm not sure if she meant when I got through pissin' or screwin', but the grin she gave me when I turned back around led me to believe it was the latter.

After Carmen said goodbye to Glenda and a few other co-workers, we took our time walking to my car, still caught up in the moment.

A few raindrops fell on us as we got to the car. Before I let her in, I turned her to me and looked in her eyes. I don't know what I was looking for, but I kept looking anyway.

"What is it, baby?" she asked as a few raindrops fell on her nose.

I planted a major kiss on her as the raindrops became heavier. Instead of breaking loose to get out of the rain, we continued to kiss.

My dick rose, ready to unleash hell on her pussy once again. I felt a stream of rain water running down the brim of my hat onto my shoulder as my tongue softly massaged Carmen's.

I looked at her and saw her headpiece was getting soaked. She had a sprinkle of raindrops on her forehead that looked like transparent freckles.

"Get in, princess, so we can go."

"I don't want to let you go yet. This feels good," Carmen said, snuggling up close to me. My hat slightly shielded her from the rain.

I held her tighter and said, "Anything you say, baby girl." I could feel her body heat through the leather of her jacket. There we were, standing in the rain kissing and holding each other like two lovesick fools.

Even though it felt good and right, I could still feel the Doubting Thomas in me trying to gain control of my feelings. Thoughts of "Can I trust her?" and "What if she gets pregnant?" were tapping on the window of my subconscious, begging for attention. Instead of letting those thoughts in, I closed the blinds. I was gonna enjoy the moment.

"Come on. Let's get you out this rain. The last thing I wanna do is get you sick after the good night we've had."

"Okay," she sighed.

I opened the door and got one last kiss for the road, then closed it behind her.

We were just about the last ones to leave the parking lot. I turned on the radio just in time to hear "Sweet Love" by Anita Baker.

Carmen's hand found mine as we began the short trip back to her place. My thoughts were on having her again before the night was over. Upon arrival, I found no parking spots in front of either my place or hers.

"Baby, you can park in my stall in the underground parking garage if you like," Carmen said.

"Good thinkin'. I'll do just that."

When I pulled up to the touchpad at the entrance to the garage, she gave me the code to get in, and then guided me to her assigned stall.

"I wish my building had parking like this. Sometimes, I have to park damn near around the corner."

"Well, now that you know the code, you can use it anytime you want." We exited the car, and I grabbed her umbrella and purse out of my trunk. It felt eerie, like we were a married couple on the way home from a night out.

Even at one in the morning, there was still the sound of music in the air and people on the streets, mingled with the steady sound of rain. I put my arm around Carmen's shoulder and ambled with her to the elevator. We only had to wait a minute for it to arrive. I pushed the six button and we were on our way up.

Carmen stood in front of me, unbuttoned my jacket, reached inside, and hugged me around the waist. She placed her head on my chest.

I held her until the chime told us we'd arrived at her floor. After the elevator doors opened, we were greeted by a Mexican couple on their way down.

All four of us exchanged smiles and then headed off in opposite directions.

"This must be a night for romance. That's my next door neighbor Juanita and her new boyfriend."

"Yeah, it feels like that kinda night."

Once inside, she stretched and took off her coat.

"Don't just stand there like a stranger. Make yourself at home. Get out of those wet clothes."

I chuckled to myself, thinking that sounded like one of my lines.

"Sure thing, baby, I'll be glad to."

Carmen hung up her jacket, kicked off her pumps, took off her headpiece, and released her hair from confinement.

"I'll be right back, okay?" I nodded, acknowledging her, and proceeded to get comfortable. I kicked off my Stacy Adams and put them next to the couch, undid my tie, sat down on the couch, and turned on the TV.

Carmen returned wearing a purple silk robe and joined me on the couch. I couldn't tell what she had on underneath, but since I could see her nipples outlined nicely under the silk fabric, I ventured a guess she was nude.

"I love your purple wardrobe more and more."

"Thank you. There's a lot more where this came from." Carmen laid her head on my shoulder and asked, "Are you going home tonight?"

"Only if you want me to."

"Good, I was hoping to hear that. Let's go to my bedroom."

"That sounds damn good to me." I clicked the red power button on the TV remote control and followed her well-formed booty into the bedroom.

She turned on the Aiwa mini component set which sat on her dresser and put in a CD. She lit a single, tall white candle that sat in a holder shaped like a woman sitting Indian style, holding the candle between her legs. In the meantime, I had stripped down to my "special drawers."

"Hey, don't turn around! Blow out the candle for a minute. I wanna show you somethin'."

"What are you up to, Rio?" she asked as she blew out the candle.

"Okay, look." I stood in the "Superman" pose, giving her full view of the glowing message on my drawers.

She laughed. "You're so bad! But that's cute!"

"I just wanna be sure you can find what you're lookin' for."

"Oh, I don't need a glowing sign, baby. Your signpost is big enough for me to find with my eyes closed," Carmen said in an arousingly sensual voice before she turned to relight the candle.

Carmen untied her belt before walking up the two steps which led to the top of her Queen-sized Mahogany poster bed. I watched as her robe fell lazily to the cream-colored carpet on her bedroom floor.

The curves of her drum-tight body were lusciously outlined by the dim, wavering candle light. She had a six-pack belly that rivaled Janet Jackson's. Her ass was round, tight, and smooth with no imperfections. Her ample breasts were firm, unabused by time or overuse.

Her areolas were coffee-colored. Her erect nipples looked like the erasers on those oversized pencils I used in first grade.

Just looking at her, I felt blood rush to my genitals.

"Damn, you're sexy, girl. Come here and lay with me."

She smiled and ascended the mahogany steps.

We lay there on top of her bedspread with me positioned on my back and Carmen on her side rubbing my nearly bare chest.

The Clark men had hardly any chest hair at all. I had just a sprinkle right between my pecks.

"I'm on the pill, Rio."

"What made you say that?"

"Well, I figured it would put your mind at ease considering the fact I have about a gallon of your sperm swimming upstream inside me right now."

I could see her white smile even in the muted light.

"Whew! That's a relief. I was just calculating when your due date would be," I joked.

"Do you have any kids, Rio?"

"Nope, not a one."

"Do you want any?"

I knew that was coming. Normally, I would have said, "Hell naw!" but the look in her eyes told me I had better come correct with my answer.

"To be honest with you, I don't want any, but who knows. If I meet the right woman, I might change my mind."

"I see. Do you think you'll ever find that woman?"

"I pray every day I will."

What a big lie that was. I was gonna have a lie bump as big as my fist on my tongue.

Carmen seemed satisfied with my answers.

"What about you? Do you want any?"

Carmen stared off into space as she rubbed my chest. "I've always wanted a big family of my own, but as I get older, the number of kids I'd like to have decreases. I believe I'm down to about two or three."

I put my hand into her long, black hair and pulled her down to me until our noses touched.

"You never did answer me when I asked you to 'go with me', you know."

"Oh really?" Carmen laughed as she recalled the day when I popped the question.

"Yes really! I poured my heart out to you and you just played with it like a cat with a ball of yarn."

"Po' baby." Carmen kissed me on the lips. "I thought you knew. You had me at the pedicure." She then placed her tongue in my mouth.

I rolled her over on top of me and felt her soft vaginal hairs brush against my upper thigh and her hard nipples against my chest. My fingers swam in her soft locks as we kissed over and over, gaining passion momentum. The sounds of our low moans almost drowned out the sounds of "Never Too Busy" by Kenny Latimore playing at low volume.

I rolled her onto her back and kissed her neck and ears as she opened her legs for me while rubbing my back. I continued my journey south, stopping only to suck on her concrete hard nipples. I licked slow circles around the areola and teased the nipples with the tip of my warm tongue and lips.

"Ohhh, baby," she murmured with pleasure.

I alternated between her left and right breast, giving each one equal attention. I ran my tongue down between the ripples in her six-pack, then stopped at her navel and played with her tiny navel ring with my tongue. Her hips undulated underneath me in anticipation of a licking by my well-trained tongue.

"I want you in my mouth. Turn over," she whispered. Without *any* hesitation, I rolled over and praised the Gods for the upcoming treat.

She took my diamond hard penis in both her hands and stroked it lovingly and tenderly. I felt one of her hands move to my balls and the warmth of her tongue on my shaft, licking it up and down as she moaned with delight. She used the other hand to rub the swollen head while licking the shaft.

"Oh, Carmen....Mmmmm...that feels...good," I managed to whisper.

Seconds later, I felt my dickhead disappear between her soft lips and a gentle sucking and licking motion took over. I lifted my head up just enough to see my dick going in and out of her mouth as she sucked me with her eyes closed, seeming to enjoy it as much as I did.

"Mmmmm, baby, turn around so I can lick you, too."

While still sucking, she managed to position her pussy right on my hungry mouth. I licked her moist pussy lips on a mission to find her clit. I could tell I found it when she took her mouth off my dick in order to gasp for air. She alternated between sucking me, moaning, and jacking me off. Carmen was so wet my chin was covered with her woman juice.

"I want you inside me now. Please, baby?" Carmen whimpered, begging for my hardness.

I joined her in her piles of pillows and lay between her spread-eagle legs. I looked into her eyes.

She placed her hand on my cheek and whispered, "Make love to me, Rio."

I kissed her right hand as she took her left hand, grabbed my hard soldier, and placed the head on the entrance to her tunnel of love.

We didn't fuck.

We made love.

It seemed to last forever. While stroking her, I sucked the fingers she placed in my mouth as she bit, kissed, and sucked my chest and nipples. There was no shortage of wetness in her. I could hear the wet smacking sound of me going in and out of her. I couldn't be sure of everything that was said in our throes of passion, but I vaguely remembered hearing the word love at some point.

I discovered she had multiple orgasms. When it got so good I couldn't hold back anymore, she grabbed my ass and simultaneously locked her legs behind mine so I couldn't escape, ensuring she got every drop of my love oil.

After unloading inside her, I fell over on my back and tried to catch my breath. She lay next to me breathing equally as hard, with her left arm across her eyes and the right on my thigh. The next thing I knew, I awoke to a chilly draft blowing across my legs and ass.

Carmen was balled up next to me in the fetal position as though she was trying to get warm. I got up, tossed the sheets back, and motioned for her to join me under the mile high pile of covers on her bed.

Without entirely waking up, she slipped under the covers next to me and we lay facing each other. I put my arm around her and she responded by scooting even closer to me. Our lips accidentally touched and our tongues followed suit.

After a few minutes of goodnight kisses, I noticed her alarm clock said 4:22 a.m. and then fell into a coma-like sleep.

Six hours later, my eyes fluttered open. I looked over my shoulder and saw my girl was still fast asleep. On her dresser, the candle had burned down to a small nub. I lay there with my hands beneath my head, staring at the ceiling as many thoughts and scenarios ran through my mind.

Where do we go from here?

How is her family gonna feel about me?

What if she's lying about being on the pill?

Can I trust her?

Is it possible that I'm in love with her?

Those were all valid questions which deserved answers.

But until that time, I'm gonna give this relationship all I have, keep on writin' in my journal, and see what happens.

CHAPTER TWENTY-ONE

A few days later, a monster rain storm blew through. While looking out the window next to my cubicle, I watched the wind blow a woman's umbrella inside out as she stood at the bus stop. Thousands of rain-soaked dead leaves and a few small tree branches stood no chance against the bully winds. *I'm sure glad I don't have to catch the bus*, I thought. I was reminded that Carmen would be out in the rain. *Too bad she gets off earlier than me or I'd give her a ride home.*

Fifteen minutes before I got off work, Carmen gave me a call. "Wassup, love?"

"Not much. Getting ready to leave the doctors office."

I heard the sound of a doctor being paged in the background. "Are you okay?"

"Yes. I just had a routine check up and now I'm on my way home. What are you doing?"

"I'm about to leave work." I looked out the window and saw the rain hadn't let up at all. "You want me to give you a ride home?"

"Sure, if you have time."

"Where is the doctor's office?"

"I'm at Kaiser on West MacArthur. Do you know where that is?"

"Yeah. I'll be there in about twenty minutes. I'll meet you at the main entrance."

"Okay. I'll be waiting. Bye."

Half an hour later, I picked her up. Before we pulled off, I asked, "Baby, when you gonna go pick up your car? I hate you having to use public transportation to get around. I heard there are more big storms on the way next week and I don't want you out in it."

"I don't know. I thought about it this morning when I got caught in a downpour on the way to work. It messed my hair up. Lucky for me, I had a scrunchy in my purse and was able to comb it into a ponytail. Since I didn't have an umbrella with me, I had to use my briefcase to cover up from the rain."

There was a moment of silence before I made the next statement. If I did offer to help her drive back from Alabama, I'm sure I'd have to meet her parents. To me, that was a major thing. I hadn't met a woman's parents I was dating in over ten years. Amanda used to practically beg me to go to her family functions so I could meet her family, but somehow I always managed to weasel out of it.

"You want me to help you drive your car back, Carmen?"

"Are you serious, Rio? Would you really go with me and help me drive back?" she asked wide-eyed.

"Yeah, I'll go with you. I have about two weeks of vacation left and I could use a getaway."

She leaned over and kissed me on the cheek.

"Thank you, Rio. I really appreciate the offer, and I do need a car to get around here and---"

Before she could finish thanking me, I lifted her chin so I could see her pretty face and said, "It's okay, baby." I held her chin and tongued her. We sat there after the kiss and hugged for a while as the rain drummed on the roof of my car.

"Can you get the time off to go, Carmen?"

"Yes, I have about a week of vacation time left I can use."

"Well, I suggest we go soon before the weather gets too bad."

"How soon can you take off, Rio? I can leave whenever. Let me know so I can get our plane tickets."

"I'll check the calendar at work and let you know. We should try to leave before Thanksgiving, though," I suggested as I drove her home. Two weeks later, it was time to leave. Carmen's sister agreed to pick us up from the airport once we got to Alabama. "Andretta said she's parking now and will meet us In front of the United Airlines baggage claim area outside in fifteen minutes," Carmen said as we walked towards the baggage claim area. "Is Andretta your younger sister?"

"No, she's the oldest girl. She's thirty-eight," Carmen responded as we stood at the baggage carousel. After claiming our four bags we went outside and waited for Carmen's sister to arrive. I couldn't help but wonder how Andretta would look.

It didn't take long for me to see her; I picked her out of the crowd instantly. I could see that the genes ran strong in her family. Andretta was so fine all the spit dried up in my mouth when I saw her. She was dressed in black slacks, black pumps, a red clingy sweater, waist length black leather jacket, full lips coated in red lipstick, hair in an immaculate French roll, eyes dark and mysterious, and a body that would stop traffic. On her ring finger I saw a huge rock; somebody had locked that good lookin' bitch down.

"Hi baby sis!" Andretta said as they both squealed and hugged. "How was your flight?"

"It was fine, just a little bumpy," Carmen said as she squeezed my hand.

"This has to be Mr. Rio!" Andretta gave me a hug. I felt her breast against me even though she tried to give me the "family hug" where you hugged without your bodies touching.

"How are you?" I asked.

"Real good! I'm so glad to see you two!" She had a much deeper southern accent than Carmen. "There are lots of people waiting to see you guys. Are you going to get a hotel room or stay at Momma's house?" Andretta asked.

"Now you know Momma wasn't hardly going to let us stay in a hotel," Carmen said with a gigantic smile.

"What did Daddy have to say about that?" Andretta asked.

"He was the one who first insisted we stay with them so he could meet my new boyfriend." They both shared a secret look and laughed like hell.

"Did she warn you about the grilling you're going to get from our father?" Andretta asked as we entered the elevator to take us down to the parking garage.

"No she didn't." I playfully squeezed Carmen's hand.

"Don't worry about him. He's all talk. He likes to play 'Protective Daddy' with his girls," Andretta said as our eyes met and lingered for a split second.

"Chester's the one. He thinks just because he's the oldest he has to play Daddy sometimes," Carmen chimed in as they once again shared the secret look and laugh.

In the parking garage Carmen and Andretta talked and laughed all the way to the car. I was impressed when we stopped at the rear of a new silver Range Rover. As soon as she opened the back hatch the smell of expensive leather wafted into my nostrils. The Rover was fully loaded including a DVD player mounted on the ceiling. When I opened the back door, there was a Houston Hills junior high gym bag on the seat.

"Just toss that in the back, Rio. That's my daughters cheerleading bag," Andretta said.

"You have a kid old enough to be in Jr. High?" I asked flattering her sexy ass.

"Why yes I do! As a matter of fact I have three children. Aquina's fourteen, she's the cheerleader. Adam's ten, and LaRell's my baby, he's seven," she said while smiling at me in the rear view mirror.

I still couldn't believe she had kids. Her body showed no signs that she had been through the rigors of child birth. She didn't even have the slightest baby pouch belly. I was overjoyed at that news; it gave me hope that Carmen would still have her sexy figure if she was to have a kid.

"Did you talk to Momma yet?" Andretta asked.

"Yes. I called her when we were getting off the plane and told her we were here waiting for you," Carmen said.

"I bet she's cooking up everything in the house," Andretta said with a laugh.

"I wonder who all's going to be there. What are the twins up to?" Carmen asked.

"You know those hard heads ain't changed; still hanging around the house driving Daddy crazy," Andretta said as we exited the garage and headed toward the freeway entrance.

I kicked back in the supple leather seat and chilled as I took in the sights. From what Carmen told me Alvintown, was the ultra small town. The population was two hundred people, only about ten percent were black.

All I could think of was the Klan, Confederate flags, and rednecks after she told me that. From what I could gather, her father was a big time dentist in Montgomery but liked the small town life of Alvintown. I'd never seen so many pickup trucks and cowboy hats in my life as I did that evening on the way to Carmen's parents' house.

"How long are you staying before you leave?" Andretta asked.

"I'd like to leave by Wednesday. We'll have at least three days of driving and a day to recuperate before going back to work," I replied.

"Damn girl, sounds like Rio has it all together," she said as she smiled at me in her rear view mirror.

"Yes he does. That's why he's my Boo!" Carmen smiled and gave me her hand. The closer we got to Alvintown the more it reminded me of the woods in the Blair Witch Project. We were going deep in the Sticks.

"How's Willie?" Carmen asked.

"He's fine. He took the kids to Prattville to his brothers' house for a birthday party for little Isaac. He turned eight today." Andretta said.

"What? He's already eight? The last time I saw him he was just turning five." Carmen said.

"Well, you have been gone for a long time, Sis. I bet you Momma's going to try to get you to stay," Andretta said with a chuckle.

After taking what seemed like the only Alvintown exit, I was relieved to see a few signs of civilization. There was a small strip mall with a Shoney's, an Amoco gas station, and a Dairy Queen. It looked like the hot nightspot for the youth to hang out at on summer nights.

As we continued through that one horse town, the homes became further and further apart. Most of them were made of brick nestled on large lots of land. It was going on 7:30 p.m. and it was dark as hell. There weren't many street lights in those woods.

We turned down what looked like a private road that was lined with trees and street lights. The road looked freshly paved. It twisted and turned for about a quarter mile before I saw Château Massey.

The place looked like the White House. The trees suddenly gave way to a lawn about half an acre long and wide before you got to the actual house. I couldn't see all the details of the house in the darkness, but what I could see told me there would be plenty of room for Carmen and me to stay.

"We're here!" Carmen said eyes full of joy. I noticed the house had a circular driveway that took you back out to the same road you came in on. The house was well lit and there were several cars parked in front of the house on the spacious driveway. Every car there seemed to have been made in Germany. The only exceptions were a Chevy Tahoe that was sitting on twenty-three inch chrome rims and the Range Rover we rolled up in.

"Dang! It looks like the entire family's here!" Carmen said.

"Surprise! We decided to have an early Thanksgiving dinner for you two since you won't be here next week!" Andretta blurted out.

"Oh no you didn't!" Carmen screamed with joy.

"Yes we did! Now you have to act surprised. You know I can't keep a secret!" Andretta said as they both laughed. At the door pleasant aromas drifted into my nose.

"Damn! Smells like somebody can cook in there," I said.

"Oh yeah, Momma can burn. I know you've tasted Carmen's cooking. Where you think she got her skills from?" Andretta asked happily. After Carmen rang the doorbell, I heard the sound of heels clicking on a hard surface on the way to let us in.

"Who is it?" A very polite southern accented voice asked.

"It's us Aunt CeCe!" Andretta said. Aunt CeCe came out of Andretta's mouth sounding like 'Ain't' CeCe. The woman that opened the door had to be in her late forties but could have passed for a woman in her early thirties. She was about the same height as Carmen, a little thicker, silver and black wavy short haircut, and had the same dark eyes as Carmen and Andretta.

"Carmen baby, is that you!" Aunt CeCe said as they hugged. "Now this handsome young man has to be Rio," she said as I offered her my hand. "Family don't shake hands here; you better give me a hug!" Aunt CeCe said as she bear hugged me. "Come on you guys! Dinner's all ready for you."

That was not a house; it was a mansion. The marble entry floor that led to the reception room had to cost five pounds of paper money. I heard voices a couple of rooms over from where we were.

"Just leave those bags there for now; you can take them up later," CeCe said.

"We're going to go wash up and then we'll be right there," Carmen took my hand and led me in the opposite direction.

"Damn this house is nice! How'd you ever leave here?" I marveled at the size and majesty of the home.

"Its okay I guess. If I hadn't left, we wouldn't have met," Carmen said as she ran a hand down my cheek.

We entered a bathroom that was as big as my kitchen. It had dual sinks with expensive looking faucets and a gray marble top. The house looked old yet new. The woodwork on the baseboards and trim was very intricately designed -- nothing like the bland way some of the new homes were designed.

"How long have your parents had this house?"

"My father bought it about thirty years ago, but the house itself was originally built in 1851. It used to belong to a rich cotton farmer, horse breeder and slave owner named Amos Underdown. This used to be called the Underdown Plantation."

"Wha? Your bullshittin' me, right?"

"Nope. It's all true. The back of the house burned down back in 1970 right before my parents bought it. They had it rebuilt as close to the original specs as possible," Carmen said as she dried her hands.

"Are you serious? There used to be slaves livin' in this house?" I was in awe.

"Yup! I'll give you the grand tour tomorrow; but right now I'm starving. Let's go eat."

I'd never been in a house that large. The staircase leading upstairs was as wide as a Buick. We passed walls decorated similarly to Carmen's place, lots of African artwork. I could hear the sounds of laughter and muttered conversations as we stepped into the dining room.

The dining room was enormous. Seated around a long rectangular solid oak table were nine people that definitely shared the same blood. The table had ten chairs, four on each side and one at each end. After doing the math, I saw that we were going to be one seat short. At the head of the table was a man with more Indian blood than black, whom I assumed was her father. On his right were three men and a woman; on his left were four women. One of them was a stunning woman the color of a Hershey bar. She had to be Carmen's mother.

The room became suddenly quiet upon our arrival. "Hello everybody!" Carmen said as she proceeded to hug and kiss everyone as they all stood up to greet us.

"Hey, Squeaky!" Her father said as he hugged her. "And you must be Rio," he said as he shook my hand.

"Nice to meet all of you," I said. Mr. Massey was about 5'9" at best and skinny as a rail. His hair was jet black, naturally wavy and gray at the temples. His skin was a rusty brown color and he had a big Indian nose. His teeth were white as chalk and were all natural. His eyes were black as frying pans and could see right through you. I knew then that the picture Carmen showed me of her Indian grandmother was her fathers' mother, not her mothers as I had assumed.

"Hello Rio! It's a pleasure to finally meet you!" Carmen's mother said as she flashed me a happy smile.

"The pleasure is all mine, Mrs. Massey," I said as I gave her a family hug. She was about 5'5" and still shapely despite the fact she had nine kids and nearly a dozen grandkids. She was a little plump, but you could tell she was the shit back in her day.

As everyone started taking their seats, Mrs. Massey did the math and also found that we were one seat short.

"Carmen, go get a chair out of the sitting room. You and Rio sit at the end of the table," Moms said. There was plenty of room for both of us on the end of the table; it had to be at least three feet wide.

Everyone at the table seemed to be cool except for this one dude who was sitting next to Carmen's father and he looked dead on him. He looked at me like I was up to something. He was about 5'8", with a thin build and short haircut like his father. His hair was also jet black and wavy. He was dressed in a black suit, yellow power tie, and was clean shaven. When I shook his hand it was clammy like a soggy dish rag. He barely mumbled "Hi" as he took his hand back.

Her other sister's name was Bethany, Bet for short. She was sexy in her own way, but looked like a straight up nerd. Her hair was in a bun so tight it made my head ache. She was dressed in a long dark blue dress with white buttons down the front. There was a split in the middle of her dress that let me know she had some seriously sexy legs.

All of her siblings were there except for the twin boys. Her youngest sister, LaKeisha, was fine, sexy and wild. That young bitch had it all; ass, tits, legs, everything. She was about 5'4", 130 lbs, and chocolate like her Momma. She had big tits, slim waist, and an ass that bought tears to your eyes. She was dressed in skin tight black knit dress that had buttons that went from her neck down to her belly button. It was unbuttoned down to her mouth watering mounds. Her black wavy hair hung loosely on her shoulders and was parted so that it fell over her right eye occasionally. When she shook my hand and said "Hi", I noticed she had a pink, flesh colored stud piercing her tongue. A small stud pierced her left eyebrow.

The food was top notch. There was a fried turkey and a baked turkey. The rest of the meal consisted of mashed potatoes, macaroni and cheese, greens, yams, ham, dressing, roast duck, corn bread, string beans, cranberry sauce, dinner rolls and fried chicken. It was a serious feast.

During dinner, the conversation went all over the place. Her brother—the hater with the clammy hands—did most of the questioning. He asked me what I did, what my parents did, how old I was, all kinds of shit. I had to basically run down my pedigree. Her father sat back like a general letting his second in command pump me for info while he analyzed it.

Her sister LaKeisha on the other hand was showing definite interest in this tall dude from California. I watched as she provocatively let her tongue linger on the corner of her mouth as she attempted to lick a drop of gravy from the corner of her mouth.

The fact that she was right next to me didn't help matters much. My mind immediately imagined her tongue stud licking my pee hole. I think Carmen saw the way LaKeisha was flirting with me when she squeezed my hand noticeably hard as I watched LaKeisha's tongue work on that drop of gravy. During that meal I found out the following about the Massey children:

"Clammy hands" real name was Chester. He owned a Chevy dealership in Mobile. Chester started off cleaning up his father's dental offices after school—her father started with two but now he has five—and he used the money he earned to buy used cars he would fix up and sell. After graduating from Syracuse University with a Masters in business, he used the ten thousand dollar graduation gift from his parents to open up his own small car lot. Ten years later, he had a very successful Chevy dealership.

Bethany was Daddy's girl. She used to come by his dentist office every day after school and watch her father ply his trade. By the time Bethany was in high school, she was able to clean teeth on her own and prep patients for dental surgery. She went to the University of Alabama and received her D.D.S. She runs most of the dental operation for her father. The brother next to Chester, Melvin, owned his own Bar B Que restaurant called "Mel's Smokehouse" in Montgomery. He looked more like his mother and was thankfully not as inquisitive as Chester.

The brother next to Melvin, Luke, had his own real estate agency following in Momma Massey's footsteps. He was a chameleon in the respect that if you looked at him once he looked like Moms; you look at him again, he looked like Pops. He wore his hair in a short, neat ponytail.

After my second helping of the feast, I could hardly move. I'd never had roast duck for Thanksgiving before.

"Would you like some dessert, Rio? We have sweet potato pie, coconut and chocolate cake, and banana pudding?" asked Momma Massey.

I patted my gut. "No thanks ma'am. I have no room left." Carmen had eaten so much she had to undo the top button on her skirt. I glanced at my watch and saw it was almost nine.

"Well, if everyone has had enough I'm going to put this away. You guys go to the sitting room and relax," Momma said. As if it was scripted, all the women got up and began gathering dishes and utensils and taking them into the kitchen, all except LaKeisha.

"I'll be right back. I'm gonna go smoke," she said as she plucked a pack of Newports from her Coach bag. Carmen looked at her and grimaced. "Girl, you still smoking those death sticks?"

"This is only my fifth cigarette all day! I've been doin' good," LaKeisha said as she switched that pretty ass out the door to the porch.

The rest of the guys walked down the hall and Carmen motioned for me to follow them. "I'll be right there. You go with Daddy," she said as she kissed me on the cheek.

"I can't hang, baby; I'm too sleepy."

"Okay, I'll take you up to my room."

After telling everyone good night, we headed to our sleeping quarters.

"Where are the twins?" I asked.

"No telling. Those fools could be anywhere. They stay in the streets," Carmen said with a slight scowl on her face as we ascended the stairs.

"Well here it is; the bedroom I grew up in," Carmen said. The room was bigger than it looked from the outside. The first thing I noticed was there were two twin beds separated by a night stand.

"What is this?" I said pointing to the beds after dropping my bags.

"All the bedrooms are set up like this," Carmen said with a smile. My parents are very religious and don't believe in pre-marital sex. In their minds sleeping in separate beds is much less of a temptation than sleeping in the same bed."

"Are you kiddin'?"

"Yes I am, silly. All of us left our rooms they way they were before we went off to college. It's like a family tradition."

As I looked around the room I saw lots of her past. There were several trophies on her dresser; a couple from team tennis, a few from swimming, and several from dance competitions.

"Damn baby, you was the bomb in high school I see!"

"Was? I still am!" She tried to flex her muscles. There were also several pictures of her in her band outfits. She was a flautist.

"Oh hell naw! I know you weren't one of those band geeks! When I played football we used to laugh at'em all the time."

She looked at me with her arms crossed on her chest. "You weren't saying I was a geek when I was playing *your* meat flute.

"I'm gonna shut up," I said as I continued to check out her room.

"Do you still have your flute?"

"Yes, it's in my closet somewhere." Carmen looked through her bag for something.

"Dammit! I left my gown," she said as she furrowed her eyebrows.

"Didn't you tell me you have a closet full of your old clothes still here?" I asked as I looked out her window at the vast backyard.

"Yeah, I may have something I can wear in there," Carmen replied as she thought about it.

I saw a picture on her wall of her and some Buster hugged up in the classic senior prom pose. Carmen's hair was in that old page boy style and she was wearing a blue satin gown with a gigantic corsage weighing down her arm. The guy was wearing a powder blue rented tuxedo with the ruffle shirt and propeller-like bowtie. He was only about an inch taller than Carmen, had a piss-yellow complexion, and had a long Jheri Curl full of juice, a thin moustache and a trail of razor bumps along his jaw line.

"When was this taken?" I asked. Carmen was inside her closet looking for pajamas at the time.

"When was what taken?"

"This picture of you and some Jheri Curl juice drippin' Negro in prom outfits."

"Oh that. That was my senior prom and that's that son-of-a-bitch Keith." She sounded mildly annoyed.

"How old is dude? He looks a little old for a high school student."

"He was twenty-one in that picture. I was seventeen."

"Damn! Homeboy was robbin' the cradle for real."

"Whatever." She didn't respond to happily to my kidding so I stopped heckling her about the picture. Instead, I joined her in the colossal closet.

"You weren't bullshittin' when you said you had a closet full of clothes," I said as I looked at a rack at least seven feet long full of clothes. There was also a built in four drawer dresser packed with more of her wardrobe.

"Ah ha! I think I found one of my old gowns. Now I have to see if I can still fit it." She emerged from the rack with a long white tee shirt like gown that had a picture of red female fox with the word "Foxy" in red letters beneath it.

"I got this back in 1986," she said as she through it over her shoulder. As she stripped down to her white undies I went into my bag and put on a pair of Oakland Athletics gym shorts and a matching Oakland A's tee shirt.

I couldn't help but laugh as I watched Carmen try in vain to get that now sausage casing tight gown over her voluptuous ass.

"Give it up baby. You have way too much ass now to get that gown on. I have a tee shirt you can wear," I said as I laughed and hugged her.

She gave me the evil eye. "I bet it would fit if you weren't humping me 24/7 Mr. Funny Man." I gave her my red FUBU tee shirt. It fit her like a skirt. While Carmen was tying her hair up in a scarf, there was a knock at the door.

"Come in!" She said. It was Momma Massey.

"I just wanted to make sure you guys were comfortable before I turned in for the night," she said as she stepped into the room. I looked at my open suitcase and saw that a pair of my tiger-striped boxers was on top in plain view. When Momma Massey saw me get up to try and stealthily conceal my draws, she saw them and immediately looked up at the ceiling then turned around to face Carmen.

Carmen missed our little embarrassing moment. I quickly shut my suitcase and sat it down next to the bed.

"We're fine, Momma. You just go on to bed and we'll see you tomorrow," Carmen said as she kissed her on the cheek.

"Well, breakfast will be at seven if you two want to join your father and me." She hugged us both and left the room. I laid on the bed and dozed off as I waited for Carmen to finish getting herself ready for bed.

"I hope you don't think you're going to sleep in that bed alone," Carmen said as she climbed into bed with me. I was so tired all I remembered was kissing her then falling into a dreamless sleep.

CHAPTER TWENTY-TWO

After a king-sized breakfast of waffles, eggs and bacon, Carmen and I began my tour of the Massey mansion which was fascinating to say the least. Carmen showed me the back of the house which had been rebuilt. I was able to see the difference between the way the original house was built back in 1851 and the rebuild in 1970.

The architects did a good job replicating the original structure but you could still see the difference in workmanship. We came upon a huge set of solid Mahogany double doors that opened into a huge den with walls lined with books from one end to the other. There was a large desk in the middle which had an Apple iMac computer on it and a presidential leather chair to sit in.

"Whose computer is this?" I asked Carmen.

"It's my father's but my mother uses it more than he does. He *hates* computers but needs it to stay in touch with Bethany regarding the dental business." She took a seat in the big leather chair. "He's semi-retired and only goes in to the office on Tuesdays, Wednesdays, and Thursdays now. The rest of the time he spends golfing, fishing, or hunting. I think I'll check my e-mail while we're here. It'll only take a minute, okay?" She fired up the iMac.

While Carmen checked her Hotmail account and work e-mail, I looked at the hundreds of books that lined the walls. There were books there that dated back to the early 1800's. There were rows of dental books, books by Dickens, Steinbeck, Poe, and practically all the other great authors of early American history.

There was also a section on Native Americans which was packed with books on the Blackfoot Indians as well as other tribes. There was a fireplace framed by a marble mantel in the middle of the wall on the south side of the room. Above it in a glass case was what appeared to be an authentic Indian chief headdress.

"Damn, that headdress is in good shape. What kind of feathers are those?"

Carmen lifted her eyes from the computer screen and looked at the headdress. "The headdress is made of white weasel skin and most of those are eagle feathers. That is said to have belonged to my grandfather, Thunder Chief. My father says we are related to John Whitecalf Two Guns, his portrait is the one used on the Buffalo Nickel."

"Damn, that's cool as hell! I have a few of those old Indian Head nickels at home. Now when I look at'em I'll be able to say I screwed one of his kinfolk."

"You have mental problems." She shook her head and shut down the computer. "Come on there's a special place I want to show you," Carmen said as we left the den.

We walked further down the hallway past a large game room with a pool table. I couldn't see everything inside because it was dark. I'd investigate it further later on. We came to the laundry room which was like the rest of the house; large. Inside, there was a top of the line Whirlpool washer and dryer; an ironing board and a cabinet full of soaps, fabric softeners and stain removers. On the wall opposite the washer and dryer was a table used for folding the clothes. In the back of the room, I noticed a door.

"This door leads to the cellar," my gorgeous tour guide told me. After opening the door she flipped on a switch which illuminated a steep stairway. On the way down, I noticed that part of the house was ancient. I could see where the original builders used the old peg and auger method of building the house. The walls were made of old Oakwood and were in good condition, considering it was damn near two hundred years old.

The cellar was cluttered with stuff from years gone by. I saw a rocking horse that had to have been made in the fifties. There were boxes of old clothes, books, furniture, toys and other stuff.

"As you can see my parents are pack rats. They refuse to throw this stuff out," Carmen said with a sigh. The basement was vast; it covered the entire size of the house above. As we navigated between boxes and furniture, the house seemed to get older and older. Straight ahead of us was an old pine door that looked like something out of a horror movie. It was barley wide enough for an average sized person to fit through. The hinges were old, large and rusty looking. At eye level, there was an opening about one foot square covered by a metal grate. There was an old padlock about big as my fist that used a skeleton key to open it, securing the door.

"What the hell is this?"

"Remember I told you this house was originally owned by a man named Amos Underdown and that he used to own slaves? This is where he locked them up to punish them."

She plucked a skeleton key off a hook which hung to the right of the door. There was also a Coleman propane lantern hanging on a hook near the keys. On a shelf next to the keys, was a box of stick matches. She took one and lit then lantern.

"Hold this, Baby." She gave me the lantern and opened the door. It creaked in protest as it swung open to reveal complete darkness.

Carmen took the lantern from me and I followed her into the dark room. Once inside, I barely had enough room to stand up. The ceiling was only about six feet high. The entire room was about ten feet by ten feet. I noticed there were four sets of shackles dangling from the solid oak walls.

The only furniture in the room was a tiny table about the size of an elementary school desk and a wooden chair which still looked sturdy, despite its age. There were no windows or electric lights in the room.

"Damn! Did this room really hold slaves?" I asked while still trying to make my mind accept what it was seeing.

"Yes. He used to lock his slaves up in here whenever they were disobedient. He was of the mind that beating a slave into submission only meant he or she wouldn't be able to work as hard," Carmen said as she hung the lantern on a hook that hung from the ceiling.

"Amos would leave them in this room alone, shackled and in the dark for days without food or water. It proved to be much more of a deterrent than his horse whip was."

"He was one evil son of a bitch," I said as I inhaled the musty air.

"My mother decided to leave it just like she found it to serve as a reminder of how far we have come as a people. She would also bring us down here whenever any of us copped an attitude because we didn't get our way or didn't get money for something." She hugged herself and tossed her hair out of her face. "Just coming into this place reminded us of how good we had it compared to our ancestors."

A chill went down my spine as though an ice covered hand had rubbed the back of my neck. "Every black kid in America needs to see this room."

Carmen rubbed her hand on the small table top. "Look at this." She flipped the table over. On it was a message scrawled in child like letters that spelled out the words, "god wil maak it rite." Seeing those words pierced the heart of my soul. I could imagine the author of that sentence carving those words in the dark with a nail pulled from the wall.

Carmen moved to the wall and began inspecting the fetters. She took a skeleton key from a hook by the door and tested the locks on the shackles.

"Do you trust me, Rio?" She asked with her back turned to me. She continued to mess with the restraints.

"Yeah I do. Why you ask?"

"Come here; let me see how you look as a slave."

"Are you serious? I ain't gonna let you lock me in those rusty things, Girl," I said as I took a step back.

"They're okay. Momma had them refurbished a few years ago. I have the key right here and there's a spare hanging on that hook by the door." She stared at me with her raven-black eyes. Carmen's smile reminded me of a Great White shark as it prepared to bite a chunk out your ass. I thought about it for a minute then stood next to the manacles.

"Okay, but when I say unlock'em, you have to unlock'em. You hear me?"

"Yes. I promise I will," her face glowed in the lantern light.

The cold weight of the irons on my wrist and ankles bought home to me how wrong slavery was. The chains from the shackles to the wall were only about a foot long and heavy as hell. The clanking sound of the chains echoed off the walls like a ghost wail.

Carmen looked into my eyes as she locked my wrist in with a solid sounding click. She then bent down and secured the locks on my ankles. I tried to move and found that I had little freedom of movement. Carmen stood up, stepped back a few feet and stared at me; a slave in Oakland A's gym wear.

"How do I look?"

"You look like my bad Mandingo slave." She disappeared into the shadows in the corner. I saw her take something off of a hook on the wall.

"Don't you leave me here, Carmen!"

"I'm not going anywhere, baby. I just need to get something." She returned with an old riding crop.

"I know you don't think you're gonna hit me with that," I said as I tried to move my arms unsuccessfully. Carmen only smiled and laid the riding crop on the table. She then took off her robe and laid it next to the riding crop.

"What you doin'?" She looked at me as she took off her tee shirt revealing her matching white lace thong and bra. My "little man" began to transform into "Big Man." I'd seen her in her underwear plenty of times before, but right then, being unable to touch her, I was stirred up.

"You've been bad, Rio." Carmen stood just inches away from me and my hardness. "I think I'm going to have to punish you." She put her lips inches away from mine but wouldn't touch them. She took her finger, lifted my chin and began licking my Adams apple.

"Mmmm, this is the kind of punishment I like!"

"Shut up! Don't you make a sound unless I tell you to you, understand?" Carmen hissed. She gave me the most evil look I'd ever seen on her pretty face. It was kinda disturbin'. I didn't trip though; I just nodded my head and hoped she'd continue her fine tongue work.

After staring at me a moment longer she lifted my tee shirt and began kissing my chest. She kissed around my pecks and nipples pausing occasionally to bite them hard enough to make me wince. She followed up the bites with soft licks. She bit me and gave me a hickey right over my heart. Normally I would draw the line there; I didn't let chicks leave marks on me. But the whole setting was so strange and erotic, I gave her a one-time exception.

After sucking until the hickey was cherry red, she licked it with her warm wet tongue until I forgot about the dull pain. She must have noticed my pleasure because she abruptly stopped the licking and went to the table and got the riding crop.

"You deserve a chastising," Carmen said as she pulled the chair up in front of me. She sat there with her legs wide open, crop in hand. She lifted the crop to the top of my head and ran the little leather piece down my shoulder to my neck giving me goose bumps. She then lifted my shirt again and began to trace my pecks and abs with it.

I could see she was getting hot; her nipples were trying to stab through her bra. She let the riding crop fall to my fully erect penis and began to lightly hit it. Carmen stared at my dong for a moment then began rubbing the riding crop on my thighs and knees.

"You want to fuck me, don't you?"

"Hell yeah I do!" I said fervently.

"Who else are you going to give this dick to?" She stood up and put both her hands on my ass.

"You know its all yours."

"Carmen kissed my left bicep. "What would you do if another woman told you she wanted to fuck you?"

"I'd tell her no." My dick was hard as times in 1929.

"Are you sure about that?" She began nibbling my earlobe and rubbing her breast against my chest.

"Yeah," I whispered. "You know it belongs to you, baby."

"Who am I? Tell me whose this is." Carmen pressed her warm body against mine and grabbed my meat.

"Baby, this is your dick."

"No, I said tell me by *name* whose it is." She was torturing me up with that talkin'. I was ready to bone!

"This is *Carmen's* dick," I replied. I tried to press against her, but the irons reminded me I couldn't.

"You want to put it inside me don't you?" She sat back in the chair and opened her legs wide enough for me to see her warm spot.

My dick jumped. "Yesssss... gimme that pussy, baby."

"You don't deserve it; I think you want to share it with other women." Carmen stood up and looked me in the eye.

"You have the only pussy I want." Desperation leaked out of my voice.

She picked up the riding crop and began lightly striking me on the arm. "If I *ever* catch you giving another woman my dick I'm going to hurt you." She began striking me a little harder. It wasn't as painful as it was sensual. I could hear the leather piece slapping against my left forearm. After the last slap she licked my arm with her pink wet tongue.

I was so damned hard it was stupid.

I don't know to this day if it was the idea of being locked up or what, but I was so turned on I would've done almost anything she asked. Moments later I felt her hand grab my taut penis. She began squeezing and letting go, squeezing and letting go.

"I would love to suck you, but you might let some other bitch do it for you," she said as she put both hands on my swollen meat.

"I ain't gonna do that. You suck me good enough," I pleaded. She popped me on the leg with the crop hard enough to wake me out my trance.

"You like that pain don't you?" She reached under the leg of my shorts to hold my balls. She massaged them gently as she kissed my stomach and navel. Her eyes closed as she rubbed her cheeks on my stomach and massaged my balls faster. She caught herself and stopped when I began thrusting my pelvis at her dying for a blow job.

Carmen then stood up, got the little table, brought it in front of me and had a seat in the chair. "How bad do you want this?" Carmen asked as she put one leg on the table top and the other on the floor exposing her thong covered pussy to me.

"Enough of this shit. I want you right now!" I almost screamed. She said nothing as she moved the crotch floss to the left so that I was able to see her wet, pink, fat, vaginal lips. I looked in her face and saw some sex demon not my Carmen. She began slowly rubbing her clit with two fingers as she opened her legs wider. I watched as she leaned her head back and began rubbing faster. I was ready to gnaw my arms and legs off so that I could get to that wet hole.

She looked at me and put a finger in her pussy up to the third knuckle. "Mmmmmm your fat dick would feel sooo good in here Rio." I wanted her so bad I was sweating. I felt a drop run down my nose and fall on my lip. She pulled the finger out, stood up and put it in my mouth so that I could taste her sweetness. "You don't want that do you?"

"HELL YEAH I DO! Stop bullshittin' and let me out!" I said loud enough that my words bounced back to me off the walls. She smiled as she pulled my gym shorts down to my knees.

I closed my eyes and waited for the blissful feel of her soft lips on my hard head. Instead, I felt something totally different; it was her silk robe. She had wrapped the robe around her hand and began stroking my erection. I looked down and could see my weenie wrapped in the purple satin material like a bizarre pig in a blanket.

Carmen caught me looking and pinched my left ass cheek making me flinch. That pain mixed with her gentle stroking of my dick was strangely pleasant.

"Close your eyes until I tell you to open them," she commanded. I leaned my head back against the hard oak wood and closed my eyes as I was being driven insane with a desire to fuck her. I heard the chair scoot closer to me then the feel of Carmen's full lips surrounding my stiffness. She sucked the head very slowly into her mouth using her tongue to add to my madness.

"Carmen… I want you," I said in a voice so low I doubt she heard me. I noticed that she was moaning as she took as much of my nine inches in her mouth she could. I began pumping in her mouth as hard as my restraints would let me. As soon as Carmen felt my dick swelling up in her mouth she stopped sucking me immediately and squeezed my dick so that I couldn't nut.

"You're not going to cum until I say so." She stood up and began kissing my neck. She grabbed my hard monster and began rubbing the head in her racing stripe of pubic hair. The sensation felt so good I nearly drooled on myself.

Carmen kissed my mouth then bit and pulled my lower lip. It seemed she knew just how far to go before the pleasure became pain. Somewhere in my mind a voice whispered, "Does she do this all the time?" I quickly shook off that thought and let Carmen continue her Dominatrix fantasy.

Her hands were everywhere; under my shirt, in my hair, behind my neck, on her clit, on my ass, rubbing my back, in my mouth, everywhere. She put her nose an inch from mine and said, "Please don't break my heart." Before I could say anything she took off her thong, got on the chair on her knees right in front of me and pushed her hot soft ass against my erection.

My dick instantaneously used its "pussy hole radar," located her wetness and was inside her in seconds. I'd never felt anything as good as it felt to be inside her at that instant. Carmen gripped the back of the chair as her long hair fell over her face. She pushed back against me so I could get all the way inside her. I could hear the sound of the ancient chains clinking in rhythm with our strokes. Carmen was moaning loudly and thrashing her head from side to side as I felt her climax. The warmth of her cum on my pole made a string of slobber spill out of the corner of my mouth.

I yearned to wrap my arms around her hips and pull her back to me so I could tear her pussy up. She began clamping her pussy muscles on my hardness as she pushed back on it. I tried so hard to climb inside her, I felt a cramp in my left thigh muscle. Carmen pushed her wet kitty back on me faster as I prepared to skeet.

"Come on baby, shoot that cum inside me, let me know how bad you want it!" She said as she let out the most erotic moan I'd ever heard her utter.

I felt an ocean of my sperm racing toward my pee hole as every muscle in my body stiffened. I let out a long continuous, "Oooooooooooohhhhhhhhhhhhh!" as I squirted my essence inside her baby factory. I shot so much I thought I was pissing inside her. Carmen practically collapsed on the chair as my semen hose slowly fell out of her.

In the dimming lantern light I saw a few milky white drops of orgasm fluid on the seat of the chair between Carmen's upturned calves. My mouth was dry as sawdust after that draining of my fluids.

"Baby, you okay?" I said to Carmen as she sat motionless on her knees in the chair.

She finally lifted her head and slowly got out of the chair and hugged me. "That was so good. I've wanted you since we got off the plane," Carmen responded as I kissed her forehead.

I rattled the chains. "You think you can unchain me now, Mistress Freakness?"

"I kind of like you restrained," she said with a drowsy smile. She seemed to be moving in slow motion as she went to the table and got the key. After being set free, I noticed my wrists were sore as hell. I could even see a thin line of blood around the top of my wrist; that must have happened when I nutted.

Carmen pointed at the drops of cum on the seat of the chair. "I see you left your mark here."

"That's all your fault. Nobody told you to mess with my snake," I replied as I pulled up my shorts.

"That's the first time I've ever done anything like this," she said as she put her tee shirt and robe back on. Her hair was a wild mess; so much for the fresh hairdo she had.

"Are you sure about that? You had things choreographed *way* too good for it to be your first time," I said, anxiously awaiting her response.

"What are you talking about?" She tried to do something with her hair.

"You mean to tell me all this was spontaneous?"

She straightened out my shirt. "Yes it was! Do you really think this is something I could have gotten away with doing in *this* house?"

"You know you used to sneak niggas down here when Moms and Pops were gone." I wrapped my sore arms around her waist.

"Ha! You must be joking. Not as nosy as my brothers and sisters are. I'm surprised LaKeisha hasn't bought her bad ass down here yet." Carmen looked around the room as I straightened out my clothes. "I have to get something to clean up that mess, I'll be right back." Carmen stepped out the door.

Not only were my arms sore, so was the rest of my body. A moment later she returned with an old rag that was choked with dust.

"I used to come here whenever I got stressed out. It always reminded me that things could be worse. This is where I came the night I caught Keith at the wedding reception. I slept right here in this chair with my head on the table. No one knew where I was." I stroked her soft hair.

"I understand baby. You can definitely feel the pain the slaves did by just walkin' in here," I said trying to show empathy for her. Comforting a woman was not one of my strong suits. I usually found an excuse to leave when that kind of situation arose.

CHAPTER TWENTY-THREE

Lula was on the phone in the living room when we got back upstairs. When she saw us, she got off the phone and hugged us both. "So what are you two doing today?"

"Not much. I'm going to show Rio around the town and maybe go get my car," Carmen said.

"I have to go to the office for a little while but I'll be back soon. We still have dinner at six so make sure you two are here on time." Lula said as she headed toward the back door next to the kitchen. We followed Lula out as Carmen and she discussed the dinner menu for that night. We exited into a carport that held a white Mercedes ML 400 SUV, a new cranberry-colored Jaguar with peanut butter interior and a well preserved 1967 white Buick Riviera.

"That sure is a nice Riviera!" I said as I peeked inside at the immaculate black interior.

"That's Abe's pride and joy. He brought it brand new off the showroom floor on April 15th 1967," Lula said as she opened the door so I could get a better view of the interior.

"Did he ever drive it? It looks brand new."

"Oh yes, he drove it a lot. His first trip in it was to Long Beach, California. He drove there and back just to break it in. He'll put it on the rode about once a month now but that's it. The twins are always bugging him to let them 'fix it up' for him, but he just ignores them." she opened the door to the Jag and got in. Carmen and I waved bye to Lula as she whipped the Jag around and disappeared around the corner of the house.

Carmen took my hand. "Let me show you the back yard since we're out here." When we walked out of the carport I saw a red 1964 Chevy and a black one in the driveway.

"Whose cars are those?

"The red one is DaVon's and the black one is LaRon's. Those are their motorcycles over there too." She pointed to the far right side of the carport. There were two Suzuki 1100 motorcycles in the carport next to the Riviera. One was red the other black, just like the Chevy's.

"Damn! Your brothers must be getting paid," I said as I checked out their low-rider styled Chevy's.

"The only pay those fools get is from working part time at Chester's dealership and what they can sweet talk Momma out of," she said with a trace of contempt in her voice.

"You mean to tell me that even with that sweet deal of getting a house when they graduate from college they aren't in school?"

Carmen shook her head and said, "All they do is get high, play that damned rap music, and run around with skanks. LaKeisha is no better; the only work she does is stripping. She tells my parents she's a freelance model."

"She strips? I thought she got her degree in Marketing?"

"She did. She has an AA degree but she keeps on making excuses for not working. She says there's no jobs her in her field. I think she just likes that fast stripper money and can't give it up. All she has to do is go back to school and get her B.A. degree and she'll have a house waiting for her," Carmen said.

"She must be making some good coin."

"I think she does. That girl was able to save enough to buy a new convertible Corvette," Carmen said as we began walking towards what looked like horse stalls.

"This is where Underdown used to keep his horses. We had a few horses when I was a kid. As we got older and weren't around to help my parents take care of them they sold them to our neighbor. I had a horse named 'Lily' that I loved."

The horse stable looked like it could hold at least twenty horses. It smelled like old hay and horseshit. There were still lots of horseshoes, bridles, and saddles hanging on the walls and on shelves. Across from the stables was the well.

"Does that well still have water in it?"

"Yes it does but it's become stagnated so you can't drink it. My father was going to have it capped off and covered over but my mother protested, saying she wanted to keep the place in its original condition. As a compromise he had a metal grate built over it so that none of the grandkids would be able to fall in it."

"Or a drunk adult," I said as I peered into the well.

"Throw a coin in the well and make a wish!" Carmen reached in her pocket and gave me a dime.

I closed her hand gently with the dime still on her palm. "Keep your dime; I got what I wished for the day you agreed to be my lady."

"Rio, I love you." She put her arms around my neck and kissed me for a full minute. I felt I *should've* told her I loved her back, but my lack of experience with true love stopped me. We continued the tour which consisted of her mother's rose garden, (it looked to have every species of rose known to man), a basketball court her father had put in for the boys, a birdbath big enough to bathe a small child, and a tool shed full of tools that I'm sure hadn't been touched in years. A small creek ran through their property. There was a swing set that looked brand new for all visiting kids, and what seemed like hundreds of trees populated the gigantic yard.

"Are you ready for a tour of my big city?" Carmen asked as we walked through the carport and back into the house.

"Oh yeah! I can't wait to see this sprawling metropolis," I said sarcastically. We passed up Abe who was in the den on the computer and talking to someone on speaker phone. He waved at us as he continued what he was doing. LaKeisha had finally put on some clothes; a pair of tight jeans that laced up in the back, a tit-hugging "Hooters" tee shirt and bare feet that showed her French manicured toenails. Now that I knew she was a stripper, I felt an urge to get a lap dance from her.

"LaKeisha, will you give us a ride to Chester's so I can pick up my car?" Carmen asked.

"Yeah, but you know my car is only a two-seater so you'll have to ask Daddy if we can take his," LaKeisha said as she sat in the "sitting room" watching TV.

At that moment the door bell rang. "Are you expecting anybody, LaKeisha?"

"Nope. Especially not at ten in the morning." She made no attempt to go to the door. After giving LaKeisha an annoyed look Carmen said, "I'll be right back, let me see who this is," as she walked down the hallway to the door.

That was the first time I'd been alone with the stripper LaKeisha. She began clicking her tongue ring against her front teeth. I could see the pink tip of her tongue poke out of her mouth with every click. My dick began to stir as I imagined walking over to her and pulling it out for her to play with. My brief fantasy was interrupted by voices at the front door, one of them sounded pissed off, the other I'd never heard before.

"Oh shit! That sounds like Keith!" LaKeisha said as she sprung up from the chair. She ran past me to the door with her hair flying like a cape behind her. It took a minute for my mind to register what was going on. She said that voice was Keith's; that was Carmen's ex-fiancée!

I heard Carmen's voice getting louder and angrier. I looked down the hall and saw LaKeisha trying in vain to pull Carmen inside the doorway but Carmen kept swatting her hands away as though she was an annoying gnat.

"You have a hell of a lot of nerve coming here to see me you son of a bitch!" Carmen spat. LaKeisha looked at me and waved for me to come and help. When I got to the door I saw Carmen visibly shaking with fury. There in front of her was the source of her vehemence; Keith.

He looked like the same Jheri curl wearing, razor bump havin', punk ass nigga that was in her prom picture. He no longer had the Jheri curl; instead he now had a short afro and a hairline that receded like low tide at the beach. He still had that thin moustache, and was as short as Carmen.

"You okay, Baby?" I asked as I touched her shoulder. At first she tried to swipe my hand until she realized it was me.

"No I am not all right! This no good bastard thinks he can just show up at my doorstep like everything's okay!" Carmen was mad enough to scratch his eyes out.

"Now Carmen this is between you and me. There's no need to bring strangers into our business," Keith said. That set me off right away.

I stepped in front of Carmen. "Hold on, Dude! She *is* my business. And if she don't want you here I suggest you carry ya ass home." I was ready to introduce that country nigga to an Oaktown beat down. Everyone got silent after I put Keith in check. Carmen stood behind me with her arms crossed and tears of anger in her eyes. LaKeisha looked at me like I was Prince Charming.

"Look guy, I don't know who you are but Carmen is my ex-fiancée. We went through a bad time but I'm here to make peace," he said as he measured me up. He saw that I wasn't some punk he could bully. He sounded like one of those niggas I couldn't stand that had been around white folks for so long he felt superior to other black people.

"Motherfucker, we have nothing to talk about! I hate your fucking ass and want you to leave me alone!" Carmen yelled over my shoulder.

"Baby, I'll handle this. Go inside with your sister," I ordered her. At first she was going to protest but when she looked into my eyes and saw that I was serious she went inside with LaKeisha. Now that we were alone and Keith had no audience, all the bass dropped out of his voice.

"I didn't come here to start any trouble, I just came to see Carmen and apologize. I thought that maybe we could start over since so much time had passed."

I took a step closer to him. "What makes you think she's gonna want to get with you now? *I'm* her new man." His face cracked when I told him who I was.

"What? I thought you were her sisters' boyfriend." He looked embarrassed and heartbroken.

"Yeah that's right, I'm her man and *we* would appreciate you not coming around here fuckin' with her anymore," I said as my blood began to boil.

The entire scene was being witnessed by Carmen and LaKeisha from an open window behind me. "Oh it's like that?" He said trying to muster up some courage.

"Just like that." I continued staring him down, fist balled up at my sides.

"All right, I'm out of here. She's not *that* crucial to me," he said as he back pedaled towards his gold Nissan 300ZX which was parked in front of LaKeisha's blue Corvette. I noticed a dozen roses on the ground that looked like they had been slammed there by an angry hand.

"Hey, you're forgettin' somethin'!" I kicked the unwanted roses towards him. He hesitated for a minute then bent down and picked them up. I felt like kicking his teeth down his throat while he was down there.

After giving me one final glare he got in his car. Once inside he rolled down his window and said, "Hey, you're welcome to my 'leftovers'. I don't need an undercover hooker anyway," and sped off while flipping me the bird.

What the hell did he mean, "Undercover hooker?" I wondered. I stood there until I could no longer see his car. When I turned around I saw my audience had grown. I was embarrassed as hell that they had to see me get "ghetto" with Keith. Carmen opened the door and immediately hugged me so tight she almost choked me.

"Thank you baby, I love you so much," she said in my ear as she continued to hold me. LaKeisha looked like she wanted to cry, the twins were laughing like hell, and Abe was looking at Carmen and me with concern on his face.

"Damn cuz, you punked Keith's sorry ass!" DaVon said as LaRon agreed. Carmen was still holding me as Abe approached us.

"Are you all right, Squeaky?" He said.

"Yes Daddy, I'm fine," she said with her face still buried in my shoulder.

"You guys come on in the house," Abe said as he herded us inside.

We all went into the dining room and sat down at the table. After a moment of silence Carmen looked up and wiped tears from her eyes. She held my hand under the table and told Abe, LaKeisha and the twins what I already knew; the truth about what happened at Keith's sister's wedding reception.

After Carmen's tale everyone was shocked but the twins. They apparently didn't like Keith very much. Abe looked like he was going to faint and LaKeisha was ready to go looking for him so she could get a piece of him.

"I'm fine everybody. I just need to go lie down for a minute I have a headache," Carmen said as she stood up.

Carmen continued holding my hand as she led me upstairs to her room. I still couldn't shake what Keith said about Carmen being an 'undercover hooker.' Maybe he just said it to piss me off, but on the other hand…

The rest of the family remained at the table in discussion. Once inside her room Carmen locked the door, sat down on her bed and motioned for me to join her.

"Rio, thank you for being there for me. I was wondering what it would take for me to wipe Keith out of my life permanently and now I feel I have."

I put my arm around her. "Good. You don't need that kinda drama in your life." I felt her shoulders hitch as she held back more tears.

"Having to hear my family always saying how good of a man Keith was and how I should get back with him was driving me crazy. He had my mother thinking he was so fucking innocent that when I first told her about you she had a fit."

"No shit? You're mother don't like me?"

She took my hand into hers. "Not at first, but she thinks you're very nice now. At first she kept telling me to give Keith another chance. I'm so glad I won't have to deal with that anymore. That's one thing my parents don't like, a no good liar." We sat on her bed looking straight ahead out the window at the white puffy clouds that drifted by. Our fingers were making love so I decide to follow suit.

I turned to Carmen and leaned her back on the bed. As I lay between her bowed legs, I looked into her eyes. I felt heat emanating off her. She put her hand to my face and rubbed my bearded cheek in silence. I wanted to tell her I loved her badly but couldn't get the words to drop out of my mouth. I think she saw in my eyes what my mouth couldn't say.

"How's your headache, Squeaky?" I said making her blush.

"You have to promise to never call me that in public or I'll have to kill you," Carmen said as she tugged my ear playfully.

"Okay Squeaky, but first tell me how you got that name."

"When I was about three my father bought me a toy rubber Mickey Mouse that would squeak when you squeezed it. I loved it so much I would run around the house with it while saying, "Squeaky, Squeaky." Her face turned red from blushing.

"Quid Pro Quo, Rio… what's your nickname?" I felt her legs lock behind my kneecaps. I told her about the origin of my nickname, "Re-Re." She laughed and thought it was cute. After our chuckles died down I kissed Carmen's ear and whispered, "I want you." She responded with, "Take me then," and we made intimate, passionate love; the kind that produced babies under the right circumstances.

We were awakened two hours later by a knock at her door. "Carmen, are you awake?" Lula asked. I immediately jumped up and scrambled for my clothes.

"Just a minute!" Carmen said as she jumped into her sweats. I gathered up my clothes and tip toed into the bathroom to get dressed. I heard Carmen open the door and her mother say, "Baby, are you okay? Your Daddy just told me what happened!"

"I'm okay, Momma. I'm just glad everyone knows the truth now."

"Where's Rio?"

"He's in the bathroom," Carmen said as I checked myself in the mirror and made sure I was presentable. I exited the bathroom and saw Lula seated next to Carmen on her bed.

"How are you holding up, Rio?" Lula asked.

"I'm good, just glad she's okay," I replied as I massaged Carmen's shoulder.

Lula led us out of Carmen's room. "Come on downstairs and eat; you're late for lunch." *What the fuck did Keith mean when he called Carmen an undercover hooker?* That thought ate at my insides like acid.

CHAPTER TWENTY-FOUR

"I don't really want to see Chester but I have no choice I guess," she said as her eyebrows came together giving her a mean look.

"I know, Baby. Maybe we can just go get the car and leave without running into him," I said as she washed the breakfast dishes.

"I hope so; I really have nothing to say to him." LaKeisha walked into the kitchen and went straight to the refrigerator. "Any food left?" She was twenty minutes too late.

"It's all gone. You'll have to cook your own," Carmen replied as she dried her hands.

"I don't have time; I have to drop my car off at Chester's so they can see why my damn top won't come down." She looked in the fridge for something quick to eat. I then saw an opportunity to be alone with LaKeisha.

"Hey Carmen, how about I go with your sister to drop her car off at Chester's and bring yours back?"

"That could work, is that all right with you LaKeisha?" Carmen asked.

"Is what all right?" LaKeisha asked as she made a turkey sandwich.

"Is it okay if Rio rides with you to drop off your car and pick mine up?"

"Yeah, that's cool."

"When we get back you can take me on my tour of your town," I said.

"Okay, in the mean time I'll take care of a few things around here." Carmen walked with me to the room so I could get my jacket. When I came back downstairs LaKeisha was standing outside on the porch stretching. She had on a pair of vintage Yves St. Laurent jeans from the eighties that clung to her round ass tightly and an equally tight white v-neck sweater.

"You ready to go?"

"Yup, let's do this." When she started the car "Lil Kim's" latest song blasted my ear drums.

"Sorry about that!" she said as she decreased the volume. It was hard to believe she had earned enough cash stripping to buy that tight ass Corvette. It was fully loaded and well taken care of.

"Nice car," I said as we started down the driveway.

"Thanks. I had to do a lot of modeling to get it," she said thinking she was fooling me with that modeling shit.

"Miss me with that modeling drama, girl. I bet you doin' more lap dances than the law allows."

"What! Why you say that?" She faked like she was shocked.

"I know damned well modelin' didn't get you this Corvette. Quick! What's the name of your agency?" She took way too long to answer.

"Okay I'm busted! I do dance sometimes," she confessed with a smile. "I work freelance and in a few clubs. I've also been in a few videos," she said as we got on Highway 65.

"What videos have you been in?" I asked, truly intrigued.

"I've been in videos for Ludacris, Outkast, Trick Daddy, and the Hot Boyz." I tried to recall those videos in my head. "Damn! You been gettin' your freak on for a while I see."

"That was all business, honey; I don't mix business with pleasure." I was hard as hell and wanted to fuck LaKeisha right then.

"What clubs do you dance in?"

"Why? You gonna come watch me?" she asked with a sly smile.

I felt my monster move behind my zipper. "Hell yeah! I want a lap dance too."

"Usually I dance in Birmingham at Charlie's Go-Go and Club Tijuana. Sometimes I switch up and go to the Platinum Club in Anniston. Those clubs are about a hundred miles away so I don't have to really worry about too many folks I know finding out. I usually make a grip at the Freaknic in Atlanta." She was clearly proud of her career. My eyes kept drifting to her breasts as we sped down the freeway.

Every porno scenario I had ever seen went through my head. I imagined us pulling over under a grove of trees and me fucking her on the hot hood of her Corvette. I had never done sisters, but I had done cousins before. The thought of a conquest of that magnitude was awesome. "So, where's your man?"

"I don't have one right now. We broke up a couple of months ago. He couldn't handle my work situation so he left," LaKeisha replied as she weaved in and out of traffic.

"Damn girl! You drive like a maniac."

"I don't want to be down there all day."

"How soon before we get there?"

"It's about a three hour drive each way," she answered.

"Three hours! I didn't know it was *that* far." That meant we wouldn't get back until after 3:00 p.m.

The more I listened to LaKeisha singing along with Lil' Kim, the harder I had to fight telling her to pull over. During the last hour of the drive we talked openly about just about everything. She reminded me of a female version of myself; she was a certified player.

When we got to the Beltline Highway exit I saw that it was Mobile's auto row. There were several dealerships lining both sides of the street. After going about two miles down South Beltline Highway Rd, I saw a large revolving sign that simply said, "Chester's Chevrolet."

"I hope that nigga's here so I can cuss him out about that Keith shit!" LaKeisha said as we pulled into the service area. I noticed he had a lot across the street which sold previously owned cars.

"Did you buy this car here?" I asked.

She checked her make up in the rear view mirror. "Yeah, a year ago and it's been giving me trouble ever since. I let him talk me out of buying the Porsche Boxster I wanted and into getting this lemon."

"Do you know where Carmen's car is?"

"No but I'll get one of these cracker boys to go get it." We walked to the service counter.

"Hello Ms. Massey! It's so nice to see you!" said a brunette white girl behind the counter. She had a horse-like smile.

"Is Chester here?"

"No Ma'am, he's at lunch right now but he should be returning in about an hour. Would you like to wait for him?"

"No, I brought my car in to have someone see why my top won't go down. I made an appointment yesterday," LaKeisha said impatiently. The white girl rushed and checked the appointment book.

"I don't see you listed here," the girl said as she desperately searched for LaKeisha's appointment.

"You mean to tell me you don't see my name there? Are you trying to tell me I can't get somebody to look at my damned car after I drove three hours to get here?" Hearing the commotion a tall, gumpy redheaded white boy came to the counter and got the story. He told the white girl to go assist another customer while he took care of LaKeisha. Rusty—as the name on his shirt said—immediately called the foreman of the mechanic shop to come assist LaKeisha.

"I'm terribly sorry about the mix up Ms. Massey. Jeff here will take a look at your care right now." Rusty said with a well practiced smile. "Can I help you, sir?"

"He's with me; he's here to pick up my sister's Mustang. Do you know where Chester has it stored?"

"Do you mean the red one that's been here for a while now?"

"Yes, that one," LaKeisha said as Jeff waited patiently for her.

"I'll go get it for you right now sir!" Jeff went to a cabinet on the wall and plucked out a set of Ford keys. Meanwhile I watched as Jeff climbed into LaKeisha's car and began trying to drop the top as she stood over him like a hawk. After messing with the switch for a few minutes he contorted his body and checked the fuse box under the kick panel on the passenger side. He unscrewed himself from beneath her dashboard. "I think you have a blown fuse Ma'am. I'll go get one and be right back."

"I can't believe the way you have these white folks jumping for you!" I said to LaKeisha.

"Hell they better! It's not just that I'm the owners' sister; I paid cash for this damned car!" She replied arrogantly.

Jeff replaced the fuse and like magic the top went down with no problem. "There you go Ma'am it's all done. I left a few extra fuses in your glove box for you just in case you need them," he said eager to please LaKeisha's snobby ass.

She still wasn't satisfied. "That's all it was, a simple fuse? It cost me more in gas than the price of the part."

"Do you have a few minutes? If you do I'll take it across the street and have it detailed for you for your trouble," Jeff offered.

"Okay, that'll be fine." Jeff got in her car and drove off. I'm willing to bet he was glad to get away from the 'Dragon Lady'.

I looked down at her short ass. "You need to quit all that shit, Girl!"

She smiled. "Oh you be quiet." LaKeisha reminded me of Yo-Yo the way she responded to a dominant man. I knew right then that I could screw her anytime I wanted her.

"Let's go across the street to Checkers and get something to eat, I'm starving," LaKeisha said. My belly told me that was a good idea. We walked across the street and I ate one of the best chili cheeseburgers I had ever had. They had fresh made lemonade and steak fries that were big as bull's horns. I was full as a tick when we finally left. When we got outside, LaKeisha had her post meal smoke.

"Well, I see they're finished with my car." She pointed to her now shiny car as it was driven back to the main car lot.

"I hope your sister's car is ready to go."

"Me too, I want to get on the road so that we don't get caught in any traffic." She crushed her cigarette out on the bottom of her expensive looking pumps.

When we got back to the service office there before me was a red Mustang GT. it looked as though it had just rolled off the assembly line. "Is *that* Carmen's car?" I was both shocked and pleased.

"Yeah that's it," LaKeisha replied.

Rusty held the keys out to me. "Here you go sir."

"Damn that's a nice shade of red." I took the keys and opened the door.

"Yes sir! That shade is Rio Red; I like it better than the Laser Red they offered for this year's Mustang."

"You gotta be bullshittin'! My name is Rio." He looked at me in astonishment. I told him and LaKeisha how I got my name.

The car was fully equipped including an after market Sony CD player and 300 watts of power which pushed the speakers. I was surprised that the car was a five speed. That only thing I didn't like was that it had the 4.6 liter engine instead of the more robust original 5.0. It had 17-inch chrome alloy rims and a dark charcoal gray interior. I started the car and it sounded nice and healthy.

"Mr. Massey sent it to the Ford dealer down the street and had it serviced a week ago. It runs like brand new," Rusty said.

I noticed it only had a quarter of a tank of gas. "Where's the nearest gas station?"

"There's a Texaco-Merri Mart less than a mile from here up Beltline Highway," Rusty replied.

"You have a cell phone, LaKeisha?" I asked.

"Yeah, why?"

"I wanna call your sister and let her know we're on the way back." She reached into the purse on her front seat gave me her phone. LaKeisha laughed. "You better check in!"

Before I could retort Carmen answered her phone. "Wassup, love? We're about to leave now. What are you doin' with a car this cool?"

"What? It's just a car; besides you know I like nice things," she replied.

"Do you know what color it is?"

"Yes, nut, it's red! I picked that color only because they didn't have a purple one."

"It's not just red; its Rio red." I told her how I found out.

"That's a trip! Sounds like I've been destined to have Rio in my life in one form or another."

LaKeisha was in her car waiting for me after I hung up. "Okay, let's roll. Don't forget I need to stop and get some gas."

"I need to get some too," she replied and started her car. I got in the Mustang, started it up and relished the power purr of the engine. LaKeisha took off, headed towards the Texaco just as I was shifting into first gear. Right when I was about to take off, a familiar Indigo Blue Tahoe on chrome rims pulled into the driveway; it was that bastard Chester. He spotted me and pulled up even with my window. "I see you found the car!" He said as though we were cool.

"That was some fucked up and disrespectful shit you pulled by sending Keith's faggot ass to the house *knowin'* I was there and *knowin'* Carmen didn't want to see him!"

"Whoa! Buddy you got it all wrong! Keith is a longtime family friend, not to mention a good friend of mine. He has every right to want to visit my family's home if he wants." He made me want to break his face.

I fumed with anger. "You know what? If I didn't care for your sister as much as I do, I'd drag you out that muthafuckin' truck and wear your ass out!"

"Get off my property now!" Chester yelled as he locked his doors. I then looked at his spotless cement driveway and knew how to fix his ass. I popped the clutch and burned rubber sideways all the way out of his driveway leaving two fat, black patches of rubber in an S shape all the way to the street and a cloud of smoke in his face.

"Yeah, Muthafucka! Take that!" I yelled as I headed towards that gas station. He was gonna be reminded of me every time he looked at those tire marks.

"What took you so long to get here?" LaKeisha asked as she stood next to her car.

I smiled. "I had a little problem with the clutch slippin'."

"Is the car okay? Will it make it back?"

"Yeah it's cool; I was just bullshittin'." I told her what happened.

"Damn! I wish I could have seen his face! I thought I was the only one that had the nerve to stand up to his conceited ass!"

I thought of the possible repercussions. "You think he's gonna tell your parents what happened?"

"Don't even sweat it; if anything my father would think more of you for being your own man," she said with a wink.

After topping off our tanks, we got back on Highway 65 and started the three hour ride back to Alvintown. We made it back in a little over two and a half hours. I went to Carmen's room so I could take a piss. There was a note on the door which said, *Hey honey! I went jogging with Andretta and should be back about three. I love you…* I looked at my watch. It was 3:20 p.m. Minutes later, I heard voices downstairs and peeked out the door. Down in the reception room was Carmen and Andretta in biker shorts and long tee shirts that hid their nice booties well.

Andretta noticed me looking at them over the banister. "Hi, Rio!"

"How did the car run?" Carmen asked as she started up the stairs.

"It ran like a champ, ask LaKeisha; I raced her all the way back here and blew her doors off!" She kissed me on the lips, took off her headband and let her hair fall. "Come on, I have to take a shower. Afterwards, I'll take you for a tour of the town." She took off her shirt revealing a purple sports bra. The combination of Carmen's hard body and lusting for LaKeisha all day made me so horny I took that pussy.

"Come here, you," I said as I began taking my clothes off.

"Rio, I'm funky and I need to shower." I pretended I hadn't heard a word she said as I walked toward her totally naked.

"Rio, I need to shower first," was all she could say as I swept her up and laid her on the bed on top of our clothes. I quickly pulled off her shorts and slid inside her. I fucked her in every since of the word. I didn't spend time with foreplay; I just rammed her twat as thoughts of screwing LaKeisha played in my mind. I vaguely remembered seeing some of the clothes fall to the floor as I bent Carmen's legs back to her shoulders and continued pushing into her guts. I kissed her deeply not letting her catch her breath as I sprayed deeply inside her. It was almost like asphyxiation sex.

When I finally uncoupled my mouth from hers she gasped for breathe. "Oh my God!" Carmen said as she continued breathing hard. "You've *never* made love to me that hard before!" She lay with her legs wrapped around my waist.

"I just missed you," I said as my dick dangled inside her.

"I bet you didn't know that the door isn't closed all the way." I looked and saw the door was open about six inches.

She wiped sweat off of my forehead. "I tried to tell you but you were inside me so fast I couldn't think straight."

"That's what you get for being so damn sexy," I replied as I pulled out of her and closed the door.

After showering and getting dressed, Carmen picked our clothes up off the floor. "I hope you don't mind that I took your clothes out so I could wash them."

"No I don't mind, I'm glad you did, Sweetie."

"After they're done washing, we'll leave." She grabbed the clothes and we headed down stairs to the laundry room.

"There's my baby!" Carmen said as she rubbed the fender of her Mustang.

"I was surprised that you had a car with this much muscle! I thought you had the V6 engine and an automatic transmission."

"You must be crazy! I love driving a stick and I like to speed."

"Oh, here you go." I handed her the keys to her car.

"No, you keep those for me, okay?" She used the set of keys on her key ring instead.

"Are you sure about that? You want me to have a set of keys to your car?"

"Yes, that way if I lock myself out you can rescue me," she said as we entered the car. Things were getting' a bit serious. I had mixed feelings about having keys to her car. It gave her a legitimate reason to see me even if I didn't want to see her.

♦♦♦♦♦♦♦♦♦♦♦

After showing me the schools she went to, places she hung out at and the house she owned in Southmont, we headed back to her parents place. Even though it had only been a few days, I found myself digging the peacefulness of rural life. I doubted I would trade life in the big city for it, but it was a nice get away from the rat race.

"Did you have to deal with a lot of racism growing up here?" I asked.

"Hell yes! I've been called every form of racial slur you could imagine and a few I'm sure you can't. Because of my background, I was called everything from nigger to Indian whore," Carmen said.

I hadn't thought of that; the fact that her father was half Blackfoot Indian she received double barreled racism. "Did you ever see any Ku Klux Klansmen?"

"Yeah, they used to march here a lot. Things have changed a little bit; now instead of hiding under sheets most of them hide in business suits," she said as we neared the Alvintown exit.

CHAPTER TWENTY-FIVE

Back at the Massey estate, Chester's Tahoe was parked in front of the house. "Looks like we have company," Carmen said as she drove around back and parked behind Abe's Benz.

"I see Chester's here. Do you think he told your parents what went down today?"

We left the car and walked toward the back door. "Oh I'm sure he did, but I bet he didn't tell them he's the one that sent Keith over here and started all the shit." Inside the kitchen I smelled greens, cornbread, neckbones, and yams in the air. It appeared that everyone had eaten but us. I heard several voices coming from the living room. "Let me tell Momma we're here then I'll fix our plates, okay?"

"That's cool," I said. Moments later Carmen returned and fixed me a plate of the best greens and neckbones I'd ever had.

After pushing back from my empty plate I asked, "Did you run into your brother?"

"No, and I don't want to," she replied as she cleaned up after us. "Would you like to watch a movie?" she asked as we left the kitchen.

"Yeah, let's do that." In the sitting room we were greeted by Abe and his son, Chester the dick. "Hey Squeaky, I was just about to come get you," he said as Carmen and Chester exchanged antagonistic glances. "I think we need to talk; including you, Rio." Chester tried giving me an evil look. In return, I mouthed the word "bitch" to him in return.

Abe closed the door and took a seat on the sofa between Carmen, me and Chester. "Chester has already told me his side of the story; would you like to say anything, Squeaky?"

"All I have to say is he was wrong for telling Keith it was okay for him to come over here when he *knew* I didn't want to see him. On top of that, Chester also knew Rio would be here. That was disrespectful to both of us," she said as Abe listened intently.

"How about you, Rio, how do you feel about this situation?"

"Everything Carmen said is true. Why would he purposely send Keith over here under the circumstances?" I asked as Abe sat back in his seat.

"Rio doesn't need to be here, this is family business," Chester said haughtily.

Incensed, Carmen said, "You're the one that shouldn't be here! *Real* family wouldn't have pulled the crap you did!"

"See what I mean, Daddy? She's defending him and she hardly even knows him."

"What are you talking about? That has nothing to do with you disrespecting me!" Carmen yelled.

"How come you're treating her like she's a child? She's a full grown woman and can take care of herself," I said.

Chester shifted his eyes to me. "I've known her all her life and that more than qualifies me to know my sister."

Carmen fumed. "You don't know everything you think you know. I wish you would stop acting like you're my Daddy!"

"Even if I was your 'Daddy' it's obvious that wouldn't stop you from picking loser boyfriends. Keith was the only decent one you have had and you messed that all up!" Chester yelled. That last remark almost made me snap. I stood up ready to knock sparks off of Chester's face.

Carmen was so mad tears had begun to run down her cheeks. Abe, having seen enough, finally intervened. "It sounds to me like there are some issues between you three that need to be resolved in a hurry. Chester, step out for a minute and let me talk to them alone," he ordered.

Chester looked liked like a 45 year-old spoiled brat the way he stormed out of the room. Abe got up to address us as I wiped tears off of Carmen's cheeks.

"Squeaky, I know your brother can sometimes overstep his boundaries when it comes to looking out for you and your sisters but he means well."

"If that's true, why does he always single *me* out? He never says anything to LaKeisha and she's had more boyfriends that the rest of us combined!" she replied as her anger simmered.

"I don't think there's a man alive that can tame LaKeisha's spirit," he said with a sigh as he took Carmen's hand. I still couldn't believe Chester had the balls to say Keith was a good man for Carmen. I wondered if he knew the truth about his friend.

"Carmen, did Chester get the real reason behind why you broke up with Keith?"

She took a moment to recall then said, "No, he wasn't there. I don't know if anybody else told him either."

Abe sat down next to Carmen. "You know that may be part of the problem. It sounds like he doesn't know the full story."

I stood and took Carmen's hand. "Let's go outside and get some air."

"That's a good idea, Rio. In the meantime, I'll talk to your brother and tell him what happened okay, Squeaky?"

"Okay, Daddy… I'll be back in little while," she said as she hugged Abe. He was one cool old dude. I walked Carmen outside into the backyard towards the rose garden. The entire yard was well lit by what looked like street lamps from the 1800's. There was a bench between the rose garden and the creek that ran through the backyard. We sat there in silence for a minute listening to the water babble.

"I'm sorry you had to be apart of this crazy stuff, Rio. I was hoping we could've just had a good time and avoided all my family drama."

"Don't even worry about it, Baby. I'm glad I came."

"I've been going through this shit ever since I graduated from high school," she said as she leaned her head on my shoulder. There was a chill in the air that reminded me that winter was on its way. It also reminded me that we are supposed to be leaving in the morning. I looked into the sky and saw the stars were obscured by cloud cover; I hoped they weren't rain clouds.

Footsteps sounded behind us. "Oh there you are! I was looking for you two," Abe said as approached. Carmen and I stood up. "I talked to your brother and he would like to talk to you if you're up to it," he said as they looked into each others eyes. I imagined that was the look Abe gave his children when he wanted them to do what he wanted without verbalizing.

She sighed. "Okay… where is he?"

"He's in my den." I felt like a third wheel. Carmen and Chester would need to have a private conversation. I remembered I hadn't called my father's cousin Earnest yet. "Carmen, can I use your cell phone to call my cousin? He lives in Selma."

"Sure Baby, it's on my dresser."

"Nonsense, you can use the house phone, Rio!" Abe offered.

Once in Carmen's bedroom, I made my call. "Hello, may I speak to Earnest Clark?"

"Who's callin'?" a seriously country voice asked.

"I'm his Cousin Romero's son from California. My name's Rio."

"Rio? You Romey's son? I'm Earnest."

"Yes that's me. I'm here in Alvintown visiting my girlfriend's family."

"Is that right? How long you been here? When you leavin'?" he asked.

"We've been here since Sunday, but we're leaving tomorrow. I was hoping to have time to stop by and visit you guys before we leave but it doesn't look like I will."

"That's too bad! I haven't seen Romey in a coon's age. How is he?"

"He's good. You should call him."

"I will. If I remember right, you were about two years old last time I visited your Daddy. How are your brother and sister?"

"Everybody's well." I heard a TV blaring in the background.

"Well, I don't wanna take up too much of your time; I just wanted to see how you and the family were before I left."

"I'm glad you called! My kids are all grown and moved out. If you had more time I'd have them call you so you guys could get to know each other. My son Ezekiel lives in Prattville. Did you say you're in Alvintown?"

"Yes, visiting my girlfriend's parents."

"I hope you don't mind me asking; is she a white girl?" He talked as though there was a slave master within ear shot.

"Nah, she's a sister."

"Really? You know there's not many of us up there. What's her last name?"

"Massey."

"Did you say, Massey?"

"Yeah, her name is Carmen Massey, do you know her?"

"I think I know her Daddy. Is he a half-breed Indian dude?" he asked anxiously.

"Yeah he is. His name is Abe."

"Goddamn! You done got you one of them Massey girls!" he yelled.

I wanted to ask him if he knew anything about Carmen being an undercover hooker as Keith had called her. "What do you mean?"

"Boy, everybody know ole Abe, I call him Chief. They are the richest black folks in Alvintown. Just about everybody in Alabama tried to marry into that family."

I stood straight up and gripped the phone tighter. "No shit?"

"Oh yeah! Chief's Daddy owned a lot of land in Virginia. The railroad bought it all and he made a fortune. He left most of it to Abe. The story goes that since Chief left home at an early age to make it on his own, that impressed his father so much, he left Abe half of his fortune and the other seven remaining kids split the rest. Word is he left ole Abe a few million," he said. *A few million?* I snapped out of my daze. "Is that right?"

"Shit yeah! You walkin' in high cotton now, boy!" he said with a laugh similar to my father's. "Your cousin Otis tried to date the one named Bethany, but he couldn't close the deal."

"Well, I guess I'd better keep her."

"You be a fool not too! I can't wait to tell the family; they gonna flip." he made it sound like I'd hit the lotto.

"All right, I'm gonna let you go, Earnest. Be sure to tell the family I said hi."

"Yeah you do that. Tell ya Daddy to call me. And Rio, keep that girl!"

"Okay. I'll catch you later. Bye," I said as I disconnected. I understood a hell of a lot more about Chester after that call. I bet he was trying to protect the family fortune from the shysters his sisters dated. I still didn't like him; but I could understand him.

CHAPTER TWENTY-SIX

Carmen entered the room as I hung up the phone. "How did your talk go with Chester?"

"It was okay. He apologized for what happened but not directly to me. Considering his ego, that was more than I thought he'd do. He also told me you threatened him and that you did a couple hundred dollars worth of damage to his driveway," Carmen said with an impious smile.

"All I did was tell him I didn't appreciate what he did," I replied, trying to sell that lie to her. She just looked at me until I confessed. "Well, I may have said something about dragging him out of his truck but that was it."

She pushed me back on the bed and lay on top of me. "Tell me this; did I fall in love with a thug?"

"Are you sure it's love and not heart burn?"

"I've been asking myself that for a while now," she said, her lips centimeters from mine.

"I didn't think 'undercover hookers' could fall in love."

I could not believe what my lips had just said.

No matter how hard I tried to mentally suck those eight words back in, it was too late; they were gone like a fart in the wind.

"What did you say, Rio?" Carmen asked unbelievingly.

"I wanted to know if what Keith said was true."

Bad answer.

Carmen immediately jumped off of me. "I don't want to talk about that right now." Anger ruled her face.

I stood up and looked her in the eye. "What do you mean you don't wanna talk about it?"

"Just what I said; I'm *not* going to get into that."

My face tightened with anger. "What the fuck you mean? Don't you think I'm entitled to know if you was a hoe or not?"

Luckily for me I had good hand/eye coordination or I would've had her hand print on the side of my face. I caught her by the forearm and held it. "Have you lost your goddamn mind? Don't you *ever* raise your hand to me again!"

Carmen struggled to escape me as tears streamed down her face. "Let…me…GO!" she yelled. There was a loud knock at the door. "Are you guys all right in there?" Andretta asked from the other side of the door. No doubt she heard all the commotion.

"Yeah, everything is just damned dandy!" Carmen said as she angrily wiped the tears from her face. It seemed she didn't want to give me the satisfaction of seeing her cry.

"Rio, what's going on in there?" Andretta asked as she slowly opened the door. Carmen snatched her arm out of my grip as we stared each other down. I turned my glare to

Andretta. "You need to talk to your sister about tellin' the truth."

Carmen's bottom lip trembled. "You....you need too--," before she could finish her sentence she began crying uncontrollably. Andretta stepped between us and held her little sister. "Let me talk to her, Rio." The look in Andretta's eyes told me she knew what was best. I left them alone in the room and went downstairs.

Fortunately, no one else seemed to be aware of what was going on. I managed to dodge everyone and went outside. I walked around the back of the house and found myself at the swing set. I took a seat on one of the swings and wondered how things had gotten so fucked up so fast.

Deep down I knew exactly what had happened; my fear of commitment had manifested itself once again. Carmen was just starting to heal from the damage done by Keith, and I of all people reopened her wounds.

I sat in that swing until my ass ached. It was going to be a long, miserable drive back to California if we weren't able to get things straightened out. I was beginning to think she was a spoiled brat and needed too much attention. After that thought, I felt a little better, maybe it was *her* problem.

I spotted Andretta's Range Rover leaving as I entered the house. Once inside, I stood outside Carmen's bedroom door rehearsing in my mind what I was going to say. When I opened the door, I saw her bags were packed and standing at the foot of the bed. She was sound asleep under the covers in the middle of the bed. It appeared she wanted to sleep alone. Before I got an attitude, I undressed to my boxers and we slept in separate beds that night.

CHAPTER TWENTY-SEVEN

The next morning I woke up and Carmen was already up and gone. Instead of looking for her, I packed my bags and got dressed. As I was tying my shoes Carmen entered the room. "What time are we leaving," she asked emotionlessly.

"I figure if we leave by nine o'clock and drive for twelve hours we should be able to make it back by Thursday night or Friday morning."

"Well, that only gives us about thirty minutes. There's some food downstairs if you want to eat," she responded coldly. She didn't sound like herself at all.

"Thanks, I think I'll have some. Did you eat?"

"No, I'm not hungry." She brushed past me and picked up her bags. Instead of saying anything else to her I went downstairs and ate.

"Good morning, Rio!" Lula said as she entered the kitchen and poured coffee into her stainless steel commuter mug. "What time are you two leaving?"

"In a few minutes. I sure enjoyed my time here."

"That's good! You have to come back when the weather's better. Abe had an appointment this morning but he told me to wish you well."

"I appreciate it; tell him I'll call him real soon." "I have a meeting to attend myself but I wanted to see you guys off first." She stirred cream and sugar in her coffee. "Rio, what's wrong with Carmen? She seems to be upset about something."

I looked out the window and saw Carmen packing bags into the trunk of the Mustang. "We had a little misunderstanding last night, but it'll be okay."

Lula joined me at the window. "Good. Because that girl can be stubborn as a mule, she got it from her mother," she said with a chuckle before taking a sip of her coffee. Carmen closed the trunk and walked toward the door.

"Rio, take care of my baby; you're all the family she has there. If you need anything or if *anything* happens, don't hesitate to call me you hear? I mean it." She gave me one of her business cards with all her contact information on it.

"I promise you I'll take good care of her Ma'am."

"That's another thing we need to bet straight; my name is Lula or Lou; don't call me 'Ma'am' anymore!" she said with a bogus stern look on her face.

Carmen crossed the threshold. "You all ready to go Carmen?" Lula asked.

"Yes, Momma. I'm *more* than ready. I'll call you while we're on the road." Carmen seemed to ignore the fact that I was only a couple of feet away.

"Well, I have to get going. You guys have a safe trip and call me!" She hugged us both and walked to her Jaguar.

"I'll go get my bags and be right back."

"I already put them in the car," Carmen said with thinly veiled hostility in her voice. Outside, the weather was as ugly as her attitude. It was gray, overcast and cold. Carmen was dressed in black Howard University athletic department sweats and her hair pinned up under a Birmingham Black Barons Negro league baseball cap. "Nice hat," I said trying to be sociable.

"It's LaRon's," she replied with ice covered words.

"You want me to drive first?" I asked.

"No, I'll get us the hell out of here and we can switch later."

I saw a side of Carmen I didn't like at all. She went out of her way to make herself as unattractive to me as she could. She wore no lipstick, she knew I liked her hair down but wore it under the cap and her oversized sweats hid all of her sexy curves from me. Once inside the car, she opened the center console and took out a pair of black Isotoner gloves and a pair of Jean Paul Gaultier sunglasses. I took one last look out my window and bid adieu to Chateau Massey.

Once we got on I-65 she set the cruise control on 70 and stared straight ahead as she drove. "You mind if I change the radio station?"

"I don't care." Her curt answers were playing on my last nerve. I scanned the radio and it stopped on WBHJ 95.7 which happened to be playing "Return of the Mack" by Mark Morrison. I listened to that song and thought, *if Carmen don't straighten up I'm gonna show her what Mr. Morrison was talking about!* We rode in relative silence through two states.

After connecting with Highway 40 in Memphis we stopped at a Citgo Mini Mart so we could get some gas and switch drivers. I went to use the restroom while Carmen went inside and bought herself some Pringles and a diet Mountain Dew. I met her at the counter after getting myself some SweeTarts candy and a bottle of Dasani water.

"Can I have twenty-five dollars on pump twelve please?" Carmen asked the clerk.

"Your total is twenty seven forty six," the clerk replied. He looked like Goober from the Andy Griffith show.

"I got it; add this stuff too," I said, making a peace offering of sorts.

"No, keep your money." She handed Goober thirty dollars and left me at the counter. My patience was growing real thin with her.

"She reminds me of my Misses when I'm in the dog house," Goober said with an understanding smile.

"She must be a real bitch then," I replied as I took my goods and left.

Carmen stood next to the car pumping gas when I got back to the car. "I'll finish it, go ahead and get in."

"That's okay I don't need your help."

"You need to check your funky-ass attitude!" I said as my temper got away from me.

"If you don't like it, don't say shit to me!" she yelled.

"Fuck it then I won't! I ain't got shit to say to ya ass anyway!"

"Well, shut the hell up and leave me alone you asshole!" she said lividly as she pulled the nozzle out the tank and hung it up. She then got in the car, slammed the door and locked it.

"Open the muthafuckin'door!"

A tear spilled from under her sunglasses. "Stop yelling at me!"

I grabbed the door handle. "Open the door or pop the trunk so I can get my bags and you can drive back on ya own!" Goober and two customers stood in the doorway of the store watching our show. Carmen reached over, snatched opened the glove compartment and pushed the inside trunk release.

"All right, fuck it then!" I flung the trunk open, got my bags and slammed it shut as hard as I could. Without looking back,

I picked up my bags and walked back into the store. "Do you have the number of a cab company around here?"

The customers paid for their purchases and quickly departed. Goober smiled nervously and pointed out the door. "No, I don't have the number here, but you can find one in the phone book in the payphone across the lot."

I reached in my wallet. "Gimme change for a dollar." As he opened the register, I heard Carmen start the car and speed out of the driveway. Goober dropped the change in my hand. "Good luck, Mister."

CHAPTER TWENTY-EIGHT

I caught a cab to Memphis international airport and booked a flight into Oakland. During the entire flight all I could think of was how many different ways to cuss Carmen out. *That's just why I don't believe in relationships.* I made it home a little after midnight. Carmen was at least a couple of days from home.

I checked my phone messages the next morning and found I had twenty-three calls, nine from Yo-Yo. *Damn, I'm tired of these broads. Its time for me to cut all of'em loose and harvest a new crop,* I thought as I listened to my messages. Not one call from Carmen.

For a week, I fought off the urge to cave in and call Carmen. I hadn't heard from her nor seen her since our fight. I felt differently than I usually did after cutting loose a woman. My insides felt funny and my heart felt heavy. On Wednesday I went to Sam's Hofbrau for lunch. Some of Carmen's friends were there, but she wasn't. On my way out I ran into Zoe.

"Hey, Zoe. What you up to?"

She stood with her mouth open. "Hey nothing! What did you do to my friend?"

"I didn't go anything to her."

"Bullshit! Have you seen her lately?"

"Nope… not at all."

"You need to. Do you know she's cut all her pretty hair off?"

My eyes widened. "What? When?"

"About a week ago. I asked her why and all she would tell me was she had to make some changes in her life."

I ran my hand down my face. "When's the last time you saw her?"

"This morning, she gave me a ride to work. Rio, what happened? She's turned into a gloomy bitch; I want my old friend back. You need to call her and straighten y'alls shit out."

I looked away from her. "She knows my number."

Zoe shook her head. "You sound just like her stubborn ass. I gotta get back to work. I'll tell her I saw you. Bye." She headed toward her office building. *Did Carmen really cut her hair?*

♦♦♦♦♦♦♦♦♦♦♦♦

On the way home from work I thought about how upset Carmen got about the "undercover hooker" thing. Hell, the way she performed in the slave room at her parents house was *very* hooker-like. "I gotta get more info on why it upset her so much," I said to myself as I parked in front of my building.

Once inside my place, I went into my wallet and pulled out Lula's business card. According to my watch it was almost

8:00 p.m. Alabama time. I dialed the number. "Hello?" It was one of the twins.

"Hi. This is Rio, Carmen's friend. Is this DaVon?"

"Naw, this is LaRon. What up, cuz?"

"Not a whole lot. Hey, you have Andretta's number?"

"Yeah. Carmen don't have it?" Shit! I hoped to avoid that question.

"She's not home from her jazz class yet and I need to catch Andretta as soon as possible."

He bought my fib and gave me the number. I hung up and dialed Andretta's number. "Hello?" A sweet young country voice asked.

"Hello, my name is Rio. I'm Carmen's friend. May I speak to Andretta?"

"Is this Aunt Carmen's boyfriend?"

"Yes."

"Okay, just a minute." She put the phone down and summoned her mother.

"Hello, Rio."

"Hey, Andretta. How are you?"

"I'm fine. Are you and Carmen still at each other?"

"Yeah. Have you heard from her?"

"Yes. She called me from New Mexico crying her eyes out. She was scared of driving alone and mad at you. I was barely able to talk her out of leaving her car at the airport and flying home."

The inside of my stomach felt frozen. "Did you know she cut her hair?"

Andretta sighed. "She does stuff like that when she's really depressed. She dyed it red after she broke up with Keith."

"Andretta, when I had it out with Keith he called Carmen an 'undercover hooker.' I made the mistake of confronting her about it and she went ballistic."

She paused. "There's a reason for that. She had an incident in college."

Awww shit! Here it comes. She was a hoe in college, I thought as I flopped down in my recliner. "What kinda incident?"

"As a part of the hazing ritual to join her sorority, the pledges had to pose as hookers and be witnessed by at least two sorority sisters getting into the car with a 'john.'"

"That's crazy! Not to mention dangerous. What if they got kidnapped?"

"The witnessing sorority sisters made sure to get the john's car plates and be ready to follow or call the police if necessary."

"But still....Damn...."

"Anyway, when Carmen's turn came, she was dropped off in an area known for prostitution. Being as cute as she was, she was approached in less than fifteen minutes." Andretta paused.

Just the *idea* of Carmen dressed as a hoe started a headache behind my temples. "Okay. So what else happened?"

"She asked if she could get inside and talk about the price. Carmen had been told beforehand to ask for an outrageously high price in hopes of making the 'john' cancel his request."

"That is fuckin' nuts... Sorry."

"No problem, Rio. It turns out he was an undercover cop. She was arrested and booked for prostitution."

A million thoughts ran through my mind, but I was unable to form any of them into a sentence. My only response was, "Shit."

"Yes... she begged and pleaded for them to let her go, but the cracker cop wouldn't even listen to her."

"What happened to the girls that dropped her off?"

"Those no good dogs got scared and left. Carmen was held in the holding cell with the *real* prostitutes they picked up that night. She was held there for six hours before she was allowed to use the phone."

I felt like a first class butt-hole. "Who bailed her out? Your parents?"

"Hell no! They would've flipped. She called me. I'll never forget how sick I felt seeing my sister in those tramp clothes." Andretta sniffed as though she was fighting back tears. "Somehow word got out and rumors spread that Carmen was a whore. Keith used to throw it in her face every time he got mad at her."

I got up and walked out onto my balcony. "I *knew* I should've kicked his ass."

"I wanted to myself, but Carmen preferred to keep things quiet. She transferred from that school and went to Howard. Even to this day, some of folks in town still think she's a prostitute. That's why she left so abruptly and went to California after what happened at Keith's sister's wedding."

It all made sense. No wonder she didn't talk much about her home life. "Damn! I wish I'd known about this earlier."

"Well, Rio, I've got to get these kids in bed. You take care."

"Thank you for the information…Thanks a lot."

"No problem."

I turned and walked back inside. "Good night."

"Oh, and Rio, she may be mad at you, but I know my sister; she's in love with you. Think about it… goodnight."

My phone rolled to the floor as I absently set it on the edge of my coffee table. I had to see her. I picked the phone up and dialed her cell phone. She didn't answer; it rolled over to her voicemail. The time was 5:18 p.m. Since it was Thursday she was probably still teaching her jazz dance class. If I hurried, I could catch her before she finished.

CHAPTER TWENTY-NINE

I drove as fast as I could to Laney College in hopes of catching Carmen. As I pulled into the parking lot, I spotted a newspaper booth across the street. In front of the counter was a rack of bundled roses. I ran over there and pointed at the red roses. "How much?" I asked the old black man.

"Seven bucks for half a dozen."

I tossed him a ten. "Keep the change!" I dashed back across the street and to the gym. The thought of seeing her pretty face made my heart grow wings. A stream of leotard and sweat-suit clad women exited the gym as I entered. *Please let her still be here,* I thought as I fought my way through the throng of women.

When I got inside, I found the gym empty. *The parking lot!* I jogged down the hall and out to the teachers parking lot. A red mustang sat twenty yards from me. *Good she's still here!* A big goofy grin grew on my face as I walked toward her car. *I'll wait there and surprise her.*

A door on the side of the building opened and a woman with a very sexy Halle Berry-ish haircut, Laney college sweats and dark beautiful eyes exited. She smiled and turned to say something to person exiting behind her: Bernard.

The pain, anger, sorrow and hatred I felt made me literally see them through a red filter. He took her hand and said something that made Carmen laugh again as a woman waited behind them with her gym bag in hand. I almost ground the stems of the roses I held into liquid.

Her laughter subsided. She then turned and saw me standing twenty feet away. We stared at each other for what seemed like an eon. When she saw the flowers in my hand, her face went from absolute shock to total confusion. I looked from her eyes to Bernard and back to her eyes.

"Fuck it… fuck this shit," I said as I turned and left. On my way to my car, I tossed the flowers into the shopping cart full of worldly possessions pushed by an elderly homeless woman. "Thank you, mistah."

I whipped an illegal u-turn and sped home. Anger poured off me like sweat. "I'm gonna fire *all* these bitches tonight!" I said to myself after slamming the door to my apartment behind me. Visions of Carmen's face stuck in my head as I paced back and forth across my living room.

I checked my calls. Among the messages I had, I discovered Amanda had called. "She *knows* better than to me!" I hissed as I hung up. The phone then rang. "That had *better* not be Carmen's ass!" I reached for the phone. It wasn't Carmen; it was Yo-Yo. "What the fuck you want?"

"Well damn! Hello to you too! What's wrong with you? Sounds like you need me to come over there and give you some," she replied.

"Look, Yo-Yo; I don't want you to call me anymore. You hear me?"

"Whatever, now quit playin' and bring me that dick. I'm way overdue for some service."

I flashed. "Look, Bitch! Don't call me no fuckin' more! I'm tired of your triflin' ass. Call your jailbird-ass boyfriend next time you wanna fuck somebody." A stream of obscenities jumped out of my phone as I hung up in her face. "That was easy. Two down, five more bitches to go, I said as I dialed Angelina's number. The phone was picked up on the second ring.

"Hello? Who dis?" Angelina asked, with her ghetto ass.

"Me, Rio."

"I'll be damned! Rio is that really you? I had better go play the lottery if my luck is that good. What's up?"

"I need to talk to you."

"That's nice. I thought you had forgotten all about me."

"Nah, I've just been real busy."

"I stopped by your house one night last week but you must not have been there."

Angelina had just broken one of my strictest rules: *never* come by my house without calling.

"I sure hope you called before you came by. I don't allow *anyone* over my house if they don't call me first."

"Why are you trippin'? I called you from my mother's house and decided to stop by on my way home."

"Still, if I don't say it's cool to stop by, don't do it." I wanted to strangle that dense bitch.

"Oh, it's like that now? You just fuck me then treat me like I ain't shit. You're a trip," she yelled.

"What are you talkin' about? If I'd known you'd be acting like this, I never would've fucked with you from the beginning!"

"Nigga, don't get it twisted. I can get all the dick I want! I don't need your sorry ass!"

I had to get rid of her before things got any further out of hand. "Look, I don't have time for all this dumb shit. Don't call me anymore and I won't call you. I don't need your immature bullshit."

"Muthafucka! I ain't gonna call your ass *ever* again! Don't you come lookin' for me next time your dick gets hard! And for your information I'm way too mature for your childish ass. You're the one playing games and not answering your phone like a punk ass nigga would do. And if I feel like stoppin' by your house I will, punk!"

Before I got into a shouting match with her, I just hung up. She immediately called back and started screaming all over again. I hung up and put a block on her number. That was one of my ultimate fears; having not only a stalker, but an angry stalker.

Listening to her brought my high down. I went to my stash box and stuffed my pipe with a piece of green Indo weed. I smoked until my mellowness returned, then I called Amanda.

"Hello, Rio. What's up?"

"I was gonna ask you that. I got a message that you called."

"Damn, I left that message over a week ago. I guess you finally got away from your woman long enough to call me back."

"Anyway, what did you want?"

"I was just calling to see how you were. Is there a law against ex-lovers talking to each other?" She sounded like she had an attitude too.

"I know you way too well to fall for that Amanda; you called to stir up some shit." I felt my high start to dissipate once again.

"Rio, you are so paranoid. I'm not trying to start anything. I was just calling to let you know that I found some of your stuff in my closet and wanted to know if you wanted to come by and pick it up."

I tried to remember if I was missing anything. "What stuff?"

"I found a pair of your leather sandals and that silk robe and boxers I ordered for you from Fredrick's of Hollywood. You remember how good it looked on you?" she asked provocatively.

"Well, thanks for letting me know, but you can keep it or give it away." I regretted I'd ever returned her call.

"That's crazy! Those sandals are almost new and I know I've only seen you wear the robe a few times. Don't worry; I won't bite if you come get it."

I had a flash back on how good her pussy was. "Look Amanda, I'm not gonna come over there for *any* reason. We are through and I'm not tryin' to start anything up. I appreciate you lettin' me know about the shoes and stuff, but you know damn well that if I came over there you would be trying to fuck me."

"I see you still have a dirty mind. Do you talk that way to your new woman, what's-her-name?"

"That's none of your business."

"I know how much you like that dirty talk Rio. Do you screw her the way we used to? Do you make her bend over the bed and fuck her in the ass the way you did me?" Amanda knew just what she was doing; trying to get my dick hard.

I visualized how I used to do her hard and rough. "Sorry, its not gonna work Amanda. I'm sure you have no shortage of dicks when you want one."

"That's true, but every now and then I think about us. Do you ever think about me, Rio?"

"Not really, I have too much other stuff going on in my world." I sensed Amanda trying to drag me down memory lane.

"Can you honestly say that you don't have any feelings for me?"

"Look Amanda, we are over, period. It was nice while it lasted but I've moved on and I hope you have also. I would appreciate it if you don't call me anymore."

"Damn, you are a cold hearted son-of-a-bitch! After almost two years you mean to tell me you can switch it off just like that? I'm glad I found out before we had any kids or got married," she spat out.

"You need to quit all this drama, Girl. You're wastin' your time and mine."

"I hope she breaks your fucking heart you no good dog! I oughta tell her how you *really* are so she'll leave your ass like you left me!" she was on the verge of tears.

I was beyond my boiling point. "You better not say shit to her and mind your own goddamned business!"

"I only have one more thing to tell you before I leave; you remember when I went to the hospital about two weeks before you dumped me? Well, I had a miscarriage."

My high vanished. I was as sober as the Pope after her last statement.

"What the hell you talkin' about?" The word miscarriage reverberated through my head.

"I was two months pregnant at the time, and was trying to decide if I was going to tell you or not when I began bleeding and checked myself into Alta Bates Hospital," she said as she tried to hold back her tears.

I remembered that day. I'd been dodging her for a couple of weeks waiting for the right time to break things off. I knew I wanted to do it before Valentines Day—no need in buying a gift for a chick your not gonna be with—and my time was running short.

As a matter of fact, it was February 1st. I remembered because I'd gotten a *great* blow job from Angelina for taking her to cash her paycheck. When I got home, I found I had a message from Amanda saying she was at Alta Bates Hospital.

She wanted to know if I could pick her up. She ended up catching a cab since she couldn't reach me. When I finally caught up with her the next day, she told me she had food poisoning and had to have her stomach pumped.

♦♦♦♦♦♦♦♦♦♦♦♦

"You need to quit bullshitting me, Amanda. You always come up with some kind of drama when you want your way."

"Fuck you, Rio." She said in an ominously quiet voice. It was somehow worse than hearing her scream at me.

"Fuck me? No, fuck you!" I said before I realized I was yelling at the dial tone. She had hung up after her last quiet fuck you.

♦♦♦♦♦♦♦♦♦♦♦♦

Two weeks after giving all my female acquaintances the heave-ho, my world began to crumble. My thirtieth birthday was ten days away on Christmas Eve. On Wednesday December 15th, my downward spiral accelerated.

While sitting at my desk, I watched my supervisor, Mr. Upchurch, approach my desk with a small white box in his hand. "Hey, Rio, how are you?"

"I'm good. Wassup?"

He sat the box on my desk. "Guess whose turn it is for a random drug screen?"

I was fucked. I'd smoked some good weed the previous night.

Among the females I'd fired, Rosa was one of them. She was a cute Mexican woman—who enjoyed rough sex with me—who worked in Human Resources. In the past, she would've tipped me off a week before the random tests were scheduled. That gave me time to purchase a product by Detoxify called "Urine Luck." I'd passed every previous drug screen with its help.

He scowled and looked at his watch, pissed off because it was his job to drive me to the clinic. "Let's go so I can get you back. We're busy as hell." Forty-five minutes later, I stared out the window of his aqua green Cavalier on the way back from the clinic. I had roughly 48 hours left before my dirty urine test results came back. Like I said, I was fucked.

♦♦♦♦♦♦♦♦♦♦♦

"Goddammit, Rio! I'm sorry to lose you. I wish there was something I could do... you're one of the best techs I have," Mr. Upchurch said with a distraught look on his face as I cleaned out my cubicle. "You have to serve a mandatory one-year suspension and attend a company approved rehab assignment before we can consider rehiring you."

I handed him my company issued laptop and ID badge. He in return, handed me my last check. "I'm sorry too." The humiliation I felt as my co-workers looked on was agonizing. I carried my box of belongings out the building as quickly as I could.

In my car, as cold rain pelted my roof, depression cracked open my soul and sucked all the hope out of it. Even with the help of unemployment and my savings, I calculated I'd be homeless by Saint Patrick's Day if I didn't land another job. Ever since splitting with Carmen, bad karma had pitched a tent and settled into my life. Of all the women I'd cut loose, she was the only one that haunted me. *I can't be in love with her. No way would love make you feel this messed up,* I thought as I entered my place and put my box of work stuff on the floor.

After moping around for three hours, the walls seemed to close in on me. The sound of the rain and my inner thoughts strained my sanity. "I gotta get out of here," I said to myself as I rose from my couch. Since it was Friday evening, I decided to give my boy Dee a call and see if he could get out the house. "What you up to, homie?"

"Shit. I just got back from the mall. How was ya trip to the dirty south?"

I looked at myself in my mirror. *Oh well, I might not feel good but I look good,* I thought. The black suit I put on reflected my mood. "It was all right. What you gonna do tonight?"

"Nothing much. But I bet your gonna be under Pocahontas tonight, huh?"

A sense of loss hit me when he mentioned *my* Pocahontas. "Nah, not tonight. I'm through with her."

"What? You bullshittin' me, right?"

"Nope, it's all over." I told him what happened between me and Carmen.

"Damn! I sure didn't expect you to let Baby Girl go; I thought she was ya wifey."

"Shit happens. You wanna go to The Spot and have a drink?"

"Yeah, but I gotta eat something first. Let's go to Tony Roma's first."

I sat down on my bed and checked my watch. "Okay. I'll meet you there at eight."

"Cool. Later."

My heart wasn't in going out after all. After Dee reminded me of how I'd usually have "date night" with Carmen on Friday nights, the little life I felt evaporated. The urge to call her made me dial the first couple of digits in her phone number before I tossed the phone on my bed, turned off the lights and left.

♦♦♦♦♦♦♦♦♦♦♦♦

"Why in the hell are you wearin' a suit?" Dee wondered as he took a seat across from me.

"I felt like it. What you gonna eat?" The restaurant was full as it usually was on a Friday night. A trio of cute sista's sat two tables down from us. Dee spotted them. "Dude, you see those hotties over there?"

I gave them a brief glance. The shortest of the three sat at an angle which allowed us easy eye contact. She was a mullatto woman no more than 5″3′, 110 pounds, neck length brown hair and pretty light brown eyes. My kinda woman.

Dee noticed my lack of pursuit. "You need to go get at that fine light-skinned chick. She might help you get over Pocahontas."

I picked up my menu. "What makes you think I'm not over her?"

He sat back in his seat and grinned. "Look me in the eye and tell me you don't miss her."

"I don't miss her."

Dee pulled the menu out of my hand. "I said look me in the eye, not read the menu."

Just as I was about to clown him, the waitress arrived. After placing my order, I thought about what Dee said. I physically *couldn't* look him in the eye and say I didn't miss Carmen.

CHAPTER THIRTY

Later that night at The Spot, I got so drunk Lola refused to let me drive home. Dee left at midnight but I stayed planted in my seat at the bar guzzling drink after drink. At a 1:30 a.m., Lola announced, "Last call for alcohol!"

I pointed at my empty glass and slurred, "Gimme another shot of Grey Goose, Baby."

She picked up my glass. "You've had about three too many already. Are you okay, Rio?"

I nodded off for a second the shook myself awake. "What'd you say?" I gazed at her with the eyes of a lush. "You're hella… fine, Lola."

Most of the club patrons began to leave. "Do you have a nail clipper on your key ring, Rio?"

I fumbled through all my pockets before finding my keys. "Yeah… right here… Lola, why… are women so full of… shit?

Why the hell... y'all so hard to... ummmmm...why y'all do crazy stuff?

She took my keys and put them in *her* pocket. "What you doin', woman?" I almost slipped off my stool as I tried to stand.

"I'm tryin' to save your ass from getting a DUI or having an accident."

I felt like I was standing on an out of control merry-go-round. "I'm all right...I've been waaaay drunker than this...for real, Lola." I was fuckin' smashed.

She placed a cup of hot coffee in front of me. "Drink that. I'm gonna take you home after I close out the cash register."

I ignored the coffee and drunkenly stared into the faces of the females as they departed; wishing one of them was Carmen. After the last of the patrons left, I laid my head on my folded arms and dozed. Malik the Bouncer tapped me on the shoulder. "Time to go home, Chief."

"Just leave him. I'm gonna take him home," Lola said as she took off her apron.

"Damn...I got fired...lost Pocahontas...I'm....all...fucked up," I mumbled as Lola shook me awake.

"What did you say, Rio?"

"I dunno..."

Twenty minutes after struggling to get me inside her Toyota Camry, she walked me into her apartment. "Have a seat here on the couch. I have to let my cat out. I'll be right back."

By the time she returned, I was snoring face down on her gold velour couch. Lola sighed. "I've been trying to get you here forever. Now that I have you, you're too drunk for me to take advantage of." She covered me with a blanket, placed a pillow under my head, turned off the light then went to bed.

♦♦♦♦♦♦♦♦♦♦♦♦

The following morning Lola dropped me off at my car. I thanked her for taking care of me, went home, showered then called Uncle Lee.

"What you up to, Youngblood?" Uncle Lee asked.

"Same old shit. Dealin' with these crazy hoes." The petulance showed in my voice.

"When you gonna learn to not let them get to you? All the game I gave you is being wasted," he said with an exaggerated sigh.

"Did you have breakfast yet, Unk? I'm hungry as hell."

"Not yet. I was about to go to get something. Let's go to Lois the Pie Queen's and eat."

After agreeing with Uncle Lee to go to Lois', he offered to drive and we rolled out. Minutes later, we were in line waiting to be seated. They had the best grits and fried pork chops in town and there was *always* a wait to be seated. The small restaurant was almost filled to capacity. The walls were lined with autographed pictures from pro ball players to members of Earth, Wind and Fire. The smell of bacon cooking and biscuits made from scratch coming out the oven made me almost salivate.

"So tell me what's got you shook up, nephew?" Uncle Lee asked. I told him about my arguments with Amanda and Angelina and he surprised me by laughing his ass off.

"I'm glad you think it's funny. I was ready to go kick both of those bitches' asses."

"How many in your party?" a cute chocolate sister asked.

"Just two, Sunshine," Uncle Lee said causing the waitress to blush and lead us to our table.

"No wonder you're always stressed out over your women. You're still into 'Gorilla Pimpin''." He added sugar to his coffee.

"What the hell is 'Gorilla Pimpin'?" I asked, totally befuddled.

"You remember when I took you by my friend Pimpin' Ken's house back in the day?"

"Yeah. Wasn't he the dude with the scar on his neck that looked like he had his throat cut?"

"Yup that's him. He was a big time pimp in Oakland in the seventies. He had at least fifteen or twenty hoes working for him. We were tight as frog pussy. We ran the streets together for years. He handled his women his way and I handled mine my way." Uncle Lee took a sip of his coffee.

"I didn't know you were a pimp back in the day!"

"There are a couple of things you need to understand. I wasn't a common pimp, I was a Sweet Mack." He sat back in his seat and studied the menu.

"What's the difference?" I asked as the chocolate cutie asked if we were ready to order.

"I'll have eggs over easy, bacon, and a short stack of hotcakes," Uncle Lee said all the while holding the waitresses hand. She smiled like a maniac.

"I'll have the same but with poached eggs," I said as I watched the scene unfold in front of me. I could barely hear what Uncle Lee said to the waitress, but whatever it was kept her grinnin'. After she finally broke her bond with Unk he looked at me and winked.

"The difference between Gorilla Pimpin' and being a Sweet Mack is simply finesse and style. I used to watch Ken beat the shit out of his girls and cuss'em out all the time when his money wasn't right."

"No shit! That sounds like some of that old school Willie Dynamite-type pimpin'."

"He used intimidation to get what he wanted from his girls. Ultimately it almost cost him his life when he chose the wrong bitch to beat."

"Damn, Pimpin' Ken was *that* hardcore?"

"Sure was. He had this new hoe from Louisiana named Belle. He'd just added her to his stable. She was always quiet, but I guess she could suck and fuck her weight in money since Ken kept her around."

"Was she a white girl?"

"Naw, she was black as coffee grounds. We were ridin' around in his 450 SL Benz checkin' his traps one Friday night when we ran across Belle on West MacArthur Blvd."

"Over by Mosswood Park where I shoot hoop?"

"Yeah, right there. I guess he tried to impress me by rollin' up on her, slappin' her around, and basically treating her like a dog. After taking all her money, he spat in her face and told her to not wipe it off until she got another trick."

"Damn! Pimpin' Ken was straight gangsta."

Uncle Lee turned his napkin into a bib and said, "I'll never forget the way she looked at him as he stood there countin' his money. We kept a couple of apartments in the Moore House projects in West Oakland that our hoes used as a bunkhouse. The only rule we had was there was no johns allowed."

I shook my head and said, "Y'all was outta control, Unk."

"Just real pimpin', youngster. Ken decided to crash in the room with Belle that night and the next thing I know I got a call from his main girl, a hoe named Spices, telling me Ken was at Highland Hospital damn near dead," Uncle Lee said as our food arrived. That was the fastest I could remember ever being served there. I guess whatever Unk whispered in the waitresses' ear expedited our getting served.

Uncle Lee added pepper to his runny eggs. "Like I was saying, Pimpin' Ken was damn near dead. While he was asleep, Belle slit his throat with a pearl handled razor."

"Goddamn! I would've killed that bitch if I'd lived," I replied, spouting machismo.

"No you wouldn't have. You would have done just what Ken did; left that country bitch alone. He was in the hospital for three weeks and to this day can hardly talk above a whisper."

I poured blueberry syrup on my pancakes. "That's some cold shit."

"He lost most of his stable after that and took his last money and opened up a car wash. He left the pimp game alone." That was some crazy shit. I couldn't see lettin' a broad get away with damn near killing me.

"So, what happened to Belle?"

"The other girls said she went into a laughing fit and walked out the apartment with the bloody razor in her hand and they never saw her again."

"Did you keep on pimpin' after that, Unk?"

"I hung with it for about another year then gave it up. I still had lots of women and many of them offered to hoe for me, but having to chase bitches down and bail them out of jail was too much like work," he said with a grin.

"What did you do to make'em hook you up like that?" I was eager to learn his trade secrets.

"Have you heard that old saying, 'you can catch more flies with honey than with vinegar?' he asked.

"Yeah. I've heard that before. But it sounds to me like you have to be a soft ass punk and kiss up to a bitch to get them to do what you're talkin' about." Uncle Lee looked at me like I had a tail.

"What the hell are you talking about?"

"I mean you gotta be a softie. Broads take advantage of dudes like that."

"You still don't get it do you?" He spread butter on his pancakes. "I got the same things Ken did—cars, jewelry and cash—without having to strike a single woman."

"You mean to tell me you never had to smack *any* of your bitches?"

He crunched on a piece of bacon. "Never. I had a knack for making women do things for me because they *wanted* to, not because I was gonna beat their ass."

Uncle Lee eyeballed the waitress who was eyeballing him.

"If you had broken things off with Amanda and at least made her feel like you cared a little bit, I bet she would have let it go a lot easier than you 'Gorilla Pimpin'' and basically slapping her in the face. In a way, you're lucky she did have that miscarriage and didn't just have the kid and stick you with child support."

I almost spilled my fork full of eggs. "She knows better that pull some shit like that." My words didn't sound convincing to my ears.

"Yeah, so you think. As far as Angelina goes, I told you about messin' with those Puerto Rican women; they're unpredictable and dangerous. When they get mad, they sometimes lash out by breaking out your windows, slashing your car tires or showing up at your house," he said while slicing up his pancakes. Uncle Lee chuckled, "What's wrong, Youngblood? Lost your appetite?"

I had barely touched my food. "Man, it sounds like you're readin' me like a book."

"Now don't get me wrong, I've had my share of females that were crazy as Jim Jones. You have to deal with each woman on an individual basis. You can't treat your main squeeze the way you treat your bench squad and visa versa."

"I know that. I keep my girls in check."

"I can't tell by what you told me. You have to have some kind of order. You have to be able to make them feel like they're special and be able to enforce your ground rules at the same time. That, Youngblood, is the sign of being a true player of the game."

I realized then that I had a lot yet to learn about women. Even though I considered myself an expert and pretty much got what I wanted from the women I'd dealt with, I could have done much better.

"How come you don't have any kids, Unk?"

Uncle Lee's face seemed to loose all its elasticity after my question. His eyes dropped from mine to the inside of his half full coffee cup. I couldn't figure out why my question caused him to become so solemn.

He took a sip of his coffee, pulled the napkin he was using as a bib out of his shirt, wiped his hands and said, "I never wanted any." He tossed the used napkin on top of his plate and signaled for the waitress. That was the end of the conversation.

When the waitress, (Ayala was the name on her badge) arrived, Uncle Lee handed me the bill and said, "That's my fee for the lessons you just received." He took care of the tip while reeling Ayala in with his pimpin' witchcraft. She had to be about my age with dark skin and a huge rack.

While Uncle Lee worked his magic, I went outside to wait for him. I still couldn't shake what Amanda had said. I wondered how many other women had gotten pregnant by me and not told me? I'd used rubbers most of the time unless I was satisfied the woman was clean and I verified they were on some form of birth control. Maybe Amanda was lying anyway. "I ain't trippin,'" I said to myself. Five minutes later Uncle Lee exited the restaurant and joined me on the curb.

"You ready to leave, Rio?"

"Yeah. Did you get baby's number?"

"What do you think?" He pulled a piece of paper with Ayala's number out of his pocket and handed it to me.

"I just got at her to keep my skills honed. I also ensured that I'll be gettin' much better service when I come here to eat," he said with a wink.

"Are you still seein' that chick from England, Wanda?" I asked as we entered my car.

"Oh yeah, she's the main course right now. I think it's that English accent and those nice tits that keep my interest."

"Do you love her?"

"No, but I do enjoy her. Shit, it's been a long, long time since I allowed *a*ny woman close enough to me to fall in love." Again he became solemn. His face briefly clouded with a mix of emotions after his answer.

"How can you tell when you love a woman, Unk?"

"You're the only one that'll know that. It's not like a Disney film and some fairy or wizard will wave a magic wand."

We pulled from the curb. "That damn sure would be easier."

"This is the first time you've brought this subject up since you were in elementary school. Are you tryin' to tell me you're in love?" he gave me "the look" like his sister, my mother, did when she looked for an answer in my face. I turned away from him and looked out the window instead of answering him.

I *wished* I could've told him how I felt since breaking up with Carmen.

I *wished* I knew why I missed her so bad.

I *wished* I hadn't lost my job. My grandma once imparted these words of wisdom on me, "Wish in one hand, spit in the other and see which one gets full the fastest."

CHAPTER THIRTY-ONE

December 24th. Happy birthday to me. The only good thing about my thirtieth birthday was it wasn't raining. With no job to go to, my days dragged on. I'd taken to screening *all* my calls. There were very few people I wanted to talk to. During that Friday, many of my close family left happy birthday wishes on my answering machine. None of them were yet aware of my job situation.

After sulking around the house most of the morning, I decided to get dressed and go check my mailbox. The phone rang before I left, it was Uncle Lee. "Hello?"

"Happy Birthday, Playboy! What you got planned? I was gonna leave you a message. Did you take today off to celebrate?"

I've got everyday off, I thought. "Yeah I did. I might go out tonight. What are you up to?"

"Getting ready to leave. Wanda's takin' me to Carmel for Christmas."

"Are you guys drivin' down there?"

"Yeah. Wanda wants to see the coastline so we're gonna take Highway 1."

Not being in the mood to hear about a happy relationship, I blew him off. "That sounds real good. Hey, Unk, I gotta make a run, call me when you get back, okay?"

"All right, Youngblood, I'll be back the day after New Year's. Check on my house for me."

"Okay, I'll go by there every couple days. Later." After hanging up, I went to the lobby and checked my mail. Bills, junk mail and an envelope which felt like it contained a card. It had no return address, just my name written in some very good handwriting. Curiosity made me open it there in the lobby.

Inside was an African-American Christmas card. *It's probably from Granny,* I thought as I stared at the black Santa Claus and sleeping black children on the cover. On the inside besides the preprinted, "Have a blessed and happy holiday season!" was the following: *Have a happy birthday also. Take care, C.*

Several minutes passed as I read and reread that card. "Nah, it can't be from Carmen... *can't* be." I thumped the card against my thigh as a smile formed on my face. Inspired, I went back to my place and debated calling her. At 1:18 p.m. I called her job. "Thank you for calling PG&E. Our offices are closed for the Christmas holiday. We will re-open Monday, December 27th. If you have an emergency, please call our toll free emergency line, 1-800-555-9111. Thank you for calling PG&E."

After hanging up, I called her house. Her answering machine let me know she wasn't home. Instead of leaving a message, I called her cell phone and got the same response.

"Fuck! Where is she?" I said to myself. I read the card one more time then felt an odd thing; I was hungry as hell. I'd skipped many meals over the past couple weeks. The picture of a big hamburger in my mind made me grab my leather jacket and head out.

As I traveled north on Broadway to *Wendy's* to get a triple cheeseburger, a familiar red Mustang sped past me and turned into the *Blockbuster* parking lot across from *Wendy's*.

Carmen!

I cut across two lanes of traffic and heard several angry car horns as I followed the Mustang. "Why are you rollin' up on me like you're the police?" Zoe asked as she got out of her car. She wore tight jeans, a red blouse and a wool-lined denim jacket. On her head sat a red Santa Claus hat.

"Sorry about that. I thought you were Carmen." I'd parked so fast I took up two parking spaces. "Have you seen her?"

Zoe smiled and shook her head. "You two are a trip!"

I studied her light gray eyes. "Why do you say that?"

She picked her purse off the seat and closed her door. "She acts like she doesn't care when I tell her I've seen you. But she always ends up asking me where I saw you."

A fist of emotion hit me in the chest. "What you mean?"

"She's stubborn as hell and she uses me as the middle man, rather middle *woman,* just like you."

"If that's true, then why is she kickin' it with punk-ass Bernard?"

She rolled her eyes. "*You* need to get your facts straight. She's not hardly 'kickin' it' with that man."

"Bullshit! I saw her holdin' hands with that nigga after her jazz class."

Zoe sat her cute booty down on the fender of the car. "She told me what happened. For your information he was there pick up his sister who is one of Carmen's students."

I thought about what she said for a second. "Then why was he gettin' in the car with her?"

"She gave them a ride to the student parking lot so they could get to his car; they can't park in the much closer teacher's parking lot like Carmen."

I cocked my head to the side and stared deeply into her eyes. "Are you serious?"

"Why would I lie?" She stood and faced me. "I haven't had a minute's peace since you guys started this lover's quarrel."

I lowered my head and studied my shoes. *Damn…if what she says is true…* "Do you know where I can find her?"

Zoe crossed her arms, looked down and kicked a pebble. Yeah, I know where she is… if I tell you, you'd better *not* say I told you."

I placed both my hands on her shoulders. "I *promise* I won't snitch on you."

She looked up into my face. "Alabama. She said I could drive her car while she was gone if I dropped her off at the airport. She flew out Wednesday night. She's spending the week with Andretta."

I hugged her tight and whispered in her ear, "Thank you, Zoe… Thank you."

We ended our embrace. "Like I told you a few weeks ago; I want my *old* friend back."

"Do you have my number?"

"No."

"You have a pen? I want you to call me if you hear from her, Okay?"

She went into her purse and got a pen and scrap of paper. After writing my number down, she turned from me and walked away. I hopped back in my car and tried to formulate a plan to contact Carmen as I entered the *Wendy's* drive through.

CHAPTER THIRTY-TWO

After finishing off my triple cheeseburger, I treated myself to the movies. I hadn't gone to the movies solo since I was fourteen. It gave me a chance to think. A chance to come to grips with my feelings and the massive changes in my life which had recently occurred. Unfortunately, there were more changes in store for me.

CHAPTER THIRTY-THREE

On my way home from the movies, for some unknown reason, I was compelled to drive past my parents house even though I wasn't up to facing them. "What the hell?" There were two California Highway Patrol cars parked in front of the house along with a KTVU channel 2 news van. After parking across the street, I ran to my parent's front door.

I banged on the door with my fist. "Hey! Open the door!" The look on my father's face when the door swung open told me there was trouble. "What happened? Why are the CHP and the news people here?" I rushed past my father. In the living room, two CHP officers stood talking to my mother. The look of pain in her face hurt me to my heart.

Standing quietly next to the fireplace was a balding Asian man holding a portable TV camera. Next to him was a short, blond woman in a dark blue suit with a KTVU microphone in her hand. In my haste, I failed to notice Damon, Yvette and her husband Mark all sitting on the couch with grim looks on their faces.

"Somebody tell me what the hell is goin' on!" All eyes turned to me. Pops walked past me and took my mothers hand. The officers took a step back and avoided my eyes. My mother tried to speak. "Rio... you're Uncle Lee..." twin tears leaked from her hazel eyes. She buried her face in Pops shoulder and wept. "Son, Your uncle Lee was in an accident this afternoon on Highway 1."

My heart jack-hammered in my chest. "What happened? Is he okay? Where is he?" I looked into every set of eyes in the living room and none of them gave me hope. One of the officers—a redheaded gentleman—removed the cell phone from his hip and walked outside.

Yvette stood. "Rio, he was killed... him and Wanda." She too began crying. Mark stood and held his wife. Damon wiped his eyes and joined Mark and Yvette in a group hug. I took a few steps back and stood in the doorway. The scene was surreal. No way could my mind accept Uncle Lee's death. No tears fell from my eyes. There was an unnatural calmness in me.

The officer with the graying temples and slight pot belly cleared his throat. "Well, Mr. Clark, if there's anything we can do, you have my card. Give me a call anytime."

Pops offered him his hand. "Thank you."

The red headed officer returned and addressed the blonde lady. "Judy, I just got word that Ms. Hobart's family has been notified."

"Thank you."

The two officers left in silence. After a brief conversation with the blond haired woman, the camera man checked the lighting with a light meter then hoisted his camera to his shoulder. "Mr. Clark?"

Pops lifted his head as he held my mother and answered. "Yes?"

"I know this is a hard time for you and your family. Are you up to giving a statement?"

He lifted Moms' chin. She just shook her head and buried her face back in his shoulder. "I don't think now would be a good time."

After another brief conversation with her camera man, she spoke. "If you like, we can film our segment in front of you house and display this picture of Mr. Swanson you gave us." She held the framed picture of Uncle Lee with me standing behind him looking over his shoulder taken at Yvette's wedding. "Yes, let's do that instead."

"Do you happen to have a photo of the Ms. Hobart?"

Pops looked at me. "Rio, do you know if your Uncle had any pictures of Wanda?"

"No, not that I know of." I'd never known Wanda's last name. The news team went outside and began filming. The feeling that I was in a play or television show freaked me out. Sadness hung in the house like smoke from a forest fire.

The phone began to ring constantly. After the first dozen calls, I just let the answering machine take the rest. By 10:00 p.m. the house was full of people. Moms had calmed enough to deal with all the questions and sympathy hugs. It was weird. After comforting my mother, I was next in line for hugs and kind words. I think it was because everyone knew how close I was to Uncle Lee.

Damon spoke. "Hey, the news is about to come on." He picked up the remote to Pop's 70-inch TV and turned it to The Channel 2 Ten o'clock News. The story that came on after the commercial break was about a couple in a red Corvette that were forced off Highway 1 and plunged three hundred feet to their death. An eyewitness said a white Saab crossed the center line while exiting the curve Uncle Lee and Wanda had entered, forcing them off the road and over the cliff. The photo of Uncle Lee and I was displayed throughout the story.

Fresh tears flowed from all but me. The same strange lack of emotion shrouded me. It seemed I wasn't capable of grieving. At around 1:00 a.m., I prepared to leave. After Pops made her take a tranquilizer, Moms fell asleep in her recliner. I kissed her on the forehead. "I love you, Momma." She stirred a little. A frown crossed her face momentarily as she slept then was gone.

Mark held Yvette as she slept with her head on his lap. "How you doin', dude?" he asked. I rubbed my tired eyes. "I'm cool… Thanks for comin', man."

We shook hands. "No need to thank me, we're family."

"Where are the kids?"

Yvette stirred in his lap. "At my mother's."

Damon's girlfriend, Rochelle, had stopped by after work and now slept hugged up with him on the loveseat. I looked around and noticed Mom's had Pops, Yvette had Mark and Damon had Rochelle. Even in death, Uncle Lee had Wanda. Every one there had a shoulder to cry on except me. *I don't need one,* I thought as I left.

There were twenty-two messages of sympathy on my machine. Dee, Lola, Mr. Upchurch, Zoe and even Amanda were among those that offered their condolences after seeing the news broadcast. Sleep eluded me. I went to my balcony and breathed the cold Christmas Eve air. Not until I felt my nose running did I go back inside. I went to my stash box. "This is for you, Unk," I said as I rolled a joint as fat as a Sharpie marker and smoked it down until it burned my finger tips.

The following Tuesday we buried my Uncle at Rolling Hills Cemetery in Richmond, California. The day started off overcast and cold. By the time he was lowered into the ground, it began to drizzle. My family members were easy to spot; most of them wore dark glasses, including me. During the funeral, I was irritated to find there were more of Uncle Lee's friends in attendance than there was family.

Even though he was despised by many of our kin because of his lifestyle, you would think that his death would've garnered at least a few more goodbyes. During the limo ride back to my parent's house, I sat with my eyes closed as the sounds of my mothers weeping drifted in and out of my consciousness.

I can't believe this shit! Out of the eleven cars parked in front of my parent's house, only five of them belong to my relatives, I thought as the limo pulled away after dropping us off. The house was full of food and people. A dozen different conversations mixed together.

"How you holdin' up, Rio?" I turned and was greeted by my player hatin' cousin, Ryan.

"I'm good."

He started at my black crocodile shoes and worked his way up my black Bill Blass suit. "That's a sweet suit, Rio. But if it was me, I would've gone with a red tie instead of that black one."

My tolerance for his bullshit was zero. "Well, if I was going to the fuckin' club instead of coming back from a funeral, I'd wear a loud-ass tie like the one you have on."

He held up his hand. "Whoa, Homeboy. Don't start trippin' with me." The conversations around us hushed. "You need to stop all that cussing in my Uncle's house."

"Your Uncle's house? Nigga, this is my father *and* my mother's house." I never could stand his arrogant ass. He thought his side of the family was better than my Mothers. "What's going on, Ryan?" His equally obnoxious older brother, Brent, stepped up behind him. "Nothing… not a thing. Just trying to have a civilized conversation with the 'Mack Daddy.'"

I tried to let it go. I really did. When I turned to leave those two assholes, I heard Brent say, "You should know better than that; he's about as ignorant as his dead uncle."

"What did you say, Muthafucka!" I yelled as I spun on my heels and grabbed a fist full of his lapel. I prepared to mash his nose into the back of his head with my upraised fist.

"Let go of me, punk!"

"Let go of my brother, nigga!"

"If you *ever* talk bad about me or my Uncle again, I'll beat yo' faggot-ass!"

A pair of big hands gripped my shoulders. "Rio, let him go… Let him go!" Pops struggled to separate me from his nephew. After I caught a glimpse of my mother's sad eyes, I dropped my fist and let go of Brent. He straightened out the front of his jacket. "I'm sorry Uncle Romero. All I did was try and stop him from bothering my brother and he tried to jump on *me*."

Pops looked from Brent's lying face into mine. "Rio, why are you bothering them? Can't you see your upsetting your mother?"

I jerked my shoulders out of his grip. "Just like always, you can't believe what I say. You take up for those punks."

"Rio, watch your mouth." The crowd circled us. I saw Mark and Damon trying to get through to help restore order.

"I don't need this shit, I'm gone." My father followed me outside into the drizzling rain. "Rio… Rio! What's your problem?" he yelled behind me. At the sidewalk in front of my car I turned and faced him.

"You wanna know what my problem is? You *really* wanna know?"

He stood two feet from me as the light rain settled on his short afro.

"Yeah, I really wanna know."

"I'm tired of people acting like Uncle Lee and me are the bad guys all the damn time! Uncle Lee's not the only man that influenced me as I grew up." All the hardness in Pops face dissolved. "Yeah, you know what I'm talkin' about."

"Rio, now is not the time---,"

"Bullshit! Now *is* the time. I remember *all* the times we went on those trips to see 'Miss Pearl." He spun around to see if anyone had heard me. Fortunately for him, we were out of earshot of the half dozen or so folks on the porch.

"Now, Rio, we can talk about this later."

I trembled with pent up fury. "Fuck that! The reason I didn't tell Momma wasn't because I was scared of your belt; it was because I was a *hell* of a lot more scared of breakin' her heart." His mouth moved but no words escaped. He looked as though he'd aged ten years. I left him standing there, got in my car and left.

CHAPTER THIRTY-FOUR

To avoid phone calls and visitors, I went to a place where I could be alone: Uncle Lee's house. *No need to do that now*, I thought after nearly pressing the doorbell. I used my key and entered. The house smelled of Uncle Lee's favorite incense: Musk. My footsteps echoed off of his shiny hardwood floors. I went to the digital thermostat and dialed it up to 75 degrees.

After removing my jacket I tossed it on his red leather loveseat. I kept expecting to hear his familiar greeting, "Hey, Youngblood!" but it never happened. The only sound was the hum of the air compressor pumping fresh air into his one hundred gallon fish tank. "Damn, Unk, what happened?" I asked the framed picture of him taken in Aspen, Colorado a couple years ago when he attended the Black Ski Club's annual ski trip there.

His house held many memories, mostly good ones. I went to the fridge and found a six pack of Heineken beer. "Just what I need right now." I took one, sat on his long red leather sofa, picked up the remote from his cherry-wood coffee table and turned on the TV. The beer bottle was empty in less than two minutes. As I got up to get my second beer, I picked up his white cordless phone. "I might as well clear out my messages."

The fifth message was from Zoe, last Sunday. "Hey Rio, I'm sorry to hear about your Uncle. It tore me up when I saw the story on the news. Well, I have a little good news for you; I spoke to Carmen last night. She found out about your uncle's accident when she logged onto the Internet and read the *Oakland Tribune* from Andretta's house. She told me to tell you she's sorry about your loss and that she'll pray you and your family. She knows how close you two were. Here's my number, 555-9428. Call me if you need anything. Well, take care. 'Bye."

I wrote her number down and hung up without bothering to check anymore messages. On a whim, I called Zoe. After four rings I got her answering machine. "Hey, Zoe. Thanks for the message. I'm okay, just here chillin' at my uncle's house, I'll be back and forth between my place and here so if I'm not home, give me a call here. The number's 555-4020. And if you talk to Carmen, thank her for me. Peace."

After hanging up, I grabbed a third beer and sat it on the counter. The trash can was too full to hold my two empty beer bottles, so I carried the can into the garage and emptied it into his garbage can. I leaned against Uncle Lee's shiny, black Cadillac Sedan DeVille. I looked at my reflection on the roof and chuckled. "No wonder it's so dark in here, I still have my damn shades on!" I'd had them on all day. I removed my sunglasses and set them on the hood.

On the floor, against the wall, in front of the caddy, was an old trunk that looked like a pirate's treasure chest. The huge silver lock which normally kept it securely locked, hung open. I looked up toward heaven. "I hope you can forgive me for being nosy, Unk." I pulled the heavy chest out into the open and raised the lid.

The top layer of stuff consisted of three shoe boxes full of very rare and very expensive sports cards. Rookie cards of Michael Jordan, Wilt Chamberlain, Magic Johnson, Hank Aaron, Barry Bonds, Reggie Jackson, and hundreds of others filled the boxes. Underneath the shoe boxes, were dozens of leather-bound journals similar to the kind I used. "Goddamn, Unk! Your whole life story must be in here."

I turned on the overhead fluorescent lights and unfolded one of the four folding chairs which stood against the wall and sat in front of the trunk. I carefully sat the shoeboxes on the floor and picked a journal from near the bottom of the chest. The leather cover had a plastic window in the center which contained a blank, removable card which you could use to write on.

The card on the journal I picked up was dated simply, 5/66. I flipped it open. Under the date Tuesday, May 10th, 1966 I read the following: *I hate Vicky! I hate her! I hate her ass! After sneakin' off to the doctor's office in Richmond because of the pain in my nuts, Dr. Evans told me I had waited too late. The Chlamydial infection I'd caught from that nasty bitch Vicky had turned into Epididymitis, which in turn, left me sterile.*

"Oh hell naw!" I said aloud. I leaned my head back, rubbed my eyes then continued reading. *I should've listened to my friend Shucky when he told me she was a prostitute. I didn't give a damn. To me, she was too fine to have a disease. The thrill of gettin' some twenty-five year old pussy was too much of a temptation for my seventeen-year old ass to care. Vicky said I could fuck her for ten dollars. I wanted her so bad, I gave her the money and fucked her, standing up, in the carport of an abandoned apartment building. Days later, my dick burned when I pissed. I was too scared to tell anyone so I ignored it for months before going to the doctor's office. When I confronted Vicky about it, that bitch slapped me! Right when*

I was gonna knock the shit out of her, she pulled a razor out of her jacket pocket and tried to cut me! Her pimp, a dude named Lonzo, grabbed me and pulled his gun on me. He told me I'd better leave his bitches alone or he would pistol whip me. All the while Vicky stood behind him laughin'. Now I'll never have a kid. I'll never trust a bitch… never.

I closed the journal. I could see the pain in his writing. In some spots, the tip of the pen—having been pressed so hard—had been pushed *through* the paper as he wrote. *No wonder he got so quiet when I asked him why he didn't have any kids.* "Damn… I'm sorry, Unk." The phone rang, but I didn't want to be disturbed so I let the machine take the call.

I returned the journal and picked up another one from the middle of the pile. The date on the cover was 9/86. The date on the page I read was Wednesday, September 3rd, 1986. *Today was Rio's first day of high school. I was as proud as his parents were that my little man was growin' up. The fact that he wanted me to be the one to drop him off on his first day is a day I'll never forget. He'll never know of the tears I shed as I watched him walk through the gates of Oakland Technical High School. He insisted on wearing some of my cologne.*

I paused and rubbed my eyes. I remembered that day well. *I must be gettin' sleepy*, I thought before I continued reading. *Rio stopped by my house after school today and talked my head off about all the fine girls in his classes. I had to remind him over and over the purpose of school was to get an education; not chase pussy all day. My words went in one ear and out the other. His eyes beamed the more we talked about the chicks in his school. Right then, I realized the nephew I wished was my son, had the eyes of a player.*

Two drops of water landed on the page I was reading. I ignored them and continued. *After years of trying to get my girlfriends pregnant, it never happened. I guess I was still in denial of what Dr. Evans had told me years ago. The thought of growing old and not having kids to share my life with haunted me everyday of my adult life. I didn't want an adopted kid; I wanted one with the same blood I had. It's funny. Many times I'd slipped and called Rio 'son' and he always responded. He never once corrected me.*

Another drop hit the page. I rubbed my eyes again then read on. *Sometimes I wish I could tell him how much I love him. I've come to realize he's the closest thing to a son I will ever have. When he tells me about how Romero cussed him out or beat him, I wanna go beat his ass. Then I remember he's doing what a father's supposed to do when his kid does wrong. A lot of the wrong that Rio does is my fault. I've shown that boy more things than any kid his age should know. When he gets frustrated because he can't get some girl to pay him, fuck him, or suck him like my women do me, I feel responsible.*

Three quick drops of water landed on my hand before I could turn the page. I sniffed then read on. Monday, September 29th, 1986. *Today Rio stopped by after school and told me he was in love with a girl named Katrina. She was a sophomore cheerleader. He was pussy-whipped with infatuation. The way he talked about her, I thought he was going to nut on himself. It was my duty to hip him to the game and not let him fall for a bitch. It was the least I could do after what that hoe Vicky did to me.*

More eye rubbing. More drops of water. I closed the journal and recalled how after kissing and feeling on Katrina under the bleachers after football practice, I'd called her a bitch after she refused to suck my dick. Uncle Lee had taught me to be hard on a bitch, no matter how fine they were. She cried, ran away from me and quit the cheerleading squad.

I sniffed, wiped my nose with the back of my hand and picked up another journal. 6/90. Thursday, June 7th. *Tomorrow Rio graduates from high school. I've watched him grow from a horny, pimple-faced teenager to the most popular playboy in his school. He'd fucked many of his girls in my spare bedroom. Hell, I might as well call it his bedroom. When I asked him what he wants to do after he graduates, he told me he was going to have his women take care of him. The bad thing about it was, I believe he's serious… when I looked at him, I saw myself at his age and it hurt me to my heart. I think I taught him the game too good. He treats his women just as I treat mine: as disposable sex objects. I'd spent most of my life taking out my anger over catching VD from Vicky on all women. Now that I'm older, I realize how wrong I was. I'd molded Rio into a woman hating son-of-a-bitch like I'd become. I didn't want my nephew, my pretend son, to grow up and never experience love. I'd give anything to know what it felt like to fall in love.*

Drops of water obliterated the 'e' in love. All the words on the page blurred. It took a minute before I realized I was crying. I hadn't cried since I was thirteen. My chest hitched then I lost it. I yelled, "WHY DIDN'T YOU TELL ME THE TRUTH! GODDAMMIT UNCLE LEE! I kicked one of the boxes of cards and the contents leaped out onto the concrete floor.

I stood crying and wailing. I cried for all the women I'd fucked over.

I cried for my child Amanda had lost.

I cried for the loss of my uncle.

I cried because I both loved and hated him at the same time.

I cried because I'd fucked off a good career at the phone company.

I cried because I had no one that really cared about me but my mother.

I cried because I was afraid of growing up alone and unloved. I leaned against the roof of his Caddy and wept until I heard the doorbell ring ten minutes later.

I looked at my reflection on the roof of the car and saw a sad, sad man. I walked into the kitchen, grabbed a few paper towels and wiped my eyes and snotty nose. After the third ring of the bell I opened the door. "Hey, Rio. I tried to call but got no answer," Zoe said as she stood waiting to be invited in. She looked into my red eyes and I turned away, ashamed.

Zoe took a step forward and hugged me. I hugged her back as tightly as I could. I felt her hands rubbing my shoulder blades. Her long hair tickled my ear. "Its okay, Rio. I know how close you and your uncle were. It's okay to grieve for him, honey."

I didn't want to let her go. Her words soothed me. The smell of her hair shampoo, the warmth of her body and the tenderness of her words were comforting.

She separated from me and composed herself. "Rio... I left my purse on the front seat of my car. I'll be right back, okay?" I looked for her car and saw the tail end of it in the driveway.

"Yeah... okay, but I'm not really in the mood for company."

Zoe kissed me on the cheek. "You don't need to be alone at a time like this." She went back to her car. I sat on the edge of the couch looking at my feet while suppressing more tears. Seconds later, I heard her car door close. She rang the bell. "Come on in," I yelled from my seat. I didn't bother to look up after the door opened. "Zoe, you don't have to stay... I'll be all right."

"Hi, Rio." My heart stopped. The voice I heard wasn't Zoe's. It belonged to someone with a slight southern drawl. When I looked toward the voice, I saw one of God's angels. I swallowed hard and stood up slowly. Neither Carmen nor I moved. Zoe took Carmen's hand and walked her over to me. She placed Carmen's hand in mine. "Carmen, I lied about needing you to come back early because your car had gotten stolen from my house. I parked it around the corner." Without another word, she turned and left.

Carmen's dark eyes looked deep into my suffering soul. I slowly placed my hand on her cheek. She lifted her hand and rubbed mine as I caressed her soft cheek. In those few seconds, I learned what love was. I *knew* I was in love with Carmen Massey. "Carmen...I ....I... love...you...I'm...sor--" my voice cracked and I released my tears. She kissed my trembling lips as a lone tear spilled from her right eye. "I love you too, Rio... I love you too, baby." I hugged her tight. I hugged her for dear life.

I cried.

She cried.

We cried.

We hugged and kissed each others tears and professed our love for an eternity right there in the living room of my late uncle's house. I confessed everything from losing my job to why I had treated women so badly. I led her to the spare bedroom I called my own and we made love. We made the kind of love that poets had written about since time began. I filled her with every seed my body could produce. We cried and kissed and made love until our body's shut down early the next morning.

CHAPTER THIRTY-FIVE

After taking her home to pack some things, Carmen stayed with me at Uncle Lee's house until New Years Day.

It's a good thing we did stay there. Relatives that didn't give a damn about Uncle Lee while he was alive, tried to come over to claim his property. On January 16th, I received a certified letter from the law offices of Tony LaBaron. I was to meet him on the twentieth at 9:00 a.m. to discuss Uncle Lee's estate.

"Carmen, I want you to come with me to the meeting," I said as I put on a navy blue suit the morning of the meeting. Carmen had spent nearly every night with me since the funeral.

She straightened out my tie. "No, baby. I don't think I should…that's family business."

I took her hands and kissed them. "I want you with me."

She hugged me. "No, you go on. You'll be fine. Besides, I've got a project at work I have to get going."

I checked my watch. "Okay. I'll call you when I'm done." We both left to start our days.

Outside the LaBaron law offices in Berkeley, there were more relatives there than were at Uncle Lee's funeral. Moms wasn't there. She didn't want to be reminded of his death. At nine sharp, a sixty-something, bald headed, clean shaven, black man with round glasses opened his office door for us. "Everyone please follow me," he said as he led us to a conference room. Only ten seats were available around the solid mahogany table. On the table in front of Mr. LaBaron was a black briefcase. I took one of the seats on the end. The leeches that didn't have a seat stood.

Tony LaBaron stood. "Thank you all for coming. As per instructions left by the late Leonardo Swanson, I've been appointed to read to you the contents of his living trust." I looked around at the faces. Most of them were mumbling and grinning. A few had the nerve to rub their greedy hands together.

Mr. LaBaron sat down, opened the briefcase and removed a red folder. He adjusted his glasses as he sifted through the papers inside. After going through the papers for a second time, he stood. "Well, this won't take long at all." They looked at the lawyer as if he was reading the winning lottery numbers and they all had tickets.

"According to the trust left by one Leonard Swanson, his estate is to be distributed as follows: One ten-unit apartment building located at 444 Southwind Road in Pittsburg, California, one twenty-unit apartment building in Antioch, California located at 10274 Wicker Avenue, one residential house located at 954 54th street in Oakland, California, one Cadillac Sedan DeVille, one life insurance policy, all of Mr. Swanson's personal effects and contents of his accounts and safe deposit box at Wells Fargo Bank in Berkeley, California, are to all be given to one Rio Romero Clark."

The room went silent. Some of the dejected throng began to leave, others questioned the lawyer.

I could neither move nor speak.

"Bullshit!" My cousin Terrance yelled. He was one of the folks rubbing their hands before the reading of the trust. "That stuff has to go into probate!"

Mr. LaBaron maintained his cool. "By law, since Mr. Swanson created a living trust, and everything is in both his *and* Mr. Clark's name, it transfers to Mr. Clark immediately." After a few more challenges, the loser's of the "Uncle Lee lottery," departed.

I sat alone with the lawyer. He took off his glasses, removed a handkerchief from his pocket and cleaned them. He replaced his glasses and grinned at me. "Your uncle was a good man, Rio. I've been his lawyer and good friend for almost twenty years. I have just a few forms for you to sign then you're free to go."

My hand shook as I read and signed all the legal forms. Just as the lawyer had said, Uncle Lee *had* added my name to every thing he owned. "Oh, before you go, I have a couple more things for you." He handed me a Settlers Life insurance policy and the key to a Wells Fargo Bank safe deposit box. I opened the policy and my eyes widened. "Am I reading this right? My uncle's policy is for 500,000 dollars?"

The lawyer pulled an envelope out of the briefcase and his grin expanded. "No, actually you're *not* reading it right." He walked over and pointed at the words, "double indemnity." "Since your uncle suffered an accidental death, the policy pays double." He handed me the envelope. It contained a cashier's check for one million dollars in my name. It took almost half an hour for my heartbeat to slow to its normal pace.

◆◆◆◆◆◆◆◆◆◆◆

After depositing the check into my new Wells Fargo Bank account, I went to examine the contents of Uncle Lee's safe deposit box. Inside the large box was the most cash I'd ever seen. There was 100,000 dollars in ten neat and banded stacks of hundred dollar bills. Also in the box were six gaudy diamond rings and the combination to his home safe. *These must be the rings he wore in his pimpin' days,* I thought as I examined each one.

I picked up the most conservative of the six—a gold ring with a flat round top about the size of a nickel—which was encrusted with at least four carats worth of half carat diamonds and put it on my right index finger. I put one of the ten-10,000 dollar bundles of cash into my pocket and left.

Back at Uncle Lee's house, I opened the floor-mounted safe inside his walk-in closet. Besides the quarter pound bag of Indo weed, two Rolex watches, 9mm Browning pistol and box of ammo, pink slip to his car and his passport was another eight grand in small bills. According to my count, including cash and property I was worth about 3.2 million.

"Its time for a new lifestyle, Rio," I said to myself as I placed the bag of weed inside another garbage bag and tossed it in the trash. I drove down to 52nd street in North Oakland and told a group of my lifelong best friends to spread the word I was selling my Impala and would give them a good deal on it. *One more stop,* I thought as I drove into Berkeley to Greer's Jewelers on Sacramento Street.

"She's gonna love it, Mr. Clark," the lady behind the glass display said after I described the red-gold, seven carat ring I wanted her to make for Carmen. "It'll be ready in two weeks." I left a hefty deposit on Carmen's ring and purchased a three carat tennis bracelet as a thank you for Zoe. On the way back to Uncle Lee's house, on a whim, I stopped by my mother's church when I saw the Reverend McKnight's car parked out front.

"My wife and I would be honored to help you out, Rio," the smiling Reverend replied to my request. I left a generous donation to his church renovation fund. Later that evening over dinner, Carmen almost had a seizure when I told her about my inheritance.

Over the next two weeks I'd cancelled my lease and was pleased when Carmen accepted my offer to move into Uncle Lee's house with me. On Wednesday, February 9th, I picked up Carmen's ring and Zoe's bracelet. On Friday the eleventh, I called Reverend McKnight and confirmed our arrangement. "Oh yes, my wife and I have been waiting for this day."

"Is the time okay for you?"

"Yes. It'll work out fine. We'll be there. God bless, goodbye." I then called Zoe. "Rio, that is the sweetest thing! Of course I'll be there!"

"Do you know how to work a camcorder?"

"Hell yeah! Don't worry bout that, I'm gonna bring mine and take *plenty* of pictures. I'll see you later. Bye."

"I damn sure hope she says yes," I said to myself after I hung up with Zoe. That night after a steak dinner and a movie, Carmen and I went to bed. I'd found out she slept like the dead since she'd been living with me. Carmen also got up *every* night at around 3:00 a.m. to pee.

At 2:00 a.m. I crept out the bed and went into the closet. I put on a pair of black sweat pants and a white t-shirt. Inside of one of my old pair of Air Jordan's was the jewel box containing Carmen's ring, in the other, was the tennis bracelet. I put the tennis bracelet and ring in my pocket and crept to Carmen's side of the bed. While she lay on her right side, dead asleep, I slowly lifted her left hand just enough to slide the ring on her ring finger then slipped back under the covers.

I lay next to her, wide awake, waiting for her "pee time." Just like clockwork, at 3:11 a.m., dressed in her oversized Prince concert t-shirt, Carmen got up and zombie-walked to the restroom. I waited for the response.

"WHAT IN THE WORLD?" When the screams started I smiled in the darkness. She ran into the bedroom and dived on me. "RIO! RIO! WHAT DOES THIS MEAN?" she yelled as tears raced down her cheeks.

I sat up and turned on the lamp on my night stand. Carmen stared at the diamond encrusted ring on her finger. Even in the muted lamplight, the diamonds sparkled like the Milky Way Galaxy. "It means…" I got out the bed, stood on one knee and took her ringed hand. Carmen literally began shaking. "It means I love you more than I can ever tell you. But if you give me the chance, and become my wife, I promise, right here in front of you and God, I'll spend the rest of my life showing you."

"Yes…Yes… Oh God yes I'll marry you… Oh Rio…I love you so much!" Her sobs made her words hard to understand, but I read my answer in her eyes. As we held each other, the doorbell chimed. I looked at my clock; it was 4:00 a.m. Carmen sniffed and wiped her eyes. Her short, cute hair stuck up all over her head, but she still was as fine as ever. "Who could that be?"

"Come on, let's go see." Carmen slipped into her purple terry-cloth robe and we walked hand in hand down the stairs. "Ah, just in time I see," I said as I opened the door for Reverend McKnight, his lovely wife Mary and Zoe. Carmen saw the bible in the reverend's hand then placed her hand over her mouth in disbelief. "What's going on? Zoe? What are you doing here?"

"Did you think you could get married without *me* as a bridesmaid?" she answered as she pointed her camcorder at Carmen and me.

Carmen tried to cover her face and hide behind me. "Don't you film me like this!" The reverend and his wife enjoyed her embarrassment. "I trust she agreed to be your wife," Mary asked.

I turned to face her. Carmen nodded as she looked me in the eye. "Yes, I would love to become Mrs. Rio Clark." Zoe removed the camera and wiped her eyes. "I'm so glad you two finally got together," she said as her tears continued.

"Where would you like to perform the ceremony, Rio?"

I pointed toward the fireplace. "How 'bout over there?"

"Fine, fine. Come on you two." After the half hour ceremony, I kissed my new wife. I then went into my pants pocket and handed Zoe the tennis bracelet. "This is for you, Zoe. Thank you for being there for me." Fresh tears rolled down her cheeks. She put the camera down and fumbled with putting the bracelet on. "Let me help you," Carmen offered as she placed the bracelet on her best friend's wrist. We all exchanged hugs at 5:15 a.m. before my wedding party left. Once alone, Carmen tongue kissed me. "Husband, take me up stairs and make love to your wife."

I did.

◆◆◆◆◆◆◆◆◆◆◆◆

On President's Day, at six in the morning, Carmen jumped out of bed and ran to the bathroom. I heard her gag then vomit. "Are you all right?" I asked when she returned.

"No… this is the fourth time I've thrown up in the past week."

I placed the back of my hand on her forehead. "Hmmm… you don't have a fever. Do you feel sick?"

She sat on the edge of the bed rubbing her stomach. "No." She looked up at the ceiling, and then looked into my face. "Rio, I stopped taking my birth control pills after I got back from Alabama after our fight. I didn't plan on having sex *ever* again." I was completely oblivious to what she was trying to tell me. "Are you on them now?"

"No."

I sat up next to her and rubbed her belly. "Carmen, do you think… could you be… pregnant?"

"We'll know this afternoon; I made a doctors appointment for a pregnancy test yesterday." At 2:26 p.m. Carmen and the doctor smiled as they walked into the waiting room. The doctor shook my hand. She was a young African-American lady, looking to be no more than a few years older than my wife. "Congratulations! You're going to be a Daddy!" Carmen held her arms out to me. My knees nearly buckled as I stood to hug her. *Me, a father!*

Carmen looked into my face. "There's more..." Carmen looked to the doctor. "Well, Mr. Clark, your wife has *two* babies in her oven. You're going to have *twins*. Her due date is Labor Day." I was so overwhelmed with joy I damn near passed out. That meant she got pregnant around the same time Uncle Lee was buried.

♦♦♦♦♦♦♦♦♦♦♦

Eleven months later, after selling Uncle Lee's house and car, I moved my family from Oakland to a new four acre, five bedroom, Spanish-style home in Granite Bay, California. It was far enough away from the memories in Oakland for us to start a brand new life. We traded in the Mustang for a new BMW X5 SUV for Carmen to haul my babies around in. Also, I sold my car to one of my homeboys on 52nd Street and bought a new BMW 745i for me and Momma. As a tribute to Uncle Lee, I bought a beat up 1969 Coupe DeVille just like the sky blue one he once owned. I parked it in the garage and worked on completely restoring it.

With the help of Carmen's financial savvy, we acquired five more apartment buildings, insuring neither of us would ever have to work again. We mutually decided to stay home and raise our kids for the first five years since we had the financial means. Carmen didn't really want to share those important years with the strangers at a daycare center anyway.

My days were spent learning to play golf and going to school to get my real estate broker's license. I still hadn't worked out all the issues between my father and me, but we were scheduled to play golf next week… maybe we could start there.

I gave my mother all the pictures of her and Uncle Lee along with a check for 50,000 dollars. She and Pops took a two month trip around the world. I split Uncle Lee's wardrobe with Damon and let him and Yvette divide up his furniture. I gave up weed smokin' and drinkin'. I had kids to raise.

♦♦♦♦♦♦♦♦♦♦♦

Damiana's tiny hand gripped my finger as she cooed. "Little girl, this is *not* play time; this is bedtime," I said to my two-month old daughter, Damiana Lee Clark. When I heard her began to cry at a little after one in the morning, I let Carmen sleep and went to feed and change her. Carmen and I agreed *not* to give the twins rhyming names. Carmen *insisted* on naming my son after me, Rio Romero Clark, II.

They were fraternal twins. Rio had most of Carmen's dark facial features and eyes, while Damiana had my hazel eyes and nose. They both had thick, long wavy hair.

Damiana's eyes locked on my face. "I'm gonna be the best Daddy I can for you guys. I *pray* you don't give me as much hell as I gave my parents. Now, you better get some sleep. Your grandma and grandpa are flying all the way out here from Alabama tomorrow to see you and your brother and spend Thanksgiving with us. Your Godmother, Zoe, is comin' over too." I picked her up and walked her around the room for fifteen minutes before she fell asleep on my shoulder. I placed her next to her brother and changed his diaper as he slept.

♦♦♦♦♦♦♦♦♦♦♦

The next day, as I was reading the last of Uncle Lee's journals in the den which we'd converted into our home office, Carmen walked behind me and rubbed my shoulders. "You know, I've been thinking… I bet your uncle's journals would make a real good book."

I closed it up and rubbed her hands. "Yeah, I think you're right… they just might."

"CRUNK" DESCRIPTION

Imagine a Thug-World divided by the Mason-Dixon Line........

After the brutal murder of four NYC ganstas in Charlotte, the climate is set for an all-out Thug Civil War – North pitted against South!

Rah-Rah, leader of NYC's underworld and KoKo, head of one of the Durty South's most ferocious Crunk-crews are on a collision course to destruction. While Rah-Rah tries to rally his northern Thugdom (Philly, NJ & NY), KoKo attempts to saddle-up heads of the southern Hoodville (Atlanta, South Carolina & Charlotte).

Kendra and Janeen, a southern sister-duo of self-proclaimed baddest b***'s, conduct a make-shift Thug Academy to prepare KoKo's VA-bred cousin (Shine) to infiltrate NYC's underground, as a secret weapon to the impending battle.**

The US Government, well-aware of the upcoming war, takes a backseat role, not totally against the idea that a war of this magnitude might actual do what the Government has been unable to do with thousands of life sentences -- Rid society completely of the dangerous element associated with the Underground-World.

Suspensfully-Sexy, Erotically-Ghetto and Mysteriously-Raw. CRUNK will leave you saying, Hmmmm?

"Get Ready For A Wild & Sexy Ride! Twists & Turns Are Abundant! An Instant Urban Classic Thriller! Tariq, Rudd & Jones Are Definitely Some BAD BOYZ! Errr'body Gettin' CRUNK!"

"Hustlin' Backwards" DESCRIPTION

Capone and his life-long road dawgz, June and Vonzell are out for just one thing.... To get rich!....By any means necessary!

As these three partners in crime rise up the ranks from Project-Kids to Street-Dons, their sworn code of "Death Before Dishonor" gets tested by the Feds.

Though Capone's simple pursuit of forward progression as a Hustler gains him an enviable lifestyle of Fame, Fortune and all the women his libido can handle – It also comes with a price.

No matter the location – Miami, Charlotte, Connecticut or Puerto Rico – There's simply no rest for the wicked!

WARNING: HUSTLIN' BACKWARDS is not the typical street-novel. A Unique Plot, Complex Characters mixed with a Mega-dose of Sensuality makes this story enjoyable by all sorts of readers! A true Hustler himself, Mike Sanders knows the game, inside and out!

"Fast-Paced and Action-Packed! Hustlin' Backwards HAS IT ALL -- Sex, Money, Manipulation and Murder! Mike Sanders is one of the most talented and prolific urban authors of this era!"

"Sex A Baller" DESCRIPTION

Mysterious Luva has sexed them all! Ball players, CEO's, Music Stars -- You name the baller, she's had them. And more importantly, she's made them all pay......

Sex A Baller is a poignant mix of a sexy tale of how Mysterious Luva has become one of the World's Best Baller Catchers and an Instructional Guide for the wanna-be Baller Catcher!

No details or secrets are spared, as she delivers her personal story along with the winning tips & secrets for daring women interested in catching a baller!

PLUS, A SPECIAL BONUS SECTION INCLUDED!

Baller Catching 101

- Top-20 Baller SEX POSITIONS (Photos!)
- Where To FIND A Baller
- Which Ballers Have The BIGGEST Penis
- SEDUCING A Baller
- Making A Baller Fall In Love
- Getting MONEY From A Baller
- What Kind Of SEX A Baller Likes
- The EASIEST Type of Baller To Catch
- Turning A Baller Out In Bed
- GAMES To Play On A Baller
- Getting Your Rent Paid & A Free Car
- Learn All The SECRETS!

BY THE END OF THIS BOOK, YOU'LL HAVE YOUR CERTIFIED BALLER-CATCHER'S DEGREE!

"CAUGHT UP!"

When Raven Klein, a bi-racial woman from Iowa moves to Atlanta in hopes of finding a life she's secretly dreamed about, she finds more than she ever imagined.

Quickly lured and lost in a world of sex, money, power-struggles, betrayal & deceit, Raven doesn't know who she can really trust! A chance meeting at a bus terminal leads to her delving into the seedy world of strip-clubs, big-ballers and shot-callers. Now, Raven's shuffling through more men than a Vegas blackjack dealer does a deck of cards. And sex has even become mundane -- little more than a tool to get what she wants. After a famous acquaintance winds-up dead -- On which shoulder will Raven lean? A wrong choice could cost her life! There's a reason they call it HOTATLANTA!

"WILD THANGZ"

Jazmyn, Trina and Brea are definitely a trio of Drama-Magnets - the sista-girlz version of Charlie's Angels. Young & fine with bangin' bodies, the three of them feel like they can do no wrong – not even with each other. No matter the location: Jamaica, Miami, NYC or the A-T-L, lust, greed and trouble is never far from these wanna-be divas. Jazymn has secret dreams that if she pursues will cause her to have mega family problems. Though the most logical of the group, she can get her attitude on with the best of them when pushed. Trina wasn't always the diva. Book-smarts used to be her calling-card. But, under the tutoring of her personal hoochie-professor, Brea, she's just now beginning to understand the power that she has in her traffic-stopping Badunkadunk.

Brea has the face of a princess, but is straight ghetto-fab -- without the slightest shame. As the wildest of the bunch, her personal credos of living life to the fullest and to use *'what her mama gave her'* to get ahead, is constantly creating drama for Jazymn and Trina. When past skeleton-choices in Brea's closet places all three of them in an impossible life-and-death situation, they must take an action that has the most serious of consequences, in order to survive! The very foundation of their friendship-bond gets tested, as each of them have the opportunity to sell-out the other! The question is, Will They? Wild Parties, Wild Situations & Wild Nights are always present for these Wild Thangz!

"Slick" DESCRIPTION

Dana & Sylvia have been girlfriends for what seems like forever. They've never been afraid to share everything about their lives and definitely keep each other's secrets ... including hiding Dana's On-The-DL affair from her husband, Jonathan.

Though Sylvia is uncomfortable with her participation in the cover-up and despises the man Dana's creepin' with, she remains a loyal friend. That is, until she finds herself attracted to the very man her friend is deceiving.

As the lines of friendship and matrimonial territory erodes, all hell is about to break loose! Choices have to be made with serious repercussions at stake.

If loving you is wrong, I don't wanna be right!

"SLICK!!! .... Ain't That The Truth! Brenda Hampton's Tale Sizzles With Sensuality, Deception, Greed and So Much Drama – My Gurrll!"

- MYSTERIOUS LUVA, BEST-SELLING AUTHOR OF *SEX A BALLER*

"HYPED" DESCRIPTION

Maurice LaSalle is a player – of women and the saxophone. A gifted musician, he's the driving force behind MoJazz, a neo-soul group on the verge of their big break. Along with his partner in rhyme and crime, Jamal Grover, Maurice has more women than he can count. Though guided by his mentor Simon, Maurice knows Right but constantly does Wrong.

Then Ebony Stanford enters Maurice's world and he begins to play a new tune. Ebony, still reeling from a nasty divorce, has just about given up on men, but when Maurice hits the right notes (everywhere) she can't help but fall for his charms.

While Maurice and Ebony get closer, Jamal is busy putting so many notches on his headboard post after each female conquest, that the post looks more like a tooth-pick. When a stalker threatens his life, Maurices warns him to slow his roll, but Jamal's hyped behavior prevails over good sense.

Just as Maurice is contemplating turning in his player card for good, stupidity overrules his judgment and throws his harmonious relationship with Ebony into a tale-spin. When it appears that things couldn't get any worse, tragedy strikes and his life is changed forever!

A Powerfully-Written Sexy-Tale, *HYPED* is a unique blend of Mystery, Suspense, Intrigue and Glowing-Sensuality.

"Buckle Up! HYPED Will Test All Of Your Senses and Emotions! LUKE Is A Force To Be Reckoned With For Years To Come!" -- WINSTON CHAPMAN, ESSENCE MAGAZINE BEST-SELLING AUTHOR OF "CAUGHT UP!" AND "WILD THANGZ"

"STILL CRAZY" DESCRIPTION

Kevin Allen, a rich, handsome author and self-reformed 'Mack', is now suffering from writer's block.

Desperately in need of a great story in order to renegotiate with his publisher to maintain his extravagant life-style, Kevin decides to go back to his hometown of Chicago for inspiration. While in Chi-town, he gets reacquainted with an ex-love (Yolanda) that he'd last seen during their stormy relationship that violently came to an end.

Unexpectedly, Yolanda appears at a book-event where Kevin is the star-attraction, looking every bit as stunningly beautiful as the picture he's had frozen in his head for years. She still has the looks of music video model and almost makes him forget as to the reason he'd ever broken off their relationship.

It's no secret, Yolanda had always been the jealous type. And, Kevin's explanation to his boyz, defending his decision for kicking a woman that fine to the curb was, "She's Crazy!".

The combination of Kevin's vulnerable state in his career, along with the tantalizing opportunity to hit *that* again, causes Kevin to contemplate renewing his expired Players-Card, one last time. What harm could one night of passion create?

Clouding his judgment even more is that Kevin feels like hooking-up with Yolanda might just be the rekindling needed to ignite the fire for his creativity in his writing career. But, there are just two problems. Kevin is married! ....And, Yolanda is *Still Crazy!*

"Darrin Lowery deliciously serves up.....Scandal & Sexy-Drama like no other! *STILL CRAZY* has all the goods readers are looking for!"
-- Brenda Hampton, Author of "Slick"

"SHAKEDOWN" DESCRIPTION

Paris Hightower, is a sexy young thang who falls in love with the man of her dreams, Tyree Dickerson, the son of very wealthy Real Estate tycoons. But there's a problem.... Tyree's mother (Mrs. Dickerson) thinks that her son is too good for Paris and is dead-set on destroying the relationship at all costs.

After Mrs. Dickerson reveals a long-kept secret to Paris about her mother (Ebony Hightower), a woman that abandoned Paris and her brother more than fifteen years ago when she was forced to flee and hide from police amidst Attempted-Murder charges for shooting Paris' father --- Paris is left in an impossible situation.

Even though the police have long given-up on the search for Ebony Hightower (Paris' mother), the bitter Mrs. Dickerson threatens to find her and turn her in to authorities as blackmail for Paris to end the relationship with her son.

Paris knows that Mrs. Dickerson means business – she has the time, interest and money to hunt down her mother. Left with the choices of pursuing her own happiness or protecting the freedom of her mother, a woman she barely knows, Paris is confused as to the right thing to do.

As the situation escalates to fireworks of private investigators, deception, financial sabotage and kidnapping, even Paris' life becomes in danger.

Just when Paris feels that all hope is lost, she's shocked when she receives unexpected help from an unlikely source.

"Be careful who you mess with, 'cause Payback is a ......! *Shakedown* combines high-drama and mega-suspense with the heart-felt struggle of the price some are willing to pay for love!"

-- Winston Chapman, Best-Selling Author of *"Wild Thangz"* and *"Caught Up!"*

BLACK PEARL BOOKS INC.

ORDER FORM

Black Pearl Books Inc.
3653-F Flakes Mill Road- PMB 306
Atlanta, Georgia 30034
www. BlackPearlBooks. com

YES, We Ship Directly To Prisons & Correctional Facilities
INSTITUTIONAL CHECKS & MONEY ORDERS ONLY!

TITLE	Price	Quantity	TOTAL
"Caught Up!" by Winston Chapman	**$ 14. 95**		
"Sex A Baller" by Mysterious Luva	**$ 12. 95**		
"Wild Thangz" by Winston Chapman	**$ 14. 95**		
"Crunk" by Bad Boyz	**$ 14. 95**		
"Hustlin Backwards" by Mike Sanders	**$ 14. 95**		
"Still Crazy" by Darrin Lowery	**$ 14. 95**		
"Twisted" by Holland Jones	**$ 14. 95**		
"Slick" by Brenda Hampton	**$ 14. 95**		
"Hyped" by Luke	**$ 14. 95**		

Sub-Total	**$**
SHIPPING: ___ # books x $ 3. 50 ea. (Via US Priority Mail)	**$**
GRAND TOTAL	**$**

SHIP TO:

Name: ________________________________

Address: ______________________________

Apt or Box #: ___________

City: _____________ **State:** _____ **Zip:** _____

Phone: _________ **E-mail:** _________________